DISCARD

The Kings of San Carlos

Also by James L. Haley

MOST EXCELLENT SIR: LETTERS RECEIVED BY SAM HOUSTON,
  PRESIDENT OF THE REPUBLIC OF TEXAS, AT COLUMBIA,
  1836–1837
TEXAS: AN ALBUM OF HISTORY
APACHES: A HISTORY AND CULTURE PORTRAIT
THE BUFFALO WAR: THE HISTORY OF THE RED RIVER INDIAN
  UPRISING OF 1874

The Kings of San Carlos

JAMES L. HALEY

DOUBLEDAY & COMPANY, INC.

GARDEN CITY, NEW YORK

1987

Principal characters in this book
are based on historical persons
now deceased. Ancillary characters
are fictitious, and any resemblance
to actual persons, living or dead,
is purely coincidental.

Library of Congress Cataloging-in-Publication Data

Haley, James L.
The kings of San Carlos.

1. Apache Indians—Wars, 1872–1873—Fiction.
I. Title.
PS3558.A3577K5   1987   813'.54   86-32974
ISBN: 0-385-15589-1

To Michael,
with love

The Kings of San Carlos

CHAPTER 1

I never will forget the time I met John Clum. I was the driver on his last visit to Arizona. The Historical Society gave a big dinner and reunion in his honor, and the next day I drove him up to San Carlos. The director would have done it himself but he had to leave town on business, so he left his car for me to take him.

U.S. 89 North from Tucson was one of those two-lane concrete roads with no shoulder and a dashed yellow stripe down the middle, the lanes hardly wide enough to fit one of today's cars on. Scrub brush and cactus grew right up to the edge, and you could see where pebbles and cobbles had been kicked up onto the pavement by tires where someone had pulled off to change a flat or cool the radiator. Tar squeezed up from the expansion joints at identical intervals and the tires would *tump-tump* as we passed over each one. More than that, we could feel them. The tires would buck just a little over each one so that we felt each *tump-tump* like a pulse deep inside the director's new '32 Chevy. I hated it, because it was so lulling and regulating that when we'd hit a stretch where the road had been repaired, the spacing of those joints was skewed and rapid, as though the car was having a heart attack. Lord, it was awful.

I was grateful it was only twenty miles to Oracle Junction where we turned off onto an unpaved grade that is now State 77. As we drove along the straight stretches I couldn't resist stealing glances at Mr. Clum. Even when he was strong and straight he hadn't been a tall man, and now his old frame seemed wasted within his loose white cotton shirt. His dark eyes had lost none of the quickness I had read about, but instead of the skin around them being taut and alert as in his pictures, his eyes rode lower on his face, nestled in soft, rippling bags below them, lapped by wrinkled, sliding lids above. I could tell, though, it was only the skin that had collapsed; the eyes were still the same, darting and comprehending.

At his dinner speech the night before, he had apologized for not being as tan as he used to be. The only exercise he was allowed now was tending his rosebushes at home in Los Angeles, and he wasn't permitted out in the sun without his hat. The downy fringe of white hair around the back of his head was still thick, but his bald top was quite tender and pale. The only color there lay in a few surfacing blood vessels and some brown age spots that seemed to sit on top of his skin like daubs of wet clay. But the most remarkable thing was his nose. I had seen the old photographs that showed he had a strong, straight, almost Roman nose, but in his old age its strength had slid flabbily down to the end, so that it hung in a bulb over his clipped white mustache. I knew that men's bodies sagged with age, but I never realized that it happened, independently, to noses.

His quick eyes caught me suddenly in my study and he turned his head to look at me, fully and searchingly. "What's the matter, son? Haven't you ever seen a legend before?" He cracked a sardonic smile and I saw he still had his own teeth. Flawed, but still his own teeth.

He wasn't the least bit uncomfortable about carrying his own fame, and I had to start laughing. "I sort of know you already," I said, and told him I was the one who had been copyediting the articles he had been sending to the *Historical Quarterly* about his days as an Apache Indian agent on the Arizona frontier. Of course, we knew he had been giving the same material to the *New Mexico Quarterly,* but we never let on that we minded it. We knew how deeply he believed in his message, and just couldn't begrudge him trying to find the largest audience he could.

"So you're the red pencil." He nodded.

I admitted that I was.

"Well, if you're the red pencil, who the hell is the blue pencil?"

I told him emphatically that the director himself edited the content. Memoirs as important as his weren't about to be entrusted to anyone less than the director. That seemed to satisfy him, because he smiled when he took his eyes off me and looked back out the windshield.

At some length we crossed a low bridge over a wide, dry arroyo. "Why, that's the Gila," he said with some surprise.

I acknowledged that it was.

The road followed the river east for a couple of miles before turning north, and there was a road sign pointing that this was the way to Globe.

Mr. Clum asked, "Isn't this dam on the Gila?"

I answered that it was.

"You mean there's no road from here to up there?"

"Nossir." I explained how the highway went up to Globe, east over to Peridot and then back down to where they were building the dam.

He looked fitfully back over his shoulder and said, "Pull over here." I eased the car off the grade at the first bare spot of level ground, and he opened his door, saying, "Come on, boy, let's take a stretch."

I stopped the engine and got out, walking around the front of the car to stand next to him. His upper body seemed engulfed in that loose white shirt; his belt rode higher across the front than the back, which made his chest seem more sunken than I figured it probably was, and he had put his rumpled gray hat on his head. He stood with his hands on his hips, looking forward up the road and then backward toward the river. "What jackass laid this thing out, anyhow?"

I begged his pardon, and supposed that Globe had overtaken San Carlos in commercial importance, and roads went where the business was. He snorted a little but didn't say anything. Back toward the river there were a couple of pretty-good-sized mesquite trees with a log underneath, and I asked Mr. Clum if he would like to rest there and eat lunch—I had brought some sandwiches and a bottle of water. He mulled the prospect with what I figured was that famous mental economy of his, then he looked down and shook his head. "No, no, we can eat on the way. If there's going to be a show we'd best not hold it up. Besides, if I get sittin' down comfortable out here I might not be able to get back up again."

I didn't want to stop talking to him, and given a choice, preferred to become a pest than to squander the opportunity of a conversation with John Clum. "How many of your old Indians do you think will be there?"

"Can't say, boy. Probably not all of them remember me very kindly. But Indians always like a good show. Blowing up the old Agency buildings will be a heck of a show."

I asked him if it didn't make him a little sad that the Apache Agency he had built was going to be demolished, and the ruins would be at the bottom of the new lake. He denied it. "Progress is the name of the game, kiddo. Apaches couldn't live in the Stone Age forever; us horse-and-buggy folks gotta move on over, too." Suddenly he shook his head. "Aw, hell, this is silly. I'm getting old and I can't remember your name. They just told me last night."

His calling me "boy" and "kiddo" had seemed so natural, it never occurred to me that he was struggling to recall my name. I smiled my biggest. "It's all right. I'm Alex."

"Damn! I knew it was something easy. Alex what?"

"Clay."

"That doesn't sound Jewish."

It addled the tar out of me that he should guess I was Jewish, and I asked him how he knew.

"Well, by golly, you were starin' at my honker, so I was starin' at yours!"

Suddenly it was hard to watch the road for fear of showing him my profile. I looked over at him and he was grinning to beat the band—but gently, hoping he hadn't given offense. "Clay, huh?" he said. "I'll call you Mudpies. That'll help me remember."

I had been given a John Clum nickname! I was so proud I could have jumped right out the window and hopped the rest of the way to San Carlos. God, I would have given anything to have seen him in his heyday as the *enfant terrible* of the federal Indian Service—to have been there when he first got off the stage in Tucson in August of 1874.

CHAPTER 2

It would have helped if he had known what he was doing—if he had some inkling of what was expected of him, what his duties were.

But, he didn't. From the time he had gotten his orders, his life had been a blur. All the clothes and belongings he meant to take he fit into two carpet satchels and a large trunk. The topmost item in the latter was a Navajo rug, his one souvenir from his trip to New Mexico the year before. He went out as correspondent with the Meteorological Survey; the trader had called it an "eye-dazzler," made for a chief. John couldn't swear to such an assertion, but it was undeniably beautiful, an undyed woolen background with a pattern of red and yellow blazes outlined in black. He folded it gently up and laid it atop his suits, then got on the train from Rochester to Cincinnati to say good-bye to Mary, then down to Elmira to see his parents.

Of them all, his mother was the only one to question what he thought he was doing, undertaking to manage an Indian Agency when he hadn't the least shade of experience with them. Poor Mama—always worrying, always looking out for him, looking over his shoulder from whatever distance, just because he had always been small for his age and got into fights when other kids called him a runt. When he would come home with his clothes torn and his face battered, he could never make her understand that he had won most of those fights.

Of course he could manage Indians. Hadn't he shown "considerable administrative skill"—their very words—when he went to New Mexico with the weather survey? That was even Apache country, and they had seen no hint of trouble. All that ghastly stuff in the eastern newspapers was just printed to sell copies.

Still, as the train rumbled its transcontinental way west, little things in the back of John Clum's mind began to pull at him. As the endless grass of Kansas slipped by, John watched from his gently rocking car the huge white piles of buffalo bones stacked by the tracks, all that remained of the bison herds wiped out by the Dodge City hunters a couple of years before. The bone collectors got paid eight dollars a ton for them, to be shipped east and crushed into fertilizer. Every several miles was a water tower, and by it a tall, silently bleached ossuary of buffalo bones.

It was little things that nagged him, paltry things, little pairs of twos in his mind's eye that he kept adding together without getting four. When he stopped in Washington, why hadn't he been allowed to meet the President? When he got his commission his name was there on the bottom, big as life: U. S. Grant. They knew that at some point it was inevitable that some Indian would ask him whether he had ever seen with his own eyes the Great White Father they kept hearing about. Now he would have to say no. Why had the Indian Commissioner steered him through the Department of the Interior like some kind of child who mustn't be left alone for a minute? Even when he got to meet Secretary Delano, it was only for the briefest introduction and then he was nudged out again. It was almost as if the Indian Bureau was trying to keep the Secretary from knowing too much about him, as though he, Clum, was some kind of embarrassment to them. And then, he was shuffled out of the building so fast that it was only on his own initiative that he went back in and searched out a clerk who supplied him with several previous years of Apache Agency reports. And why did the Assistant Commissioner, the official with whom he would have the most contact, when he saw Clum with the volumes under his arm, why did he register just the faintest flicker of a frown before commending his determination to make a quick study of his new position?

Ah, the books. John glanced down at his lap, to the green cloth bindings of the Government Printing Office. *Secretary of the Interior: Annual Report for 1871.* John had worked his way up to reading about the horrors of the Camp Grant Massacre, where, only some three years before, a hundred and thirty Apache women and children under army protection were butchered by a drunken mob of Arizona citizens. A hundred men had stood trial for it, every last one of them acquitted by a jury in Tucson.

By the time the train reached San Francisco John had read through the reports and agency returns. He had looked out only infrequently to see the Rockies roll by, becoming increasingly absorbed in the aftermath of the Camp Grant Massacre. The questions multiplied. The army officer who had given the Indians sanctuary was court-martialed ruthlessly, not once but three times, and then transferred out of the area. Why? Then, when the federal prosecutor brought charges against the citizens responsible, the army refused to aid in the trial. Again, why?

John Clum knew he could not fathom the answers, but he sensed that behind the questions loomed the mysterious figure of George Crook, Colonel of the 24th Infantry and commanding general of the army in Arizona.

When the train reached San Francisco John spent one evening in a hotel, writing three letters—one to his parents, one to Mary, and one to the Commissioner, outlining his thoughts on what he had learned from the reports he had read. The next morning he boarded a steamer for San Diego, and the morning after arriving there boarded the stage for Arizona.

After climbing over the coastal hills the coach dropped down into the Imperial Valley and then entered the flat, searing immensity of the Mojave Desert. The driver stopped to change horses at the stations every twenty miles, the coach leaping and lurching between outposts like a rabbit trying to get from shade to shade before the desert sun could finish it off. By the middle of the afternoon John had grown so sleepy in the hot, rocking stage that just before he closed his eyes, the feeling swept over him that it was the coach staying in place and the white desert earth that flew beneath them. He awakened with a start just as they pulled into the ferry station on the Colorado River, opposite Yuma, Arizona.

They spent the night in Yuma and boarded another stage in the morning. When the driver told them at breakfast that they would reach Tucson that evening, John dressed in his best brown duck suit, expecting to make his round of official courtesy calls at the same time, and get an early start for San Carlos the next morning. They made good time, and the coach pulled to a stop at the Tucson station almost before John was aware they had entered the town. One minute they were in the desert, watching Sentinel Peak slip by the windows, the next minute they were in town—nothing like outlying ranches or neighborhoods to inform them of its nearness. Even the town lots that had been cleared for building were scarcely distinguishable from the cactus-studded pebbles of the desert.

At the station the driver jumped down and shook hands around with the men who had gathered. "Go get Mr. Oury," he said, "I got a mighty important passenger." John opened the coach door for himself just as he heard the driver continue, "That young feller there is going to be the Indian Agent at San Carlos."

John just began to smile at this recognition when it was rubbed from his face by a smattering of chuckles. One of the men, a big, burly, bearded fellow, hooked his thumbs under his belt. "Just how you figger you're gonna tame them Indians, sonny?"

"By treating them fairly, and letting them know I expect the same from them, and rewarding them for good behavior."

The bearded man laughed, making a noise like a handsaw biting through pine lumber, and John drew himself up. "Perhaps if such a method had been tried before you wouldn't have had the trouble with the Apaches that you have."

"But, young man." John turned to see a middle-aged woman, one of two ladies in dark dresses who had stopped to listen to the conversation, shading themselves with parasols. "Do you really expect you can keep your scalp long enough for your plan to work?"

"Madam, any Indian who expects to lift my scalp would be wasting his time."

John doffed his bowler, and there was an explosion of guffaws. "Why, he's bald as an egg!" The heavy fringe of hair over his ears and around the back of his head had concealed that fact until he removed his hat. Theirs was a reaction that he had come not just to expect, but to use with some talent; at least now they were laughing with him instead of at him.

A third woman approached, a strikingly handsome lady in green and gold velvet. As she neared, the first two ladies looked away and walked off without speaking, but she seemed to take no notice. "Howdy, mister," she said with friendly huskiness, holding out her hand. John took it. "My name's Titania. The boys here call me Titsy for short." John felt his crest fall about two inches. "I got a little hotel establishment up the street there. If you don't have other plans for lodging we'd be mighty happy to put you up and give you a good night's sleep."

"Uh," John stammered, then smiled. "Thank you. I shall certainly, ah, consider it."

"I gotta be goin'. You come by and see us, now."

When she was out of hearing one of the men slapped John on the back. "You stay at her place, sonny, you'll get a restful night, all right, but you won't get a wink of sleep."

John scratched at his nose. "So I gathered."

"You must be Mr. Clum." The voice was deep and sonorous, the words spoken slowly and with a grave kind of dignity, but not without a touch of theatrical feign, in the manner common to preachers and politicians. The knot of men parted and John beheld a man he might have pictured as the town undertaker; tall and gaunt, made taller by an old-fashioned stovepipe hat that was as black as his suit and the narrow black velvet tie whose strings curled down into the bright white maze of ruffles that fronted his shirt. The tall man nodded. "Hello, boys."

The coarse men with whom John had been speaking seemed reduced almost to schoolboys as they chorused, "Howdy, Mr. Oury," it seemed with one voice. It was friendly enough, but John detected a distance, a deference. They did not offer him their hands, and he stepped through them, holding out his own two hands to John. "Welcome to Tucson. I am William Sanders Oury. Perhaps you've heard of me."

John held out his hand. "Indeed I have," concealing for the moment the wave of revulsion that surged out of his recent memory that Oury, he had just read on the train, was a principal though murky figure in the Apache massacre at Camp Grant. There were those who suspected him of masterminding the whole plot, but nothing could be proved.

John looked up—far up, for he was short and Oury was very tall— into a face that he was sure now should be the undertaker's, with sunken eyes and hollow cheeks, a thin beard. The face was vaguely reminiscent of Abraham Lincoln's, but without Lincoln's compassion and humility—as though when the sainted President died, a malignant counterpart or caricature continued to walk the earth in his guise. John's wariness was visceral; it made the hackles rise on his neck, but it was instinctive. Of facts he knew none on which to base his distaste, or speak of it.

"Thank you," he said calmly. "That is very kind. And if I may say so, I hope that my work at San Carlos will help make Arizona a better and safer place to live for all its people—red and white." He said the last three words slowly, the way a man leaves his hand on a chess piece until he is certain of the move.

"Indeed." Oury smiled, showing long yellow teeth that lapped each other crookedly, streaked with the brown stains of teeth that had sucked too many chaws. It was a smile not, as John sensed, at the sentiment, but one that recognized his words not as a greeting, but a move. They understood each other. "Some other prominent gentlemen and I will be dining this evening at the Excelsior Hotel. If you will be pleased to join us, you will find that it can also accommodate you comfortably for the night."

"I will look forward to dinner with you and your friends." John squeezed Oury's hand with finality and withdrew his own.

"Shall we say eight o'clock?"

"Suits me fine."

Oury bowed and turned away, not seeing one of the boys poke John familiarly in the ribs. "What about Miss Titania?"

The man's breath nearly made John faint. "Well, I guess one of you fellows will have to stand in for me. Think you can manage?"

The spread of chuckles left John figuring which of them to ask for help in getting his bags to the hotel, but he left off that thought when out of the corner of his eye he saw Oury press a coin into the stage driver's palm and gesture up the street. At once the driver and the man who had ridden shotgun the last leg of the trip hefted John's two satchels and trunk. Hastily John excused himself from the others and followed after the two to the Excelsior.

The sun was barely up the next morning when John paid his hotel bill and ate breakfast, then sauntered into the nearby livery stable and found the proprietor forking hay. "How's the federal credit?"

A ruddy-looking Scandinavian looked over his shoulder. "You army or Indian Bureau?"

He was startled to be taken so literally. "Indian Bureau."

"Well, I don't know. You got vouchers?"

"Of course."

The entry of a third voice in the stable caused them both to adjust their gaze, the same, solemn preacher's voice that greeted John at the stage. "It's all right, Sam. He's genuine."

"Whatever you say, Mr. Oury. Just list up what you need and write it down."

John walked over to Oury and with an unease he still couldn't explain, took his hand again. "Thank you once more. I am indebted to you for your help."

Again Oury laid his other hand atop John's. "You are welcome to my help. And you must remember when you are at your duties, and discover what a truly isolated place San Carlos is, that you must come to me for any other service I can give." He turned and left with a heavy airiness, almost flowing out the door like a ghost.

John turned back into the livery stable. "Well, let's see. I'll need to rent a good strong horse from you, and I guess this buckboard here will do admirably. When I get to San Carlos I'll have them sent back down to you."

"Oh, very well." Sam acted as though he didn't want to give up the buckboard, walking slowly over to it and then pushing at a dark brown blanket lying lumpily in its bed. "Up, Edwin! Up!"

The blanket was so particled with bits of straw and stable matter that John hadn't noticed it before, but then it made a movement, like a rat in a feed bag, and syllables issued from it. "Wha— What?"

The far end of the blanket curled back and the sleepy face of an unkempt young man appeared, more bits of straw sticking out from his fine blond hair and the thin, scraggly beard that patched his face. He blinked his bloodshot, watery brown eyes. "What is it?"

"This gentleman here has commandeered your bed for government business. You gotta roll up and go elsewheres."

Edwin pushed himself out of the back of the buckboard and began rolling up his blanket; one of the times he pulled on it an empty whiskey bottle rolled off the wagon and hit the ground with a clunk. When he was done, John pulled two quarters out of his change pocket. "I am sorry to have discommoded you like this. Please go have some breakfast for your trouble. But mind you, make sure it is a solid breakfast. Nothing to drink but coffee or milk."

Edwin looked confused. "Milk?"

"No whiskey, or I shall take the money back. Is it a deal?"

Edwin stared glumly at the coins and then nodded, closing his long white fingers around them. "Why, I shall call forth a veritable banquet upon your generosity." He swaggered out of the stable, tripping only once, over an iron wheel hoop lying in the yard.

John pulled an octavo voucher out of his coat pocket and began to fill it out as Sam hitched the horse to the buckboard. "That was a sure waste of four bits, young fella. You don't really think he'll go eat ham and eggs on it, do you?"

John handed him the voucher. "Yes, I do."

"Why?"

"Because he looked hungry. Besides, if I see him drinking, I will break the bottle over his head. Then I will give him another fifty cents, and if he knows what is good for him, he will be hungry." John patted the horse on the withers. "Why don't you toss his feed bag in the back so I can feed him properly on the road?"

"Oh, well, sure." Sam's surprise was the only indication that John had offered more than the customary care.

"Just add the cost of his oats to the voucher."

"Oats?" Sam began to chuckle. "Lord help me if you ain't the greenest thing to pop up since last spring. You won't find oats within a hundred miles of here."

"What do you feed them?"

"Barley. You roll it like oats, 'cept it's barley."

John shrugged. "Well, barley then."

Sam hefted a bucket of grain into the wagon bed directly behind the seat. "No, I won't charge you for it. You know how to drive a horse?"

"Same way I'd drive a man: kindly. You want to tell me where the general store is?"

"Up this way," Sam pointed, "second street on your right."

"Pleasure doing business with you; I'll send your outfit back down to you in a week or so."

John returned to the hotel long enough to collect his trunk and satchels, and in another couple of minutes reined in before the general store. He stayed a moment on the seat, writing up a list of what he would need to get as far as San Carlos. He paid for the goods with another voucher, this time without Oury's presence, but with a remark from the proprietor that Oury had approved his credit. Suddenly the spillage from Oury soured, as John recognized what it was about it that made him uncomfortable. "If Mr. Oury has been approving my credit, I imagine he could disapprove it just as easily, if he chose."

"You betcha." The proprietor nodded.

Next to his luggage in the buckboard John loaded the beans and coffee and flour and bacon he had bought, some canned goods, and the water barrel, which he filled with buckets from the pump behind the store.

He was almost ready to set out when he noticed across the street what appeared to be the principal restaurant in the town. Casually John strolled up to the corner before crossing over, then spied into the restaurant over the curtains as he walked by. Edwin sat at a near table, a knife in one hand and fork in the other, a gingham napkin stuffed into the throat of his shirt. Both cheeks bulged out like a chipmunk's.

John hadn't meant to be seen, but Edwin caught sight of him looking in, smiled hugely, and waved with the fork. John smiled and nodded, touching the brim of his bowler. Then he returned to the buckboard, released the brake, and headed north out of town.

CHAPTER 3

The road he took soon led more east than north, through the pass between the Rincon and Santa Catalina mountains. It was here John stopped to eat and to rest the horse, offering him water from the bucket before tying on his feed bag.

The desert was different from what he remembered in New Mexico—lower and hotter. Out of Tucson the thin brush consisted mostly of palo verde and creosote bush, the low cactuses like prickly pear and cholla towered over by the high-ribbed saguaro, their arms spreading like crosses on which to crucify the thirsty. Ocotillo, too, were common, their long, languid stalks bending in the hot wind like so many buggy whips rooted in a single pot. As he got up into the pass he began to see bear grass and sotol, but of trees there were none save the occasional mesquite, the thinness of whose branches was the only evidence of the struggle of their life's work, carried on grimly, underground, the continual root-probing to find enough water to keep going.

The road he was on led to Fort Grant, and after resting he drove twelve or fifteen miles farther on, passing the fork in the trail that led up to the old Camp Grant, which had been abandoned not long after the massacre. He made camp for the night in a small, rocky vale whose profusion of shrubs told him that water must lie near the surface. In the center of its floor was a dry wash, with rocks smooth and rounded from bearing the sudden freshets of the thunderstorms. In a kind of grotto at the head of the wash he found a few rocks damp to the touch, covered with a patchy carpet of moss. Below them was a small bowl-like hollow, dry now but with a light-colored water ring like an unscrubbed bathtub. During its season it must be a tolerably refreshing spring.

John drove as far up the wash as he could, which wasn't far, before cooking dinner and bedding down in the back of the wagon. He slept wonderfully that night, breathing in the dusty, spicy desert fragrance like a tonic, and awakened at first light keen and refreshed.

He raised Fort Grant that afternoon, the windowpanes and white-painted porch trim glinting distantly from the rock houses on Officers'

Row. As he drew near, all the buildings in the post seemed stoutly built and well maintained; nobody took notice of him until he stopped at the edge of the parade ground and inquired of a white-haired sergeant with a neck like red leather where he might find the commanding officer.

"Where did you come from?" he demanded in astonishment.

"Tucson."

The sergeant pointed back up the road. "You rode through that country alone?"

"I did, yes."

"Boy, you're not lookin' to watch your grandchildren grow up, are you?"

"You apparently believe that I was in some danger." John's voice assumed a lofty tone that annoyed the old sergeant.

"Let's just say that your living presence here will be regarded as something of a curiosity. The lieutenant's house is the big one on the left of the row down there; it's past quittin' time now so he ought to be there."

John thanked him and headed the wagon down a manicured, rock-lined drive that surrounded the parade ground. Officers' Row was well kept, with curtains visible in the windows and each little yard fronted by a brightly whitewashed picket fence. The largest house was one story of rock and a second one of mansard dormers; there was a full-width front porch sparingly trimmed in gingerbread. It looked so much like the house of Mary's parents in Cincinnati that it jarred him to see it transported to this place.

He braked the wagon and entered the yard through the tightly hinged white gate, mounted four wooden steps up to the porch, and knocked on the door as he took off his hat. Presently it was answered by a robust-looking man in a partly unbuttoned officer's tunic; he appeared in his prime, with bright blue eyes and short brown hair just salted with gray. The only incongruity was his beard, trimmed in an out-of-fashion imperial. "Yes?" he asked.

"I am looking for the commanding officer of this post."

"You found him."

John extended his hand, which the lieutenant took. "My name is John Clum, I came to pay my respects. I'm on my way to San Carlos to take up duties as the new Apache Indian agent."

"Really? Well, welcome, but I wasn't aware that any change in administration was being contemplated there."

John smiled as disarmingly as he could. "I guess I am a pretty well-kept secret."

"Come in, my name is Abner Merriman." He led John into a parlor generously furnished with a rosewood suite, and poured two shot glasses of whiskey from a tray on the sideboard. "Cut the dust," he said, handing one to John and downing his in a gulp. "You're traveling alone?"

"Yes, my survival seems to have already drawn the admiration of one of your sergeants."

"Sit down, please. You must understand that there has been quite a lot of disruption on the Tucson road in the past few weeks. You didn't see any sign of trouble?"

John shook his head, as much from the bite of the whiskey as in denial. "Not even a smoke signal," he said.

"Have you ever been in this part of the country before?"

"I was in New Mexico last year with the Meteorological Survey, but this is my first service with the Indian Bureau."

The last remark seemed to provoke a scowl, but the officer was too courtly to jump on the point. "Perhaps," John went on, "if you could fill me in on recent events and conditions here, I would be very glad to have your advice."

"Forgive me." Merriman gave a little wave of his hand, then began to button his tunic, which when he was done made him look much more formidable. "I didn't mean to look so stern. It's just that, with things so unsettled out here, one must question whether a change from military to civilian administration would be well advised at this time."

"Yes, please go on."

"The new agent." Lieutenant Merriman repeated the phrase with an importance that seemed patronizing but not caustic. "Well, come with me. I've been keeping a guest here you'll want to meet." He headed out the door in that robust way some officers have, the good ones who prefer riding horses to riding chairs. When he dropped down off the porch he turned to make sure John was following in his wake. "You ever hear of Eskiminzin?"

Instantly John recognized the name from the books he had read on the train. "He was the chief who went into Camp Grant to make a treaty with Lieutenant Whitman."

"Yeah, that's what he said. Of course, you know he's a lying, thieving cutthroat."

"Is that a warning?"

"If you come out here ready to believe anything he tells you, it is."

All his unanswered questions surfaced in John's mind as they strode across the beige, packed, sandy earth. "Well, I'll just wait and hear him out."

Merriman didn't let the subject drop. "Of course, the trouble was as much Whitman's fault as the Indians'. He had no authority to reach any kind of agreement with those Apaches and shouldn't have led them on."

"But I thought his job was to control the Indians in his area."

Merriman had hit a stride and John was working to keep up, but the officer shot him a glance that was disdainful and sidelong. "Control of Indians has never been assumed to mean the same thing as peace with them, Mr. Clum. You will come to learn that." They passed between two buildings on the opposite side of the parade ground, then down a hot sunny slope to a fenced compound with a small rock hut in it, like a dog run or chicken coop. Outside its gate a sentry stood at ease, tiredly sweating under his felt campaign hat, leaning on his carbine. As the two men approached he formed up into a kind of attention, not unlike how a thirsty cactus swells after a rain, and saluted the officer. "Good afternoon, sir."

"Good afternoon, Corporal." Merriman returned the salute. "I have a visitor to see your prisoner. This gentleman is to be the new Indian agent at San Carlos."

The corporal had set his rifle aside and was slipping a key into the padlock on the gate. "Is that a fact," he smirked, and then added almost as an afterthought, "sir."

The gate did not swing on proper hinges; when the corporal lifted the gatepole out of its hole and held it back it was more like opening a passage in a fence. When the two were inside the compound a stocky, middle-aged Indian emerged from the rock hut, shackled at both the wrists and ankles. He walked forward a few paces but then stopped, apparently embarrassed by the rattling of his chains.

"Chief," said Merriman when they drew near, "this man's name is Clum. He is the new Apache agent at San Carlos."

"Hello." John offered his hand and left it hanging there as Eskiminzin looked from Merriman to him with no discernible expression; he lowered his eyes for a second to see—and be seen to see—John's open hand.

"You agent now?" he asked placidly.

"Yes, I am."

Eskiminzin held out not his hands but two fists, with the arc of the chain hanging beneath. "You tell me, maybe, why Gray Fox do this to me?"

"Who?"

Lieutenant Merriman interrupted at John's elbow. "That's what they call General Crook."

"Crook." John nodded.

"You're in chains, Indian," Merriman continued, "for starting a war against the government of the United States, and for killing innocent citizens."

"Soldier make big talk when he got Injun in chains—tell bunch of lies. Take chains off, maybe have to speak true when Injun free."

Merriman snorted an obscenity, and John thought he better speak up. "Eskiminzin, the President appointed me your agent because he wants to help your Apache people. I came to this place because I wanted to meet you, and I want to hear your side of things. Will you tell me what all has happened between your people and the government?"

Eskiminzin had let his hands fall down to his thighs, his gust of defiance having passed like one of those little dust devils that throws sand in your eyes and then disappears without a trace. But his misery was unfeigned as he looked from one to the other. With an odd kind of measure he said, "Injun can't talk. Got chains on hands and feet, just like chains on tongue." He held out his hands again to John. "You agent now, maybe you take irons off, then we make good talk."

Instinctively John knew it was a loaded question, not just asking for the chains to be removed but testing his new agent's power with the military. If John had influence, the chains would come off; if not, then he was like the other agents and need not be listened to with any great attention. The sheer subtlety of it was wonderful.

"What do you think, Lieutenant? Can't you take his chains off while he talks to me?"

Merriman looked around the perimeter of the enclosure and then beyond. The guardhouse and yard sat in a clearing, so called not because any trees grew on the hot flat, but because the brush had been cut away and the larger rocks removed to form a bare yard of some size. It was a gesture of respect for the skill with which Apache warriors could stalk utterly undetected to within spitting distance of the wariest sentry, using for cover only the bushes and boulders of the natural desert. Some of the rocks had been used to build the guardhouse itself; the others had been carried or rolled some distance away and left—a condition, Merriman quickly realized upon assuming command, that created only increased cover for Indians to approach that far. "No, no, I'm afraid not. There are probably four or five of his people within the sounds of our voices at this moment, only we can't see them, just waiting for a chance to help him escape. While I have him, he stays in shackles."

Up to this point Merriman had seemed less erratic and irrational than John had been led to expect from army officers, and he suspected his request would not have been denied unless there truly were some danger in it. John swallowed. "Then why don't you wait outside until we're through?"

Merriman's eyes widened for a second. "Very well. I have work to do in my office. The guard will let you out when you are ready."

Once he was gone, John and the chained chief stood, sizing each other up. Eskiminzin was a short man, shorter even than John, but stout, with a barrel chest and short strong arms, stubby like the branches of a Joshua tree. His face was round and regular, not bony or angular like an Indian's was supposed to be, the copper-bronze skin as void of expression as a wooden mask. "You crazy?" he asked. "Stay in here with Injun alone, maybe kill you."

John hung his head and smiled. "No, you won't. During my whole trip out here I read as much as I could about you and your people. I read everything Lieutenant Whitman wrote about you."

"You know Whitman?"

"No, but he wrote reports to the government about how hard you were working to settle your people down."

Eskiminzin's lip pulled up; if he were an animal it would have been a growl. "Injun get big reward, this place."

"I am sorry that fellow wouldn't take your chains off, but it could be that since you are in trouble with the army, the Indian Bureau can't help you."

The Indian shrugged.

"My word, it's hot out here."

"Not bad. Gets hotter."

"Do they give you enough food and water?"

"Yes."

John shifted his weight uneasily. "There's a little shade over here. May we sit down?"

Eskiminzin turned and stepped toward the thin line of shade along the north wall of the hut, swinging his feet out to the sides so as not to foul his ankle irons. He folded his legs easily under himself and sank to the ground, looking up at John who removed his hat and seated himself. Eskiminzin's face suddenly went slack. "You got no hair!"

John made a little show of nonplus. "Well, you have plenty. Why don't you give me some?" The corners of Eskiminzin's mouth twitched up into a smile and the bronze crow's-feet at the corners of his eyes deepened, but he made no reply.

The silence grew into such a length that John remembered something his mother used to tell him, that when you don't know what to say, just go with the truth and let everything else sort itself out. "Well, Eskiminzin, I really don't know how to begin, except to say that I don't believe that any of this is your fault. But maybe you better tell me about the man you killed."

"Charlie." He nodded sadly.

"Yes." That was his name, Charles McKinley, he remembered.

"Injun not want to kill Charlie." Eskiminzin stopped to think, then heaved a heavy sigh. "Trouble, start long ago. Soldiers always chase us, shoot us up, kill people. Whitman come to Camp Grant—not this place, but old Camp Grant—my people say, go in there and see if you can make peace with those people. We did that. Whitman damn fine man, good friend. Feed us, give people work, tell ranchers, give people work. Made money, bought things. Then white people come from Tucson, bring Mexicans and Papagos, try to kill all my people. Shoot, stab, club, burn. Those not dead, I take, run away to mountains.

"Not Whitman fault. He come out with soldiers, bury my people, cry, chase killers. I tell him, all right, we still friends. We move back down, women make new wickiup."

"Wait a second. What is that?"

"House where Injun live." John nodded and the chief went on. "Pretty soon more soldiers see us, shoot up camp, chase us off. I tell Whitman, you people crazy, we leaving. We go back to mountains.

"My people say, you no good chief. Most of us dead now because you chief. Look, you still got white friend over there, Charlie. People say, you kill Charlie, or you not chief anymore. Make up your mind. So I go see Charlie. He glad see me, feed me good dinner. After that we shake hands and smoke, then me take gun and blow belly out."

"So you did kill him."

Eskiminzin nodded, expressionless. "Me chief again. Hide families in mountains, take men to war. Gray Fox beat us. I bring people in to surrender, Gray Fox put me here, people still out there." He looked up beyond the fence. "War not my fault. White people break the peace, white people to blame."

"What about Whitman? Wasn't he your friend, too? Why didn't you try to kill him?"

"Gray Fox punish Whitman because he my friend. So, we still friends. He know that, somewhere."

"You don't know where he is?"

The Indian shook his head.

"Perhaps I could try to find out for you."

He looked at him, incredulous. "You do that?"

"Yes, of course I would. Eskiminzin, tell me, if another agent came and tried as hard as Whitman did to do right by you, would you cooperate with him and do as he asked?"

"Yes."

"Well, that is what I am going to do. I am your agent now, and I am going to try my hardest to do what is best for you. That is what the government sent me here to do. The problem, as I see it, is that Washington is so far away that they don't always know what the best thing is when they give me orders. But you will know, and I will know what the best thing is, and that is what we will do, even if Washington doesn't always understand why. Will you help me in that?"

Without anger Eskiminzin held out his wrists and rattled his chains. "You not helping me now."

"I know." John reached out and tangled his own hands in the shackles. "But because I am your agent, as long as you are a prisoner part of me is a prisoner, too. After I get to San Carlos, I will go see Gray Fox and try to get him to release you. I can't force him to, at least not right away, but I will get you out as soon as I can."

Eskiminzin moved his hands together, enclosing John's in his own. "You go now, and we see."

Both men stood up, and John fixed his bowler back on his head. "The lieutenant told me a few minutes ago that the roads are dangerous and I shouldn't be traveling by myself. Is that true?"

Eskiminzin shrugged. "South," he gestured, "my people pretty good, doin' right. Chiricahuas pretty bad though. They not my people, they shoot you maybe. North," he inclined his head the other way, "you go San Carlos and not worry. My people watch out for you." He looked John up and down in a brief inspection. "Wait," he said.

John followed him to the door of the rock hut; Eskiminzin entered briefly and emerged with a stubby white feather. "You travel, you wear hat. Put feather in hat. People know you, you be safe."

John took the feather and nodded to the sentry to open the gate. He shook hands with Eskiminzin again. "If you are sincere in what we have talked about, then once you are free, we will talk many times over the years and we will be friends. I give you my word on that."

The shadows were lengthening and the day cooling as John strode back up the rise and across the parade ground to Merriman's quarters; he found the lieutenant seated on the front porch, his feet on a rail and a drink in his hand. "Well, Mr. Clum," he said, "how went your interview?"

John mounted the steps up to the porch. "He admits his crimes, but he is more sinned against than sinning, I daresay."

"You daresay. I daresay, it's getting pretty late. Why don't you accept the hospitality of our post and get a fresh start in the morning, if that is your intention. Or, if you prefer to wait a few days for the next patrol to go out, they can escort you as far as halfway to San Carlos." Merriman gestured to an empty chair beside his and John sat down.

"No, thanks, I'll head on tomorrow."

The officer looked at him evenly, finally sniffing with a twitch of his nose. "I can see how a civilian might regard this assignment as something of a feather in his cap, but don't you think that's a bit obvious?"

He had forgotten about the feather and laughed, removing the hat and regarding it. "Just a little gift from him to me," he said.

Dinner that evening was the best he had since leaving San Francisco, attended by Fort Grant's other two officers, whom John probed for particulars of the local terrain, conditions, Indian relations, and politics. He didn't know what was at the bottom of the trouble with the Apaches, but he felt certain that if there were matters of greed involved, politics could not be far removed. After he retired he discovered that the guest room of Merriman's quarters came with a huge zinc bathtub, and the services of an enlisted orderly to provide buckets of hot water. John couldn't imagine when such an opportunity might present itself again, and he indulged liberally.

Merriman saw him off the next morning, leaning on the wagon brake long enough to say, "Mr. Clum, I do not consider myself a cowardly man, but I tell you I would not care to travel alone or even in a small party in the country through which you are going. Are you certain you won't wait for an escort?"

"No, but thank you, for everything." John offered his hand and Merriman took it. "I'm sure I'll be quite all right."

The officer backed off. "Good luck to you, then."

John wished he had meant his parting words as calmly as he had said them. Once beyond the protection of Fort Grant, he found himself endlessly fingering his bowler to make sure Eskiminzin's feather was visible, and even then scanning the countryside continually for the most minute sign of danger, like a deer who senses the unseen presence of a mountain lion.

The trail led roughly north until it dropped down into the shallowness of the San Simon valley, which it followed northwest before splitting off north again over a low divide to the Gila, and San Carlos.

To pry his mind off the danger of lurking hostiles John turned his thoughts to dinner the night before, turning over in his mind the clay-like shards of conversation, trying to reconstruct a whole vessel of sensibility of how the last war had started. That it was touched off by the Camp Grant Massacre was certain, but when he asked the officers what had provoked such barbarity they answered with what he began to perceive was an official army version: that Eskiminzin's people had been using Whitman's protection to sneak down to Tucson to raid ranches and steal stock, and the citizens there took matters into their own hands to end the depredations and punish the guilty.

But, no, that didn't add up. John had read the transcript of the trial, and every time that line was given the U.S. Attorney shredded it with evidence beyond dispute. Eskiminzin's people had been nowhere near Tucson. Indeed, the trial itself of the Camp Grant murderers was undertaken only because eastern reformers forced President Grant into it; there wasn't a dime's worth of support for it anywhere in Arizona. It showed every sign of a stage play whose mass acquittals were a foregone conclusion. Yet, it was not clear who stood to gain from such a horror.

The miles passed quickly. He raised San Carlos in late afternoon of the second day, soon after the road had descended into the flats of the Gila and turned upstream. As pebbles as regular as paving stones—only smaller—crunched under the iron-rimmed wagon wheels, he noticed the river flowing low and tepid for short stretches, before disappearing underground for longer stretches. After a couple of miles he discerned a large adobe barn-like structure, surrounded by corrals and outbuildings, and a smaller, residential-looking building, also of adobe and fronted by a low veranda flanked, as he could tell by standing in the wagon seat, by a rock-bordered flower bed. That must be home, he thought, and that's what he steered for.

CHAPTER 4

As he pulled up close to the main building John's eyes got big as he discovered that the flower bed was marked off not by rocks, but by heads—seven Indian heads with long black hair and no eyes and swollen, stinking tongues that stuck out past their teeth. John's stomach contracted and he felt dizzy. He reined in and slapped on the brake, then leapt down and bounded through the exact middle of the porch, as though he were afraid one of the mummifying caputs would bounce up and bite him. He burst through the door and pushed it shut with his back, his hands grasping the latch behind him.

"Can I help you, son?" He heard after a few seconds a voice that sounded like a rake dragged through wet gravel, and looked up. There was a large, stocky man about sixty years old standing foursquare in an interior doorway.

"What are those out there?" John croaked.

"What, now?"

"The heads!" He had to calm himself. "The heads."

"Ah. Criminals—murderers and such like. Executed a couple of weeks ago, they were."

"Beheaded? You behead people out here?"

"Mercy, no." The older man smiled a little. "Fugitives, they were, with bounties on that part of their anatomies you see lyin' out upon the ground. They were chased down by their own people. And, the desert bein' too hot and rugged to tote back a whole body, they bring in just the heads to claim the rewards."

John continued to stare.

"It is the only way to identify the wanted," the older man insisted.

"Well, that may be, but I want them taken away and buried as soon as possible."

"And who might you be to say so?"

"I'm John Clum, the new agent," he said, straightening himself.

"Well, then, I'm Martin Sweeney, soon-to-be drifter but temporarily a guest of the Agency, earnin' my keep as adjutant to the actin' agent,

Major Babcock." He came fully into the hall and they shook hands. "Why don't we go into the office and have some coffee?"

The building in which John found himself was an adobe dogtrot, whose breezeway had been enclosed to form a middle hall. There were no floorboards; what furniture there was sat upon packed earth. The flimsy pole roof covered, as he learned, four rooms, each with a door into the hall, two on a side.

As Sweeney opened the near door on the left side John stopped to examine it. "I can't say I've ever seen an invention like this before."

"Wood is at a premium out here. When you need lumber, the first rule is, consider what else might do and use that instead."

"So I see." John held the door by the outer frame, which was the only wood in it; thin lumber, one inch by four, with a diagonal brace. The body of it was made of canvas, stretched across the frame, the hinges cut from rawhide. There was no latch; the door just naturally swung toward the wall. "What if the wall leaned the other way?"

"Then we'd have hung it from the other side. Here." Sweeney had poured two cups of coffee from a pot on the stove at the opposite end of the room, and he handed one to John. " 'Tisn't much of an office, but it serves. Do sit yourself."

John took a seat on a rude parson's bench against a side wall, but had no sooner gotten comfortable when they heard someone enter the back door. The steps grew louder on the dirt floor and in strode a uniformed major, ordering before he caught sight of anything but Sweeney, "Sergeant, whose wagon is that?"

Sweeney swept his arm from one to the other. "Major Babcock, allow me to present Mr. Clum, the new Apache agent from the Indian Bureau."

John rose, but the officer's hand froze almost in the act of being offered. "How do you do. You must have come here at some little trouble. However, we have no need of a new agent here."

"But you must have been notified I was coming."

"I am responsible for this agency and its Indians; Sergeant Sweeney performs most of the routine duties. I see no need for a change in administration."

As he reached into a jacket pocket John planted himself where he stood, his feet a little wider apart than his shoulders. "My commission was approved at the highest levels of the government, although I was warned I might encounter some . . . purely local . . . opposition from the military. My papers."

At the veiled insult Babcock fixed his eyes hard on him, their tiny black pupils and steel gray irises making John feel as though he was looking into the barrels of two Winchesters. Babcock was perhaps fifty, but lean, with short gray hair and a beard closely trimmed to a point beneath his chin. He snatched the paper with tough, hairy fingers, finally breaking his irritated gaze to open and glance it over. "Have you any experience?"

"I interviewed for this position already, thank you."

Babcock snapped the paper back out to him. "My orders are to extend the hospitality of the Agency to you, and assist you in an orderly transition of authority. I am also to prevent you from undertaking any program or activity disruptive of the peace and safety of the Agency or my command, which frankly I interpret to mean that you will stay out of our way."

"Well, sir, it seems to me the most orderly transition of authority would be for me to hire Sweeney there out from under you."

"You may *request* that I assign Sergeant Sweeney to begin training you in agency duties."

"Oh, very well, if that makes you feel better about it. My instructions are to cooperate with the army insofar as I can do so without compromising the authority of my department. So, yes, I would appreciate his assistance." The concession was made in such a patronizing tone that the muscles stiffened in Babcock's neck.

"Carry on, Sergeant." He spun on his heel and left.

"Now look what you've done," scowled Sweeney. "You've gone and made him angry, and sure he'll take it out on me."

"Then for your sake I'm sorry."

Sweeney's belly started to bounce up and down in a laugh that was silent until he opened his big square mouth in a basso chuckle. "By God, nobody your age has sassed him like that in twenty years. I'm glad to have seen it."

"Are you going to tell me to stay out of your way, too?"

"No."

"Why not?"

Sweeney sank back deep in the leather cushion of his chair and set his cup of coffee on his belt buckle. "I can tell you, if you want to know. I was in the infantry at Chickamauga. The bugler in my company, he claimed he was seventeen, but everybody knew better. He was fourteen, maybe. He saw his best friend get killed. He threw down his bugle and picked up his friend's rifle and side arm and went ravin' toward the front. I saw him shoot six or seven rebels before they got him. Since that day, if a man tells me he can do a job, I might not always believe him but sure I don't ask to see his birth certificate."

John found himself liking this barrel-trunked old man with his shock of short white hair and big chin, and his wide mouth that turned down at the corners—turned down, curiously, even when he smiled. His tough face with its sad blue eyes was honest; Sweeney was a man who would tell you the truth, and tell you where to go if you didn't like it.

John ambled across the room and slid his cup onto a shelf beside the stove. "Think you could show me around the place?"

Sweeney kicked his feet off the table as he swallowed the last of his coffee. "Sure, though you'll be seein' most of it right around you. This here is the office and sittin' room, and the kitchen is here in back of it. We keep the stove out here, the winters bein' as cold as they are. You ever been out here in the winter?"

"No, not in the winter."

"It'll surprise you, how cold it gets." He looked askance at John as he headed into the hall. "I'm not sayin' you'll last that long, mind, but if you do."

"You taking bets?"

"Nope. I never make wagers with hard-earned money. It's a fool's waste of time. These Apache Indians don't see it that way, though. Son, I've seen an Indian bet everything he owned, lose, and walk away in nothing but a G-string. Seen that happen more than you'd care to believe." Sweeney had passed out through the front door and they stood on the packed earth of the veranda; he pointed over to the left. "That largish building about fifty yards off there is the commissary where we store the rations that we hand out on issue day to the Indians. It's also sort of a meetin' hall when the weather's bad."

"Is it often bad?"

"Nope. Next to it you see the wagon yard and corral; usually if there's a meetin' the Apaches just congregate about the wagon yard. Then beyond that you see the barn, then that little adobe house with the wire fence around it—that belongs to the agency interpreter. His name's"—Sweeney exercised his lips a couple of times to say it right—"Merejildo Grijalba."

"Oh Lord, I'd better just call him Mary Hilda and let it go."

"You do and you might be eating soft food for a few days."

"Is he on the army payroll?"

"Aye, but it doesn't matter. He lives here; he'll do the job for whoever runs the Agency."

"He's it? No other staff or workers?"

"Nope. They all got run off when the army took over the Agency. Troops have been doin' it all. You're goin' to have quite a job to get it all reorganized without 'em."

"What's that little hovel out there by itself?" John pointed off to the right.

"Ah, that'll be the guardhouse, where the bad eggs go to rot for a little while."

"No block for the headsman?"

Sweeney held the door for him to go back inside. "Don't be flip with your elders." He passed straight through the hall. "These two rooms are for sleepin', but Major Babcock prefers to stay out with his troopers. I sleep in the back one, here."

They passed through the rear door and walked out several paces. "That's the army camp over there." Sweeney pointed off to the right a little, and John saw in the middle distance several dozen white conical tents standing in rows like the neat, straight bumps of a waffle iron. Near them were supply wagons, picket lines of horses, and a short flagpole under which reposed a Parrott gun.

"What's out that way?" John swept his arm out toward the northeast, indicating a mountain range made lavender by the distance.

"El Diablo," said Sweeney.

"The devil?"

"He's about the biggest of all the chiefs in Arizona, exceptin' Cochise himself, and he just died, down south."

John pursed his lips and mused briefly. "When can I meet him?"

"He doesn't come down here anymore," answered Sweeney tightly. "He never did care much for white people, and he hasn't come down at all since the army put his nephew Eskiminzin in the hoosegow at Fort Grant."

"Does he cause trouble?" The connection registered but he didn't let on.

"Nope. Matter of fact he was the first Apache to make a treaty in Arizona, back in sixty-eight. He just don't believe in mixin' with them."

"Does he belong to this Agency?"

"Aye, he draws his rations here, if that's your meanin'."

"Perhaps Diablo ought to learn to come in when he's sent for."

Sweeney spit sullenly into a sagebrush. "Now, son, I'm goin' to tell you this and you better take it to heart. Don't move in here and go stirrin' things all up before you even know how it is. These Indians are wild, and capable of anything, even the friendly ones. When anyone wants to see Diablo, he goes out there"—he jerked his head in the direction of the mountains—"even General Crook."

"No fooling, even Crook?"

"Aye."

John thrust his hands into his pockets and looked out again at the distant mountain range. The intervening desert was so flat and featureless that the distance to it was impossible to judge. The thin, scrubby brush got smaller and smaller before fading into a wash of light brown and gray-green, and the low-lying hulk of mauve sat perfectly on the horizon, neither above it nor below it, dividing the earth from the pale blue of the sky. Such an Indian was a wonderful mystery to file away for investigation. "Tell me about Crook," he said.

"How much do you want to know?"

"How much ought I to know?"

"All of it, if you're to stay out here. Let's go back inside." Sweeney turned back toward the headquarters building and John followed, listening. "The Apaches call him Nantan Lupan. That means Chief Gray Fox. He is the only officer ever to beat them down head-on in a war. They fear him, but he's the only white power in the territory that they fear. They respect him, too. He keeps his word to them, and they respect that."

"I'll have to pay him a call soon."

"He'll not welcome you, I can tell you."

"Why not?"

The two men had regained the rear entry of the adobe dogtrot, entered, and pulled open the canvas door of the office. Sweeney sank into his large, leather-cushioned chair. "How did you prepare for this job, son? What do you know about this place, or what's . . . gone on here?" There was a sting of acid in Sweeney's voice that hadn't been there before.

John poured them both a cup of coffee and sat back on the parson's bench. It surprised him to stand examination, but he submitted to it. "I read the agency reports, and the yearly returns of the War Department and Indian Bureau."

"So you know there is some disagreement within the government on how to manage Indians." ·

John shrugged. "The War Department wants to kill them, and the Indian Bureau wants to feed them. Seems simple enough to me."

"No, it isn't at all simple. When you arrived in Tucson, I'm guessin' you met most of the official-type people."

"Yes." John nodded.

"Oury and the rest."

"Yes."

"And they all smiled and warmed you up and said you must come to them if you ever needed any help, did they not?"

"Of course. What else would they do?"

"Stay away from them, son! Vipers and Gila monsters, all of them, and they'll make you their instrument, if they can."

"Maybe it's time I heard a more complete explanation, Mr. Sweeney."

The older man chuckled for an instant. "Please, just Sweeney, like a butler. That's what I'm used to."

"Not Sergeant Sweeney?"

"Nope. Not no more. That's just his way. Now, tell me what you've heard so far about what they call the Tucson Indian Ring."

John shook his head. "Not a thing."

A restive noise issued from Sweeney's jowls, at once annoyance at having to begin at the beginning, but also an oddly paternal tolerance of being John's first source of enlightenment. "While you were in town," he rolled slowly, "I'll not suppose you made the acquaintance of a certain Mr. Junior." He nodded, confident.

"I didn't, no."

"That's because they ran him out of town. Or rather, he left for reasons of his health, as they say. He spoiled their party, don't you see?"

"How?"

"It's not all as simple as you come out here and say the army wants to kill Indians and the Bureau wants to feed 'em and civilize 'em and whatnot. The Bureau people out here have been crooked as a barrel of snakes, and the last agent they sent out here was the worst one of 'em all, he was."

"Dr. Wilbur was a temporary acting agent from Tucson, not from the Bureau."

"No matter. He was a civilian. You want to know how he ran things? He owned a store over in Globe. When the issue rations and supplies would come out for the Indians he'd send 'em over to his store and sell 'em cut-rate to his friends. The Apaches never saw the stuff. Elijah Junior worked for the beef contractor that supplied the reservation. He knew the weight reports had been falsified so the government would pay for more cattle than they got. He knew a lot about it—everything, practically. Nobody ever thought he would turn state's evidence. He was a mousy little fellow, but he sang like a canary bird and blew the whole operation sky-high. That's how the Ring works; the Bureau people help keep up the army contractors until they can get a war a'goin', then the army contractors remember their friends until things settle back down again. It's like a damn reciprocatin' steam engine. When General Crook heard about it he went on a rampage, he did, rode into San Carlos with three companies of cavalry ready to shoot anything that moved.

"Wilbur got out just in time, but managed to convince some of the chiefs that Crook was comin' to kill them. Started the worst war in ten years, and Crook had to put it down. After that, he sent Major Babcock over to administer things properly, and you're the first Bureau man to dare show your face around here since. Now do you see?"

"Why did Junior turn on them? Weren't they paying him enough?"

"It was his conscience. Lyin', cheatin', stealin', connivin'—got too heavy for him to bear."

"Don't you think I could convince Crook I'm not like that?"

"Doesn't matter. It's the Indian Bureau system you represent to him; that is where the fault lies."

"How high up does the corruption go?"

"High. Certainly some of the bureaucrats in Washington are involved, but we can't know who."

John swallowed, took a long draw from his tin cup of coffee, and swallowed again. Slowly, the behavior of those Indian Bureau men in Washington began to make sense. He swirled his coffee around in the cup. "This is a pretty cold feeling to find out I've been had."

"Must be."

"You're an army man, what about you? Why are you talking to me like this? Aren't you giving me more help than Babcock intended?"

"I don't know. Maybe. I've been chasin' Indians since the Civil War. I know 'em pretty well. To them it's a man's heart that makes the difference. Maybe I feel like you could do some good out here. I don't know."

"What do you think I should do?"

"Son, I've been mustered out and I'll be leavin' within days. It isn't up to me to tell you what to do."

John nodded, thinking fast. Here was one man, at least, who wouldn't turn on him. He mustn't let him go. "I gather you know the local Indians better than Major Babcock—you're the one who deals with them day to day."

"Aye. Myself, and Grijalba."

"Can I ask you to stay long enough to arrange a meeting between me and the chiefs?"

Sweeney smiled slowly. "You don't think the major will throw me out if he finds me helpin' you so much?"

"On the contrary, it is I who will be throwing him out."

Sweeney's lips formed a sarcastic "O" as he nodded gravely. "I'll ask around in the mornin' and see what the natives say to it. For now"—he gulped the last of his coffee, then raised his feet from the floor and kicked out, using the momentum to get to his feet—"why don't you toss your bedroll and gear into my room, then go bed your horse down. I'll get over to the mess tent and fetch us back some supper. I'll not speak for you, but I'm starved."

He was gone before John could gather further particulars about the meal, and finding himself alone he poked into the rooms across the hall. The front one he found closely packed with boxes and crates. In the second he found Sweeney's cot, its bedding neatly made up—which struck him as odd, for he hadn't picked Sweeney as much of a house-keeper—and a small, rough-sawn chest of drawers, or lowboy, with a basin and pitcher on top. A small mirror with a flaking, blue-painted frame hung by a string from a nail driven into a crack in the adobe.

His eye followed the wall up to the roof of carrizo reeds, laid across and weighted on willow poles, and then back down to the dirt floor, which gave birth to the adobe wall as easily as it might a rock or cliff wall. Much of his budget, he mused, should go into construction.

He went back outside under the mesquite-trunk porch, his senses assaulted again by the stench from the rotting heads. He jumped into the wagon, holding his breath until he rounded the corner of the building, then pulled around to the back door. He was unrolling his blankets in the wagon bed when he looked up and saw Sweeney returning with two large plates laden with stew, beans, and hard biscuits. "What's the matter, I'm not good enough to eat with your friends?"

Sweeney would have taken offense if he hadn't seen John smiling. "Nope, let us say I'm doubtin' whether you're seasoned enough for their company." He handed John one of the plates and they entered the right rear room, the kitchen, that had its own door to the outside. Sweeney poured them two cups of water from a bucket pegged to the wall, just flavoring each cup with a dribble of whiskey he got out of a closed cabinet, and they sat and ate. "Those soldiers have no use for a civilian Indian agent, and their brand of humor can play mighty rough on a tenderfoot, beggin' your pardon." He toasted him. "Between those two considerations, they might have you ridin' out of here before you ever lay eyes on an Apache."

The stew was thick and hot, and went down pleasantly; it was dark outside by the time they were through. From the same cabinet where he got the whiskey Sweeney pulled out a jar of jam for the last of their biscuits. Before he sat down again he went into the front room long enough to slide a pot of coffee onto a stove lid to boil. When he returned John saluted him with his cup. "Sweeney, you look after me like a perfect gentleman. You're hired."

The corners of his wide mouth turned down and he laughed, showing a full complement of big square teeth. "No," he shook his head. "No chance of that, son. Six years I've been lookin' for a ticket out of this territory. I'll not be turned aside now."

"Well, whatever you say." The moment was too conducive to contentment to worry about that now. There would be time enough tomorrow to plot how to keep him. "It's such a beautiful night I think I'll sleep out tonight."

Sweeney nodded. "I saw you makin' up your bed." He hesitated with some discomfort before adding, "I could move back out to the camp, if you want the room."

"What? Absolutely not, I wouldn't hear of it. You stay here where you're comfortable. I can move my stuff in tomorrow—unless you'd rather not share the room."

"No, no, that's fine with me." Sweeney's mouth then screwed up in response to some interior amusement. "Besides, having somebody twitchin' around on the floor at night might scare off some of the crawlin' things."

In the wagon that night John slept like a log, lulled by the night sounds from the distant army camp and only occasionally disturbed by an errant vapor from the front porch.

CHAPTER 5

John was more tired than he thought, and the coming of first light made no impression on his reverie. When he finally woke up it was all at once after a booming explosion, whose concussion hit him like somebody slapping both ears at once. He awakened sitting bolt upright, having been oblivious to his own yelp and flailing of limbs to the four directions. He turned one way and saw Sweeney standing in the whole width of the kitchen door, laughing at him from a throaty depth John couldn't reach even when he tried to sing baritone. He turned the other way and saw a curl of smoke rise from the Parrott gun beneath the flagpole. There was a few seconds' silence before Old Glory snaked smartly up the pole to a bugle salute and military commands half shouted and half shrieked that he couldn't make out.

John shook his head. "Oh, mother dear." He looked back at the kitchen door but Sweeney was gone. He ambled over to the outhouse behind the commissary, stretching as he went, and on returning found the kitchen empty and Sweeney in the front office with ledger books laid out on the desk in front of him. "Is there coffee?" John ventured.

Sweeney leaned his head toward the stove. "Help yourself." John's eyes cleared with a couple of swallows, before Sweeney continued, "I pulled out the books so's you could see how we keep shop. Give you something to do while I ride out and talk to the chiefs."

"You don't think I should go out with you?"

Sweeney considered it. "No, it'll make a better impression to wait, and introduce you tonight like you're a real somebody."

John snagged for a second on the intimation that he really wasn't a somebody, but let it go.

Sweeney reached out to the edge of the desk and took up his hat, a battered blue kepi left from the war, and stood up, turning a last couple of pages in one of the ledgers. "It's all here. The more you can figure out for yourself the less I'll be havin' to explain to you. You'll find your breakfast in the warmin' bin there; we'll be back around noontime."

John had just started to ask who was going to accompany him when they heard the front door open and shut, and a short stocky Mexican strode into the room. With broad courtesy Sweeney exaggerated, "Are you ready, señor?"

"*Sí.*" The man was wearing a dun-colored poncho and a sombrero that hid all of his features above shaggy gray eyebrows; and most of the rest of his face, from just beneath the eyes on down, was obscured by a beard that looked like short, thick, curly black-and-white wool. Only his nose protruded, short, crooked, and deeply pored. He looked at John, his eyes dark, sharp, and animated. "And so, you are he who cannot say my name. I am Merejildo Grijalba." He held out his hand, strong and hairy.

John shook hands with an embarrassed shrug. "I'm afraid your linguistic skills leave mine behind."

"Can you say *gringo?*"

Sweeney started to roar, but managed to stifle it into something like an elk's bark until he could see how John reacted.

"No," said John evenly. "I thought I was going pretty good with Mary Hilda."

Grijalba smiled. "Well, you keep tryin', you get it right."

"How much do they pay you?"

"Twelve dollars a month, and rations."

"Well, if you want to work for me, I'll give you fourteen, and a food allowance as well. Does that suit you?"

"*Muy bien.* Let's go, Irish."

On his way out the door Sweeney told John to stay out of trouble, an admonition that, curiously, he didn't mind. He found comfort in the old man's rough, paternal interest, and his familiarity with a setting in which, John knew, he might otherwise feel quite alone. Once Sweeney and Grijalba were gone John sat down at the desk, nearly spilling his coffee when he caught himself against falling into the depth and lowness to the ground of Sweeney's chair. It was the first time he had sat in it, handmade of yellow-gray mesquite, rude but solid, with big, square, stuffed cushions, seat and back of tanned calfskin. He sank in until it embraced him like a bear hug, a big chair made by a big man, which John appreciated, but from which he was too short to work at the desk.

He pulled a little octavo notepad out of his shirt pocket and wrote a reminder to have a new chair ordered in Tucson when he sent Sweeney back with the rented wagon. Only as he finished did the fault of the plan occur to him, and he wrote on the back of the preceding page "Hire Sweeney."

John laid the pad and pencil on the wide arm of the chair and pulled the open books down into a pile on his lap as he swung his feet up onto the desk. The most complete accounts were of the weekly issues of rations to the Apaches who resided near the Agency. Their numbers vacillated from five hundred to seven hundred, with frequent notes logged that this family or that one had complained bitterly at being refused rations in midweek because, they said, they could not come in on issue day, or for the absence of the family head. Only one exception was made; each week's entry contained the line "Issued to wife of Eskiminzin in absence of chief." Some of the other names he recognized: Casador, who had been referred to as a chief in army reports for as long back as John had read them, and Sanchez, and intermittently Zele, whom John recalled reading about as something of an old high horse and troublemaker.

The financial leavings of the Agency were sparse. John assumed that what few pages remained of the last Indian Bureau tenure were so doctored as to be of little use. Since the army took over, the rations had come out of the military appropriation, and soldiers had done the labor. He found incidental expenses tallied monthly—a few dollars logged "Gifts—Important Indians," which made him smile. A little judicious bribery could be a good thing. At the end of the first month's ledger he read "Interpreter's Salary, $10.—" He flipped forward to the most recent entry, July 1874, and saw the entry repeated exactly, as it was for each month in between. He smiled again as he decided how to handle the discrepancy. John closed the ledgers and set them aside, and brought in from the wagon one of the carpet-bag satchels from which he took a box of writing paper. As he passed the stove he looked into the warming bin and saw a tin plate of bacon and gravy. Sweeney had set the biscuits aside so they wouldn't get soggy. As he ate, John found his pen and inkwell in the satchel, and underscored across the top of one of the sheets *San Carlos Apache Agency, Proposed Budget, Remainder of 1874.* His own forty dollars a month came directly from the Bureau, and was not part of his operating budget. He dipped the pen in the well again and hesitated, finally writing "Military Liaison." That would be a good title for Sweeney, and he followed it with $20.—/ month." Grijalba's salary he set down at thirteen dollars, and then on the octavo pad played with a number of figures estimating the cost of occasional labor before it hit him to follow the army's example. If they could use soldiers, he would use his Apaches. John listed down a number of his known allowances, like six thousand dollars for issue goods and rations, and eight thousand dollars for construction, before his mind returned to the idea of using, perhaps even hiring, Indians to do the jobs other agencies hired out to whites. The novelty and its possibilities were enormous.

After finishing breakfast John lugged his big trunk from the wagon into the storage area that was the front bedroom, pulling his key ring from his pocket and clicking open the locks. He raised the lid with a creak, then reached in and laid his Navajo rug across his arm and returned to the office. He had just finished draping it across the back of the parson's bench when Sweeney entered from the kitchen. "What's this, now?"

"You back already?"

"Aye, we rode out to Casador's camp and Grijalba told him what was up. Chief said he would send out runners to the other camps and save us the trouble. That just beats the band, that does. Where'd you get that thing?"

John smoothed out the rug and stood back to admire the red and yellow blazes that formed a pattern across the back of the bench. "You like it? Makes it just like home, sweet home. Bought it off a trader in Santa Fe last year."

"Navajo?"

"Yup."

"Well, you probably didn't pay him more'n twenty times what he paid some poor old drunk Indian for it." Sweeney rounded the desk and eased into his big mesquite chair. "Still, it's a nice piece o' work. I'm sure the woman who made it still wonders what happened to it; probably gave the old man Hail Columbia for sellin' it."

"Sweeney, that's my pride and joy you're talking about. Please don't make me feel guilty for owning it." He poured himself another cup of coffee. "What shall we put on the agenda for today?"

"Well, I'd suggest you prepare a suitably pretty speech for tonight."

"Will Diablo come?"

"Don't go bettin' on it."

Sweeney got up again and went into the kitchen to pour himself a drink. John followed him. "His name isn't on the ration list. How come?"

"He lists some of his relations as heads of households and they ride in to collect. It's sort of an arrangement we worked out—gets him out of havin' to come down himself."

"I gather that's a concession that wouldn't be made for just anyone."

Sweeney plopped on one end of the parson's bench and stretched a big leg along its length. "He's a powerful man." He pointed his cup at him. "Don't you even talk about him around other Apaches unless you do it with a lot of respect."

John handed him the budget he'd been drafting. "Tell me what you think."

Sweeney held it out to arm's length and perused it, tilting his head back even a little more in the fine focus of the farsighted.

"You shorted Grijalba a dollar a month. I'm takin' it you noticed he overstated his salary somewhat."

"Somewhat, yes. Why didn't you stop him?"

"He's a grown man. 'Tisn't my business to stop a man tryin' to get a boost up in this world."

"Yes, well, if he asks you about it you can tell him I docked him four bucks a month for trying to trick me, and raised him three for almost succeeding."

Sweeney made an amused harrumph and returned to the list. "Construction?"

"Gonna fix this place up."

"Uh-huh. What's this 'Military Liaison'? Who you got for that?"

"Nobody yet but I'll need somebody pretty quick." John leaned his head to one side, idly regarding his fingernails. "It does sound like something for which you would be admirably qualified."

With his head stretched back to read, Sweeney's sudden glance at John showed much of the whites of his eyes, giving him that look of walleyed wariness that you see in a man being stalked. "Uh-huh. Well, if you had a 'Military Liaison' he could tell you one big mistake you're about ready to make. You invite a couple of dozen Indians in for a smoker without tellin' the army about it, the boys might start loadin' up for some action when they see 'em comin', you know."

"It is not my intention to set a precedent of asking Major Babcock for permission to carry out my job."

"Well, when he sits next door with two companies of infantry with artillery support, you'd do well to extend him a little courtesy."

John was never fond of being called down, but he was glad Sweeney had not, as he might have done, told him outright he was too big for his britches. "You think you could go over and square it with him?"

Sweeney sighed and let his leg fall to the packed-earth floor. "Oh, all right."

"And while you're over there you might discuss this with him; I'm going to need an accounting of all the agency equipment and stock and everything. Otherwise when the army pulls out I won't know what is theirs and what is ours."

Sweeney chuckled. "Oh, he'll like that."

When Sweeney had left him alone John finished emptying the wagon, setting his baggage in the storeroom and spreading his bedroll on the ground in the bedroom, along the wall opposite Sweeney's cot. He took up his notepad and went out to the barn, an ill-fitted piece of construction whose four outer walls seemed to lean in together for support. With wood so scarce it did not surprise him that boards of varied widths left long chinks in the walls, providing an airy kind of shelter for two sunk-browed old sorrels he found inside. He made a quick list of the implements he found in and around the corral, to compare with the inventory the army gave him. He found the commissary door unguarded but padlocked; he had just tried the latch when Sweeney came up behind him. "The major was not highly thrilled to learn you'll be havin' Indians come into the Agency on a day they aren't getting issue. You'll have to give them presents or something."

"Really? What will they want?"

"Oh, I don't know. Tobacco's good. Got plenty inside here."

"Do you have the key?"

"Aye." Sweeney pulled it out of his pocket and opened the door. The time passed quickly, making notes of inventory, asking what to anticipate from the Apaches when they came. Before leaving the commissary Sweeney hauled out into the yard before the door a large card table and three small chairs that he arranged behind it.

It was about sundown when the Apache headmen began to gather about the wagon yard, quietly, leaning against posts or sitting on the rails. John watched them intently from the window of the office, men mostly middle-aged, some old, smallish but lithe, moving with perfect posture. A couple of dozen of them collected, most shirtless, some in white Mexican blouses, a few in good store-bought shirts, but without collars. They wore buckskin moccasins of different lengths, some to mid-calf, some over the knee, and long, full breechcloths that hung down past the knees front and back, exposing bronze flashes of flanks and hips that even in the oldest of them appeared firm and well muscled.

"You about ready?" John turned and saw Sweeney and Grijalba entering from the kitchen.

John had put his good suit on and pressed his bowler with Eskiminzin's feather down onto his head. "Let's get to it."

As they walked toward the wagon yard Sweeney nodded his head to
the corner post. "Don't ever point at Indians. It's rude. But that old
fellow standin' there is Casador. He's the biggest chief here and he's a
friend. I'll introduce you to him first. Then you can make your talk and
meet the others after."

Grijalba built up a fire about fifteen feet in front of the table and
chairs as John shook hands with the chief. Casador was quite an old
man, thin but spry, his face having not wrinkled so much as settled into
that look of androgynous wizardry peculiar to old Indians, as though he
might at any moment turn into a bat and fly away. When Grijalba came
over to interpret Casador said, "We haven't had an agent here in a long
time."

"I know." John nodded. "Has the army been treating you right?"

"Yes, they give us our rations on time. They don't let us go hunting
when we need to, though."

"Well, we will work on that."

"The last agent we had cheated us."

"I know. That's why the government ran him out. Why don't we all
go have a seat and we'll talk about it."

Casador strode over and sank to his haunches a comfortable distance
from the fire, followed as if by signal by the other chiefs and headmen,
each of whom stole a glance at John as he passed by, but didn't stare.
Sweeney and Grijalba sat in chairs at the card table, as John stood in
front of it and reclined back against it. Sweeney reached out suddenly to
stabilize it, hissing, "Easy!"

John took some of his weight off it, silently thanking God that the
meeting had not begun with him crashing to the ground in a heap of
curses from Sweeney and spindly table legs. "The government in Washington has been very busy," he began, deciding to stop after each sentence to allow Grijalba to render them into Apache. The sound of the
language struck him, its profusion of short vowels and soft combina-
tions of consonants beautifully unlike anything he had ever heard.
"They have been thinking a lot about you. They want what is best for
you. They want you to be happy and well fed and living in peace. They
know there are bad white men living in the country who try to harm
you. They know what happened at Camp Grant and they are sorry
about it. They know the last agent here was no good, and when they
find him they will punish him. They have thought it all out from the

beginning, and sent me here to be your agent." He walked around the table and sat down. "I want you to speak now and say whether you will work with me."

As ranking chief it was Casador who rose to respond. He stood close by the fire, his left hand down at his side and the right holding gently the throat of his buckskin garment. It was the same pose that one might see in the Congress, or Parliament, a stance of dignity common to all men of thought. "No agent has ever talked to us in this way before," he said. "You talk to us like men, not children or dogs. Now I am asking the old soldier whether or not you are the new agent, and whether you have the authority to talk this way and do as you say. Let him tell us." If Casador had been younger he would have sat without bending his back, but his age forced the concession of hunkering a bit as he resumed his seat.

Sweeney pushed up from the table and hooked a thumb under his belt. He knew Apaches respected strong, fit men, and he sucked in the stomach he had been allowing to grow, telling himself that the time had come to lose weight. "He is," he said, "and he does. He isn't like the others who have been here. He means to do right by you. I trust him and I think you should, too."

Still seated, Casador folded his arms across his chest, and his face assumed the expression of one who had early learned what an inexpensive commodity words are. Through Grijalba he said, "You no longer wear a blue coat. I want to know what you are going to do now. Where will you go?"

The acumen of Casador's question took even Sweeney aback, and his face blanked for a few seconds. "I am not going anywhere," he said finally, then looked at John. "Mr. Clum and I think the same things and believe the same things. What he wants to do, the soldiers won't like and they might try to stop him. He may need me, and so I will stay. I know he will need all of you. Will you help him and do what he says?"

John watched Sweeney resume his seat, his joy that Sweeney was staying rising like a fountain that he quickly capped. When Sweeney was settled John leaned over to him. "Boy, you sure have a sneaky way of asking for a job."

"I had to, don't you see? That question was the chief's way of saying, 'If you go, we go.' "

John nodded. The silence that followed was long but not without meaning. It was his first exposure to the unnerving Apache telepathy that is not even common to other Indians. There were no words or gestures; only the men's heads moved, and even then almost imperceptibly, as their eyes incised deeply into one another's hearts until a man determined whether the encountered thought was a counterpart of his own. First the men within each circle exchanged these terribly silent debates, and then the leaders of each clan.

Finally Casador got to his feet again and stood by the fire. "We are agreed," he told Grijalba. "This agent is young, but when a kitten gains experience he becomes a bobcat. He has trusted himself to us. If he wanted to trick us he would not have ridden alone through our country where we could have killed him. If he were lying he would not have talked to Eskiminzin as he did. We will do anything he asks of us."

John cupped his hand over his mouth and leaned over to Sweeney. "How did they know about that?"

"They know many things," he answered in a hoarse whisper. "You'll never know how much. Always assume they know it all."

John looked around the gathering of serious-looking Indians. "I am sorry to see that Diablo is not here. Did he not know we were meeting?"

"I sent my nephew to tell him about it," said Casador. "His camp is two days from here, and there was not time for him to come in."

John nodded. "Then let's go to work, shall we? What do you want me to do about the soldiers? If you think they are protecting you, we will have them stay. If they make you nervous and you would feel better without them, tell me, and we will have them withdrawn."

As Grijalba interpreted, the seated chiefs broke their silent code and stared at each other in candid amazement. Casador rose again. "In the past, many of our people were killed by soldiers, or else were killed by other whites while the soldiers were supposed to be watching over us. Maybe they were watching over us. I don't know. But it is hard for us to trust them. It is better for them to go. If you need someone to guard the storehouse there, tell us, and we will do it ourselves."

John considered this, sensing the opportunity to blend the Apaches into running their own Agency. "All right," he said, "I will take you at your word. When you go home tonight, I want you to pick four good young men, strong ones, who will take turns guarding the commissary. They will be your police, and when the army sees that you can do this yourselves, perhaps Gray Fox will feel easier about taking the soldiers away."

When Grijalba finished a few of the Apaches nodded, all of them murmuring a word that prompted John to lean over and ask Grijalba what it meant. "Is *enju,*" he said. "Means all right, good idea."

John rapped the table lightly with his knuckles. "Now, in the next few weeks we are going to have many, many things to talk about and settle. But before we do that, I have to go over to Fort Whipple and see Gray Fox. I promised Eskiminzin that I would try to get him released. Don't you think I should do that first?"

When Grijalba interpreted there was another low chorus of the word *enju.* "I want one of you to go with me," John said as he stood up. "I don't know the country between here and there. Who among you knows Gray Fox the best?"

Casador stood, without hesitation. "I have spoken with Gray Fox many times. I will go with you."

"The sooner we leave the better. Can you go tomorrow?"

"Yes."

John was sobered as he resumed his position in front of the table. "I want to thank all of you. You have shown much confidence in me before you even know me. I want you to know that I will try my very best for you. From now on we will have much to do, so I want you to go home and get a good night's sleep. Now, we have a little pouch of tobacco for each of you to take home, and I want to shake hands with each of you before you leave. It isn't much of a gift, but when you smoke it I want you to think about me and believe that I want to be your friend."

When Grijalba finished talking the Apache men stood up and formed into a line. Grijalba stood at John's side introducing each one, who shook hands first with John and then with Sweeney before striding beyond the circle of the firelight, grasping a little pouch of tobacco.

When all the Indians were gone Grijalba excused himself. John and Sweeney kicked out the fire and walked back to the office. "Well," said Sweeney, "you haven't said I'm hired."

"Are you serious? Of course you're hired. I want you to stay."

When they regained the headquarters John turned into the office as Sweeney continued down the hall. "I'll be turnin' in now. It's been a mighty eventful day."

"I'm going to sit up and write a letter. How often does the mail go out?"

Sweeney stopped in the door of his room to answer, "Well, you're the agent. How often do you want it to go out?"

John held up his hands to accept the correction and entered the office, recounting everything to Mary.

They barely had breakfast downed in the morning before they heard the snort of a horse out front, and discovered Casador sitting patiently on him. John had already packed one of the little old sorrels in the barn with enough food for the trip, and had only to quickly saddle the other. They submitted to the handling with a tired passivity, John breathing some thanks that they would cause no problem.

Sweeney took hold of the bridle as John swung into the saddle. "Watch Crook, young fellow," he said. "It isn't for no reason that the Apaches call him the Gray Fox. He'll have your lunch and eat you for dessert before you've even had a good look at him. But he is a fair man, if you can match him."

John leaned forward on the pommel to settle in more comfortably. "I guess we'll be back in eight or ten days. Whatever else you do, keep things quiet here. Nothing could ruin me like a bad incident before I even get my feet wet."

Casador had already turned his horse to go, and John turned to follow, along the north trail toward White Mountain.

CHAPTER 6

There were two ways to get to Fort Whipple. One was down the Gila to the Verde River, then upstream and over; the other was to head north, get atop the Mogollon Rim, and then head west on the trail that Crook himself had blazed a few years before. Casador guided him along this second route, past White Mountain, at which John could not gaze without wondering about the great chief Diablo whom he would surely meet soon.

They rode vigorously all morning, at a fast walk up the hills and sometimes at a canter on the downslopes, Casador silently in the lead, showing little concern for the condition of the horses—or his agent, either, for that matter. John could ride, but being unused to the vicious terrain he depended heavily on the sense of his horse to keep up with the chief.

At close to midday John hailed him, and Casador stopped and turned his head. "Don't you think we should rest the horses a little bit?"

Casador's face showed no more reaction than if John had not spoken at all.

"Oh, you are going to be mirthful company, aren't you? All right, um—" John patted his horse on the neck. *"Caballos."* He dredged the word out of his memory of New Mexico, but not remembering how to say "tired" he drooped his shoulders and panted hard a half-dozen times, and pointed to a shaded cleft in a nearby bluff.

Casador rolled his eyes, grudging, but tolerant. *"Siesta por las caballos aquí,"* and pulled his reins in the direction of the little glen. When they reached it, before John could dismount, Casador pointed at him and said, *"Tú,"* and drooped his shoulders and panted in mimicry.

John laughed out loud as he dismounted. "No. Just the horses."

Casador slid from his horse, little crow's-feet at the corners of his eyes betraying the tiniest hint of amusement.

John sat on the ground, holding up a cigarette and match to Casador, who took them with some air of surprise, as John began to understand that to Indians, small gifts are of a larger significance, and large gifts of a lesser significance, than to white people. Casador sat on a rock nearby, lit the cigarette, and took a long draw at it as John studied his face—one, he thought, that should be on a coin. The old chief's nose was long, but flattened and slightly pugged, the nostrils wide but sensitive. His lips were thin and stern, but not cruel, his eyes curiously almond-shaped without appearing oriental, seeming now in their restful gaze to have as their natural state an imperturbable serenity, yet capable of great emotion. His tight red headband kept in place coarse hair that showed more salt than pepper, draping to the middle of his back.

Casador looked at John impassively. *"Tú habla mexicano?"* He was perhaps aware and perhaps not that his own Spanish would barely pass for pidgin.

John shook his head. "No. You speak any American?"

Casador didn't need to understand the words to curl his upper lip against the thought. "No."

After a time Casador stood and inclined his head toward the north, and John nodded and rose. As he unscrewed the cap from his canteen and drank he noticed Casador also, unplugging a tight-necked wicker jug that hung from the rope that secured the saddle blanket. John pointed to it. "What do you call that thing?"

Casador waved him off with annoyance, as if to tell him to drink his own water.

"No, no. In Apache."

"Tus," said Casador.

John repeated the word, careful when he pronounced the "s" to extend his lower jaw beyond the upper to get just the slightest whistle of an "h," the way Casador had said it. Casador's astonished stare was enough to tell him that probably no other white man the chief had ever met had thought the Apache language worth learning. John approached Casador and patted the wicker jug. *"Tus?"* he repeated.

Casador, mounted, looked down at him, all trace of surprise vanished from his face. *"Sí."*

John held up his hands. *"Un moment, por favor."* Before mounting his horse he dug into a saddlebag until he produced his pencil and notepad, which he flipped open, and printed *"tus = jug."*

The effort was now on, and the journey no longer silent. Anxiously John tempered his enthusiasm for learning Apache with the caution not to become a pest, and the instinct that to keep the chief's approval he had to approach the subject with respect, not like a child playing with a new toy. Casador answered everything but volunteered nothing, weighing his commitment to be helpful and his kind feeling, almost gratitude, toward an agent who wanted to understand their language, against the danger of having an agent who might come to know too much, and from whom they could conceal little. The miles passed quickly.

They gained the Mogollon Rim at the end of a second hard day of riding, but once on top, some two thousand feet above the desert, the pine forests were open enough to allow them good time. On the fourth morning they passed Camp Verde without stopping, and by afternoon reached their destination. As they approached Whipple across the broad meadow that had been created by felling the timber to build it, Casador reined in his horse outside the gates and stared suspiciously at the high, straight pine log walls and little houses that jutted from on top, and the sentried gates that opened and shut like a mouth to the underworld. It was architecture from another universe. John pulled up beside Casador and found himself curiously pleased with the sight. The two army posts he had seen so far, Lowell and Grant, were as open as small towns, approached as easily from one direction as any other. Whipple alone was stockaded and fortified with blockhouses. John sensed a touch of the medieval about it; perhaps that was why it seemed to live up to his expectation of what a fort should be. In any case it seemed entirely appropriate for housing the commanding general.

John looked over and saw Casador's dark old eyes, reflecting like mirrors the consternation of the walls. He reached over and patted the chief reassuringly on the arm. *"Es la casa Nantan Lupan,"* he said. *"Enju."*

Casador surveyed the massive wall of pine bark for a second longer, and then with no change whatever in expression or posture walked his horse through the gate, preceding John by three or four steps.

John took a quick account of the activity around the parade ground, then turned and looked back up over his shoulder. "You there, sentry. Which building is the general's office?"

"Last on the right of this line," he answered, pointing.

"Obliged," John said, and the soldier touched the brim of his hat in acknowledgment.

The headquarters building was the largest in the compound, with a half story of board frame continuing up from the porch roof, its windows tucked into the gable ends. Simultaneously John eased down from the saddle and Casador slid from his blanket. They secured their horses to the rail, and John stepped up onto the wooden porch as Casador unfurled a smaller blanket that he'd had wrapped about his waist, and draped it regally over his shoulders before following. They passed through a transomed door into an otherwise unlit hallway that contained a rough lumber stairway up the right side. On the left was a door beyond which they saw a uniformed man busily writing at a desk.

They entered, and as John indicated a chair to Casador he said, "I'm John Clum. I sent General Crook a message that I would be here to pay my respects."

The soldier was a staff lieutenant whom John judged must have been newly arrived from the academy. He had short, fine black hair and black eyes that looked up without expression as he said, "One moment."

The lieutenant got up and rapped sharply twice on the low door of an anteroom before opening it, and John heard him say, "Excuse me, General, the new agent from San Carlos is here to see you. There is an Indian with him."

A voice from within, gruff but not deep or terribly strong, replied in a tone that sounded almost weary. "Well, send him in, and send for Mr. Free."

As John passed through the doorway Crook had already pushed himself up from his desk to receive him. He was not a tall or husky man, but his body was suspended admirably from square, erect shoulders. He was about forty-five, his blond hair was very short, just glistening with gray at the temples. His throat was hidden by a fine, blond beard at least eight inches long, deeply forked all the way to the chin and combed away to the sides.

John tried to assess Crook's face but found it was rendered unreadable by its contradictions. He had a low, square forehead that seemed doomed to scowl, but his smallish blue-gray eyes were remarkable for their clarity and animation. His cheeks were a bit sallow and weak and the ears were rather too large, but his mouth was small, tight, and resolute. The only clear declaration was his nose, large and straight except for a slight downward bend at the end. It was, like John's own, thick and strong across the bridge, as though underlain by strap iron. It was a feature that could weather anything, and as Crook leaned across his desk to shake hands, the nose preceded the rest of his face like the prow of a warship.

Crook bade John to sit down and then leaned back in his own chair, folding his hands across a stomach that was remarkably lean for a man his age, with an impassive look on his face. John pulled an old spindleback from a side wall and seated himself on the opposite side of Crook's desk, crossing his legs and setting his hat on his lap.

Crook's mouth barely moved as he said, "You're a little young to be losing your hair, aren't you?"

"Perhaps I'm older than I look, in experience."

After about ten seconds Crook shook his head sadly. "My God."

"Nossir, just John Clum." He smiled nervously.

The little mouth beneath the granite nose creased into a slight smile, and Crook nodded. "You will forgive me if I expected an older and more substantial, well, *man.*" When John made no answer he continued, "How old are you?"

"Twenty-two."

"From New York?" He continued to nod, disparagingly.

"Yes."

Crook grunted softly as he rested his left temple on the knuckles of his hand, then sighed. "Well, I guess I see their game this time."

"Who?" By this time John knew full well who, but had to make his impression.

"The Ring, boy. Who else but the Ring?" Crook's lips tightened and he looked as though he was chewing a little at something. "Who do you suppose was responsible for getting you appointed?"

"I was selected by the Dutch Reformed Church. You know that."

"The Church submits a list. San Carlos is the most explosive Indian Agency in the country, and you never even saw an Indian till you came out here. Who picked you, of all people? I'll tell you who; it was the government contractors and profiteers who started the last war, that's who. They couldn't wangle another accomplice into San Carlos, so they got some innocent, doe-eyed do-gooder full of trust and piety and love of his fellow man."

John's gaze was downcast. "I could have a worse résumé."

"They'll use you."

"I don't think so."

"You're a puppet, young Mr. Clum." Crook leaned forward. "Out here you don't know your backside from a gopher hole. They'll steer you right into a new war and you won't even know how they did it. San Carlos is a dangerous place. It just crawls with murderers and cutthroats."

"Cutthroats, yes," swelled John. "I saw the heads you had set out to . . . decorate the flower bed."

"So," Crook nodded, "you think it's me that's the warmonger."

"I think you're a soldier, and soldiers make a business of war. I represent the Church."

"Oh, do you, just?" Crook's eyes widened, and the fanlike crow's-feet disappeared, so that the shadowed little wrinkles became fine white lines feeding into the light blue eyes that flashed from beneath those thick blond brows. "Well, you just shut up and listen to me, boy, 'cause I'm telling you something. I'm telling you the Apache wars go on because the city people who fill your churches on Sundays found out there's money in it. They make—" Crook spluttered for a second, lost for words, but then recovered. "Look here; look out here." He leaned back in his chair and drew aside a thin muslin curtain from a paned window. "What do you see? Troops. Troops that need to be supplied. Out there every bale of hay and every sack of flour and side of bacon was bought from somebody who made a buck."

Crook dropped the curtain and leaned forward. "It's the common citizens—the bankers and businessmen and respectable people, them and their fancy women all feathered up like a bunch of birds." Crook wiggled his fingers at his temples derisively, then dropped his arms and paused. "You were in Tucson, what other commerce did you see there? Mills? Factories? The only money that comes into the towns is what the army spends there, or what comes from the mines, and it's the army that keeps the mines open. They need the army, and they need the Apache wars to keep us here." Crook leaned back and folded his hands again. "It's the city people, young Mr. Clum," he repeated. "They take the blood and dead bodies and turn them into velvet furniture and Saturday night cotillions.

"You've seen the desert. What else is there out here to make a living on if it's not other people's corpses?" General Crook leaned forward suddenly and clenched his fist. "Like vultures, it's their sustenance!" John looked on with wide eyes, but said nothing. "Shall I tell you about the last agent the Indian Bureau—and your Church—sent out here?"

"You mean Dr. Wilbur."

"Yes, Dr. Wilbur."

"I know about Dr. Wilbur."

"Thanks to the war he started I had to kill seven hundred, maybe even a thousand Indians, counting those that froze or starved. Since then I've had an army agent taking care of San Carlos. He is managing quite adequately, thank you very much, and if you think for one minute that I am going to let those profiteering scum use *you,*" he veritably shouted the last word and pointed, "to get their noses back in the trough, you are wrong, young Mr. Clum, and you might as well go back where you came from."

John nodded, gathering his wits. "So, you figure I'm too young and pretty to be a monster like Wilbur; I haven't been here long enough to know the ropes, so I must have been appointed because somebody figures to . . . control me. That it?"

Crook was unwinding, but wary of the frank agreement. "Something like that, yes."

"That is well thought out, General, and I even sympathize, but the unfortunate fact of the matter is, you're stuck with me."

"We'll just see how stuck I am with you."

John took a deep breath. "Like me or not, I am a federal Indian agent. I carry a presidential commission, signed with the President's name in the President's hand over the President's seal. If you try to shut me out, I can cause you a lot of trouble and you know it. You've tried for two years to get Washington to let you have permanent control of San Carlos. If they wanted you to run the reservation, you'd have it by now."

"You threaten me, young man," Crook nearly whispered, "and you'll discover fast enough that I can have six companies of cavalry mounted and on the road to your San Carlos at two hours' notice."

"Yes, but you wouldn't dare."

"And why in holy thunder would I not? I'd be done with you before Washington even knew I had left."

"I've done homework. For you to get this Arizona command, the President promoted you over forty colonels of the line who ranked you. The War Secretary opposed you, Sherman opposed you, Sheridan still opposes you—in addition to thinking you're an idiot—and every one of those colonels would like nothing better than to see your head on a pike so they can fight over your star."

As he spoke John watched as the veins in Crook's neck stood out farther and farther, but he remained coldly civil. "Who's been telling you that kind of stuff?"

John tilted his head to one side. "I have friends; we talk."

"What else do they tell you about me, or am I to know?"

"Surely. They tell me your sense of honor is unbendable, and once you give your word to any man white or Indian you won't break it, and the Apaches know it. They tell me you're one of the few officers in the army who won't go out killing Indians just to get a promotion. They tell me the Ring—I know all about the Ring—will try to get the better of me, but if I follow your advice we can beat them out. They even tell me—" John lowered his voice almost to a whisper and leaned forward. "They even tell me that if you want peace, and I want peace, and the Apaches want peace, if we all work together we just might do it."

John leaned back and regarded the wrinkled, astonished face across the desk. "Real peace, General Crook."

Crook was quiet for several seconds, then shook his head. "How can you fight the Ring? You don't know who they are or what their tricks are. I can't stand over you all the time."

"Oh, I know who some of them are; they were lined up at the stage-coach in Tucson offering me their help. My friends know what their tricks are."

"And you trust them?"

"Yes, I do."

Crook was quiet for a longer pause. "What do you want?"

John's heart soared almost into his throat. "Two things for now. I want your troops withdrawn from the Agency, and I want the chief Eskiminzin paroled to me from Fort Grant."

Crook's hands flew skyward. "Oh, you're going to make a fine agent! That's crazy! The last time I pulled the troops out I barely got them back in time to prevent a massacre." The texture of his voice changed suddenly when he said, "Lieutenant Almy was killed as a result. To the day I die I will blame myself, and I will not repeat the mistake."

"I have talked to the chiefs. They have promised to police the agency with their own men."

"And you trust them, too." Crook gestured with exasperation.

"So do you, when you have to."

"Never!"

"I heard how you cowed Diablo with that show of force last year. He allowed you into his mountains with a—ten-man escort, wasn't it?"

Crook made a dissatisfied noise deep in his throat but said nothing.

"General, the Apaches respect you because you have trusted them a little. You enlist them as scouts, you let them go out to hunt when the rations run short, but they'll never feel stable or secure as long as your soldiers are breathing down their necks. You yourself wrote that insta-bility and insecurity are a greater threat to peace than renegades and whatnot. That's in your Annual Report for—"

"Don't quote me to me, young man. Who watches you while you watch the Indians?"

John exploded, slamming his open hand down on Crook's desk. "The same gentlemen in Washington who will watch us watch each other! For the love of God can't we help these Indians just a little? Is this all we're good for?" He slumped back in his chair, breathing more slowly. "That was intemperate. I am sorry. I will be reporting to the commissioner, not you. Military rule at San Carlos is to be ended, General, that decision has been made already." He permitted himself a smile. "But I'm sure you'll keep an eye on me. You have ways; your spy network is famous."

"Yeah, well, I'm sure you'll have a few confidential sources of your own."

The idea had never until that instant occurred to John. "I'd be foolish not to. You haven't said you'd release Eskiminzin."

"That man is a renegade murderer who was involved in the last war."

"Really?" John raised his eyebrows, opening his expression like shutters flung back from a window. "I heard you jailed him for playing up to General Howard over you."

The corners of Crook's little mouth turned distinctly down, a flush of red spreading out from his eyes. "Well, that's a lie," he hissed.

John shrugged. "The story goes around."

"Don't you know he killed the last white friend he had? Shot him in the belly with the man's own twelve-gauge."

"He told me all about it," John said evenly.

"Yes, I heard you two had quite a little tête-à-tête when you went through Fort Grant."

"Not much is said in this Territory that you don't hear about. But his people want him back with them, and I am familiar with his history. I am satisfied I can use him in keeping order."

"And he has his uses for you, no doubt."

"Frankly, General, I don't care how we use each other, if the results are good."

Crook peered at him intently for what seemed like thirty seconds, tapping the knuckles of his fists together, before he stopped and pointed at him. "Young man, I have spent three years cleaning the Ring out of San Carlos and making these Indians respect me. If you show the first sign of undoing my work, I will smash you without fear of consequence or losing my command. That is my promise, and I am a man of my word. When I see the Ring getting back into San Carlos, if it's the last thing I do as commander in Arizona, I will destroy you."

"Don't you see I'm on your side?" John rose from his chair and placed his hands flat on Crook's desk. "General, we have to be friends.

If you put me out another agent will come, maybe not as good but that won't matter because you'll be out, too. Then there won't be anyone left out here but the Ring, and the Indians, and a general more eager to shoot them down than you are. The only winners will be the buzzards. If we don't work together we'll both lose everything."

Crook stood up and folded his arms. "My aide said you brought an Indian. Let's see him."

As John and Crook emerged from the anteroom, Casador rose and walked halfway across the room. "Nantan Lupan," he said finely, and raised his arms wide with the blanket still entwined in his fingers, like a great symbolic bird spreading his wings.

Crook took him in full embrace, left cheek to left, then right to right. "Mr. Free, tell the chief I am very glad he has come to see me."

The interpreter, a short, ugly young man with reddish auburn hair, spoke in crisply accented Apache to Casador; after there was a reply, Free told Crook, "He says he did not realize you lived so far away. It is no wonder things got out of control before."

Again John saw Crook give that tight little smile. "Yes, but you saw my soldiers come and set things right. My reach is very long. My soldiers are my arms."

After another exchange, Free said, "He says that is in the past, and he is glad to see you again. He came with the new agent to keep him from harm on the trail."

Crook nodded. "I know you. You have always done right." He looked askance at John and continued, "You will always have my soldiers to protect you from bad men. You have only to send for them."

The redheaded Free broke into a crooked-toothed grin as Casador replied. "He says his people wish they had to send maybe a little farther to reach your soldiers."

Crook crossed his arms and scowled at John. "Did you rehearse this, did you?"

John shrugged vapidly. "Oh, I'm much too innocent to be so designing. You said so."

Crook grunted and gave Casador his attention again. "Thank you for coming to see me. Now I want you to go with Mr. Free over to the commissary and take some tobacco home with you. About five tins, Mr. Free."

Casador and Crook exchanged hugs again before the chief followed Free out the door. John smiled and extended his hand. "I'm glad we met, General."

Crook took it without smiling. "We'll be talking again, I'm sure."

John started out the door into the hall but turned suddenly in after-thought. "Lieutenant, how old are you?"

The aide looked at John, then at Crook and back again. "Twenty-one," he said.

"Thank God. I was afraid I was the only *boy* out here." He gave a satisfied look at Crook and was out the door.

"You trust him, General?"

Crook was quiet for a second. "Would you?"

"Jake Almy and I were close. I'd never trust a Bureau agent again."

Crook headed into his office. "Lieutenant, come take a letter to Major Babcock."

CHAPTER 7

It was afternoon of the eighth day when John and Casador rode back into San Carlos. At the edge of the compound the old chief reined in his horse and made a motion from his chest out to the northeast.

"Of course," said John. He took Casador's hand, gnarled and long-nailed as a hawk's talon, in his own, and laid his left hand over it. *"Muchas gracias."*

Casador nodded and went his own way.

Lookouts had already brought in word of the arrival, and Sweeney met him on the veranda of the headquarters, backed by four young Apaches wearing an assortment of breechcloths and moccasins, but with matching carbines and *bandoleras* of cartridges slung from their shoulders; they stood at attention, expressionless.

John dismounted and exchanged greetings with Sweeney, then with Grijalba, who came up. John gestured at the Indians. "What's with the honor guard?"

"Well, you said you'd be wantin' policemen. Here's what they came up with."

"I guess they look fierce enough."

"Aye, well, listen to this. They were all scouts for Crook in '72, they came with their own guns and ammunition, and they speak English."

John looked over at them again, lined up as stiff as if they were standing before a cigar store. "My!" he said. All four were smallish but very tough-looking, eyeing him through dark almonds that had an almost preternatural squint.

"Come on, then. I'll introduce you."

Three of them had names that John found beyond his ability, and, bantering through Grijalba, joked them into accepting mimicking substitutes—Nosy, Sneezer, and Goody-Goody. Only the fourth, the smallest and most withdrawn, seemed unamused and insisted on keeping his real name, Tauclee. They had already set up a duty station by the commissary, where one of them would be found at all times. When

John dismissed them, one went there, the other three back to their camps.

Sweeney brought some dinner in from the military camp that was still out back. "What do you think I ought to do about hiring a work force?" John asked over the stew and hardtack. "The troops will be leaving if I have my way, but even if they stay I wouldn't trust them."

Sweeney chewed emphatically. "Hire your own people out here. These Indians are able to work. Don't start off hirin' white guys the contractors in Tucson send up. That's just what the vermin want, and it's for certain the root of most of the trouble out here." John looked up quizzically and Sweeney went on, "Once they get you to depend on 'em, they'll have their way with you from then on. That's what happened in Camp Grant in '71."

John's ears pricked up like a rabbit's when it hears a twig snap. "What do you mean?"

"I mean, up until that Whitman fellow took over, all the needs of the fort—firewood, hay for the horses, that kind of stuff—were supplied by workers from Tucson. Whitman fired them and gave the work to the Apaches so they could earn some money. I know that resentment had a lot to do with the massacre. They haven't been up here in two years. Don't let 'em get their feet back in."

John nodded. "All right, I'll put you in charge of hiring some of the Apache boys as soon as you get back."

"Where'm I goin'?"

"We need to return the wagon I rented in Tucson. I'll give you a voucher so you can buy it, if he'll sell it, then I want you to pick up some supplies."

It seemed forever before the wagon rolled back into San Carlos, with Sweeney sitting foursquare on the left side of the seat, reins firmly in hand. Beside him, Edwin sat, blankly absorbing the bumps and lurches of the road. Behind them in the bed of the wagon, sitting with Mandarin dignity amid the sacks of beans and flour, was a skinny Chinese, middle-aged, in a black silk tunic and long black pigtail.

John waved a hello. "Have any trouble buying the outfit?"

"Nope." Sweeney pushed down on the brake with his foot and climbed down, jumping heavily from the step. "Of course, he had to check with the big boys to be certain it was all right with them."

"Anybody suspicious about Edwin?" John whispered, pretending to look over the wagon.

"No, I gave him the dollar, and said come up to me in front of some witnesses and ask for a ride to Fort Grant. Nobody knows any better."

"Good. Who is your extra cargo in the back there?"

"Came up to me while I was loadin' supplies, he did. His English isn't what you'd call grandiloquent, but I gather he wants a job as our chef, if you please." Sweeney faced out across the valley, but sidelong kept his eyes on John. "Just insisted on comin' along, he did. Just couldn't keep him off the wagon."

"I'll bet." John reached up and took the Chinaman's cool hairless hand. "What is your name?"

In reply came syllables that John took to be Chou Sun-lee, and a pidgin assertion that he had worked for a swank hotel in San Francisco and come out with the railroad.

John nodded. "Well, give us a few minutes to consider your proposition. Edwin, climb down and take a walk with me."

Edwin got down off the wagon with the care of a man twice his age, but seemed better once he got his feet on the ground. John put his hand on his back and steered him over to the headquarters. "Tell me, what is your last name?"

"Hyatt. Least I think it was."

"You think?"

"Nobody in Tucson ever knowed me before. Haven't heard my real name in a long time. People just call me Edwin—'less they call me something else."

"How have you been making your way?"

Beneath the thin blond beard John perceived a blush of embarrassment, not at Edwin's situation, but that John would have to ask. "Just about ever'body has give me a job at some time or 'nother. I help out near ever'where now and then."

"Why hasn't somebody given you a steady job with steady money?"

Edwin shrugged. "People don't tend to think of me and steady at the same time."

The interest, warm but ill-defined, that John felt for this specimen began to make sense when it came to him that they must be the same or very nearly the same age. "How old are you?"

"I don't know. I reckon twenty-one. Maybe twenty-two."

"Where is your family?"

"All dead. Cheyennes killed 'em in Colorado when I was a boy. My uncle in Denver didn't want me so I went to an orphanage. I ran away from there before long—made my way down here."

"Can you read and write?"

"Not too good."

"Well, Edwin, I have a job for you that you might find to your liking. I cannot pay you much, but it will be steady."

"You don't want me to move out here, do you?"

"No. Please sit down." They had reached the veranda of the office and John indicated a couple of old ladder-back chairs sitting on the ground. "Now, I want you to keep this confidential. Just between you and me. Can I trust you?"

"Yes."

Like a cold breath John feared that Edwin's reliability might at any moment hang on his need for a drink, but decided that what he was about to do was no more than the gentlemen of the Ring would expect of him. They just wouldn't know who.

When they were done talking they went back over to the wagon and found the Chinaman still selling himself to Sweeney, who saw them coming and edged toward them. He pulled at his chin and said in a soft grumble that was as close as he could get to a whisper, "What about the Chinaman, now? Think you can give him a job? 'Tisn't like we couldn't use a cook around here."

"Yes, all right, hire him. It isn't every day you get the chance to hire a cook with a name like Chow Soon. Now, Edwin here is going back to Tucson. I want you to round up one of the policemen to go with him and bring the horse back. Travel at night; sneak him into town. Now, Edwin, remember all we talked about. I'm depending on you."

John worked late that night, long after Sweeney had gone to bed. He was sure he could get the Apaches to plant crops in the spring, but they would have to spend the winter digging irrigation ditches to make the ground worth anything. There would be implements to buy, wages to pay. They would have to make improvements to the Agency—he wanted a floor in the office, and a fireplace; eventually he would want a telegraph in the back room that was now the kitchen. Arranging the program took hours. He felt a little like an outlaw, alone in his desert shack, plotting, but by sheer isolation safe for the moment.

When he had finished, he turned the lantern down to its lowest possible setting and left it on a table in the hall. If this place were as dangerous as Crook and everybody seemed to think, it would be a good policy to have a light immediately at hand during the night. The little oak table in the hall looked simply too queer sitting on bare dirt. The floor would have to come first.

John had crept halfway through the bedroom door when he heard Sweeney's voice mutter tiredly from his cot, "Don't bother now bein' quiet. I'm not sleepin'."

He spread his bedroll on the opposite side of the room, but the space was so small that when John had pulled his boots off and stretched out they were only a few feet apart. "Be sure now," said Sweeney, "to shake the scorpions out of those boots before you put them on in the mornin'."

If he had been looking he would have seen the whites of John's dark brown eyes. "Thanks. I will." He made himself comfortable above his blanket, taking in a deep breath of the musty room to air the work out of his head. "You know, you never did tell me why you agreed to stay on out here."

"And won't that wait for another time, now?"

"Sometimes a man can talk more freely if he doesn't see who's listening. It's like we're more honest in the dark, maybe."

There was a few seconds' silence. "Like at confession, you mean."

John hadn't thought of that, but saw it was true. "Yeah, that's right."

Sweeney rolled onto his back like a tired old lion and ran a hand over the top of his head. "Oh, I guess I've come to have a lot of feelin' for these people. It's not that I'm doubtin' our way of life is better, mind, but—we've had no regard for what they had before. To be fleeced in the name of progress, and be used as a doormat by people who say they're better than you are. That is something an Irishman is in a peculiar position to understand."

The acid in Sweeney's last sentence caused John to gulp. "Sorry."

"Will you leave me alone, now, and sleep."

"I didn't mean to pry."

"You managed." He raised up on one elbow. "Son, you can't start off nestin' deep in the thoughts of people you hardly know, certainly not these Apaches out here. Now me, I don't care, but these Indians will resent that kind of familiarity like the dickens, and they'll give you cause aplenty to regret it. You've got to give things time, let them come to you. They will, but you can't press them. Like Diablo. If you give him time, he'll watch and make up his mind. But if you go ridin' out and come on like his long-lost nephew, he won't give you the time of day."

As John lay on his back his eyes adjusted to the dark enough for him to see the pole roof overhead, its layer of not very straight willow saplings overlaid with carrizo. He rolled his head a little from side to side and saw a couple of stars searching him out through gaps in the reeds. At least, he thought as he dropped off, it doesn't rain very often out here.

It was early the next morning, John was shaving on the porch of the headquarters, when he looked away from the mirror at the sound of a horse walking up, and dried off his face. "Well, look who's here."

The chief Eskiminzin slid off a bay horse with no blanket.

John strode out and shook hands with him, the towel draped around his neck. "You're free."

"Yes." Eskiminzin stood there short and squat and open-faced. He took John's hand and said an Apache word that sounded almost like a sneeze—"*Asoogd.*"

"The army let you go?"

"No. Injun ran away."

"What? Didn't they follow you?"

"No."

John tried to add it all up but couldn't so quickly. "Where'd you get the horse?"

" 'Pache horse. Not American. Better you keep him here, though. Gonna need more horses around here."

The magnitude of such casual generosity took him aback. "That's very thoughtful. Thank you so much. Sweeney," he called out suddenly, "come out and say hello to our company."

The big Irishman came out in a few seconds and shook hands with Eskiminzin. "Hello, chief. You look pretty good. Are you all right?"

"Yes. Been a long time, Old Soldier."

"Aye, that it has."

Eskiminzin looked from one to the other to make sure there was nothing else to talk about, then handed the bay's reins over to John. "Injun goin' home now." He shook hands again and repeated emphatically, "*Asoogd.*"

John nodded gravely and watched him walk away. "What does he keep saying that word for, I wonder?"

"Does he, now?" Sweeney put his hands on his hips. "Why, he'll be thankin' you kindly for all you've done for him. And a right remarkable thing that is for an Indian, too."

"Just to say thank you?"

"Aye, indeed. Words don't mean much to Apaches; it's what a man does that counts. When they accept a favor they remember it away and keep an eye on you. The next time you need help, they'll show up. You don't know how they know it, mind, but they do."

"Then why did he thank me?"

"You did him more than a favor. He's a chief and you put him back over his people. Sayin' thank you was extra, so you'd know how much it meant to him. It was a profound thing, indeed. You made a friend for life, I'd say." More softly in his harsh voice he concluded, "Cherish that, son, you'll have a great use for him out here."

They watched Eskiminzin walk farther away, not duckfooted like a white man, but with one foot straitly before the other, as if he was walking a beam. "How does he know where his people are camped?"

"Oh, he'll find 'em. They don't believe in askin' things they can learn for themselves."

John tugged the horse by its bridle toward the stable. "He said he wasn't released. He ran away."

Sweeney followed. "Ah, they let him escape, you can be sure. If they released him, don't you know the citizens would all make a rumpus? But to let him escape, no one is the wiser, and then if he gets into trouble they can pursue him as a fugitive."

"It still seems like they would have let him ride up with you and Edwin."

"Naw, that would have been too obvious. This way it's a sort of parole durin' his good behavior, you might say."

They stabled the horse and headed back toward the headquarters, when John stopped in his tracks. "Now what?" Through the space between the commissary and the barn they could see part of the army's camp, and out of the corner of his eye John caught sight of one of the pointed white tents as it puffed out at the sides and collapsed airily to the ground, followed by a second and third.

"Well, I'd say you'll be gettin' your wish."

They covered the intervening ground quickly, as it became increasingly obvious from the activity that the troops were breaking camp. They found Major Babcock, in front of his tent, dictating dispatches, facing away from them and unaware of their approach. "Did you intend to say good-bye?" John got his attention. "Or just slip out quiet-like?"

Babcock turned in his canvas chair. "Of course, I was going to pay my respects, but thank you for saving me the trouble."

It nagged at John like a growl in his stomach that he ought to make some statement or peace offering, but he didn't know how to put it. "Listen, I hope you don't take this personally. I am sure you are an exemplary officer; Sweeney here assures me of that. But please try to understand my position. My job is to settle these Indians down, and I can't do that if they're always looking over their shoulders to see if some of your boys are pointing guns at them."

John looked at him anxiously to see how this was taken, and Babcock gazed at him evenly. "We'll be back when you get yourself in trouble and send for us. You will, you know, when Geronimo and his boys show up killing and looting and tearing up the countryside. I only hope we can get here in time to save your neck."

John saw it was useless. "When are you pulling out?"

"At once."

"Back to Whipple?"

"Yes."

John extended his hand. "Well, good-bye. Please give my compliments to General Crook and tell him I will be keeping in touch."

Babcock pushed out of his canvas chair and shook hands coolly. "I will." He gave a curt nod in Sweeney's direction, acknowledging, "Sergeant." He resumed his seat, facing away from them again.

The two headed back toward the Agency. "You know, that's the second time somebody's mentioned the name Geronimo to me," said John. "Who is he, exactly?"

Sweeney hooked his thumbs under his belt as they walked along. "Geronimo is an old Chiricahua war chief. Been around for years, but nobody heard about him till recently. I suppose he's been carryin' on down in Mexico all this time. Far and away he's the most vicious of the lot—makes Cochise look like Little Bo-peep. I can't swear to the truth of this, but the story is he lost his whole first family, wife and kids, in a raid by a white posse. He's had no use for white people ever since. I do know he made a foray once, hit a ranch one morning on the other side of the Catalina Mountains from Tucson. Killed the whole family, then found a little baby inside the house. Now, most Apaches take infants and raise them as their own, or at least sell them back for a ransom. You know what he did?"

John looked at him earnestly, his step matching Sweeney's own. "What?"

"Geronimo, he took that baby and threw him out in the middle of a patch of cholla cactus. Some troops happened by later in the day an' started to bury the bodies, and they heard this squawlin'. Found the little guy thrashin' around, thorned up like a hedgehog."

"Are you sure that isn't a playbill from a dime novel?"

Sweeney pushed the corners of his mouth forward, wrinkling his lips like a mummy. "Son, I was there."

John felt sick, and took a deep breath. "I can imagine what he does to grown people, then."

"You don't want to hear it. He hates white people more than any other Indian on the continent, I'd bet."

"So, he runs mostly in Cochise's old range, down by Mexico."

"Aye."

"That's good, anyway." They regained the back door of the office. "Do Eskiminzin's people camp far out?"

"No, not usually."

"Why don't you send out one of our new policemen and ask Eskiminzin to come in for a chat in the morning? We need to start laying some ground rules for this place."

"All right, but mind, don't be high-handed about it when you do."

Sweeney left and John worked at his desk. It took him a long time to get the image out of his mind of a tiny baby flailing and screaming in the middle of a cactus bed.

At dawn John looked out back and saw empty desert where the army camp had been, and fought down a tiny surge of fear and isolation. The increasing light of the morning had just sent the kangaroo rats skittling into their burrows when Eskiminzin appeared at the hall door of the office. John looked up in surprise for he hadn't heard him come in. "We were just having breakfast. Are you hungry?"

"No." Eskiminzin crossed the room, but stopped about halfway, turned to the side, and held a hand up in surprise. *"Yei, ao!* Where you get a rug like that?"

"It's from New Mexico. It's a Navajo rug."

"Navajo!" Eskiminzin scowled and grimaced, almost the way a mountain lion does when it crosses the scent of a rival. "Navajos no good. Fight like coyotes, not men." He ran his hand down the back of his head, admiring the bright woolen blazes. "Women make mighty good rugs, anyway."

"I'm glad you like it."

Eskiminzin stood in place, and shifted his weight. "Sure wish I had mighty fine rug like that."

Sweeney pushed a stack of papers across the desk at John. "You need to take a look at these."

He took them up, and saw on top a penciled note. *He wants you to give him the rug. Do it quickly.* John blanched, but Sweeney glared him down with a face that seemed suddenly as if it were made of granite, until John gave in. "Well, I guess if an Indian made it, an Indian ought to have it. Would you like to take it with you?"

"Yes, I can use it." Eskiminzin removed the rug with its red and yellow blazes from the back of the parson's bench and draped it over his shoulder.

John tried hard to mask his grief. "Take care of it."

Eskiminzin nodded, sitting down. *"Enju.* Why you want to see me?"

John folded his hands in his lap. "I've been thinking about some things, and I want to ask you about them."

"All right."

"Now, I've moved in here to be your agent, but I can't just start off giving everybody orders of how it's going to be, like I'm the king or something. I need your help, and Diablo's, when he comes down, to make things good here."

Eskiminzin harrumphed. "You want us be three kings."

"Yes, if you like."

"Three kings go see baby Jesus." He observed this with a simple kind of incredulity, as though that held some meaning for him.

"Well, yes, although most people think they weren't really kings, but just wise men."

"That even better."

"Yes. Well, now, one thing I've been thinking is that you Apaches go out raiding and stealing to get things you can't make for yourselves. If you had money to buy these things, you wouldn't need to take them from other people. That is wrong and cannot be tolerated."

"You give us money, maybe?"

"There is a lot of work that needs doing around here, and I will hire your people to do it. White people won't have to come in here to do it, and I will pay money to the Apaches that work for me. Will you influence them to agree to this?"

"Yes."

"And there is one thing that we simply have to agree on before we can go any further out here."

"Nantan say that, means no drinkin'."

"Yes, I'm afraid that's exactly what I mean. You know as well as I do your people don't get themselves in trouble until somebody gets drunk. The Church that sent me is going to insist that the Apaches stay sober. Can we do that?"

"Not easy."

"Tell them we will make life so good here they won't want to get drunk."

Eskiminzin rose, scowling like a bear whose kill has been tampered with. "All right, but Injun don't know what they say." John showed him to the door and Eskiminzin's mood eased. "Soon you come out my camp. We feed you dinner."

"Yes, I will. Thank you."

Back inside John fixed his eyes on Sweeney. "Why in the devil did you give him my blanket?"

"Simmer down and listen. You can buy a rug like that for ten dollars anywhere. The chief admired it most particularly and wanted it. Apaches admire nothing on this earth like generosity, and within three days every Indian from here to Mexico will hear about what you did. That's an investment like no other you could make. Now get mad if you want to, but it was the right thing to do."

John sat down, swinging his feet up onto the desk and slamming his boots down on it. "I'll get over it. Just let me sulk for a while."

"Mr. Clum?" John had spent the afternoon looking over some low gullies along the river above the Agency, spotting out the best places to begin the irrigation ditches. He turned when he heard the voice over his shoulder and saw a small man in a dark suit, about forty, with a weak chin that came almost to a point, and large, slightly protruding eyes. "My name is Reeble." He held out his hand and John took it. "You contacted my firm about our handling of the beef contract for this Agency."

"Yes, that contract was let by the commissioner before I got here, and now I get a letter from you saying the deliveries may be delayed. What is the problem?"

"Well, we feel we have to bring it to your attention that the present method of beef delivery is not in the least way satisfactory. The previous agent had agreed to a new arrangement, but the Indians staged the last break-out before the change could be effected."

The fact that Reeble blamed the last war on the Apaches set a suspicion working in John's mind, but he had no facts. "What was that?"

"We recommend that you let us build a new corral across the river, over there. We'll even offer to pay for it. The cattle will be safer from theft, and we can drive them across the river when you are ready to weigh them and make the beef issue."

John pulled his chin, stalling, trying to see the trick in it. "I don't see why I couldn't just put an Apache guard on them."

"I'm afraid our experience has been such that we don't share your faith in the Indians' honesty."

John began to rankle, sure now that there was a scheme afoot, but the two men turned at the sound of footsteps and saw Sweeney come boiling up to them like an ironclad. "Might you be askin' about the cattle again, sirrah?"

Reeble drew himself up. "I wished to speak to the man in authority, not an employee."

Sweeney planted his hands on his hips, his knuckles curled into fists. He would much rather have laid into Reeble, that desire pulling his square upper body forward a few inches beyond where he had rooted his feet. "The man in authority is it! Well, as for authority, sir, we suggest you fulfill your contract as it stands, or the federal government will take such vigorous exception to your performance that you will learn the real and true meanin' of authority, if you please. Now, good day to you, sir."

Reeble slapped his hat on his thigh, turned, and left, without further words. When he was gone beyond hearing John looked at Sweeney blankly. He had never seen him like this. "What's come over you? You were pretty rough."

Sweeney was adamant. "He'd be rough enough on you if you'd given in, and found yourself payin' the new price for his beef."

"What new price?"

"Aw, for the love of— Look here." Sweeney whacked him on the shoulder to turn him around. From where they stood on a rise they could look out across the Gila. "There's water in the river."

John waved his hand. "Of course there's water in the river."

"Do you know how much water weighs?"

"No. Five, six pounds to a gallon, maybe."

"Do you know how much water a thirsty steer can drink? Cattle over there," he pointed, "weight scales over here."

John's eyes bugged as the scheme sank in. "So they let the cattle go thirsty a few days, then drive them over here for the beef issue and they fill up—"

"Ah, they do more than let 'em go thirsty. They feed 'em salt, they do, and you pay twelve and a half cents a pound for steer bellies just a-squelchin' with river water."

"Why, those dirty dogs."

"I warned you. Son, they'll do anything. But now look you here, you had better guard the cattle you've already got day and night. Right now I'd lay mighty favorable odds that within a week somebody is goin' to try and steal those animals."

John nodded. "And blame it on the Apaches so the contractor can get his way."

"Uh-huh. And you needn't bother thinkin' that he'll come to you again. He'll just wait till the whole episode is over, and you've got to replace what was taken, and he'll send a letter to the commissioner, with the suggestion, don't you know, that your wasteful habits are not servin' the Agency well. If you take my meanin'."

John's face took on a profound sadness at the ready glibness with which the contractors were willing to use him, but it hardened as soon as it surfaced into a resolve to fight them with everything he had. "You know," he said, making thoughtful little pointing gestures at the river, and after a few seconds his mouth twitched up into a grin. "You know, that might be just the ticket. Just the ticket. Sweeney, you sure earned your pay today. Now, go round up the cops. We've got work to do."

It was nine days after the confrontation with Reeble, at about midnight, when John heard the coded rap on the bedroom door, and saw Sneezer enter without a sound. John sat up on his bedroll and Sneezer said, "Cattle going now."

"How many men?"

"Five."

John nodded. "Well, follow them and let me know where they take them. Don't hurt them or anything."

Sneezer turned to go but stopped. "Can we scare 'em a little?"

"Well, maybe just a little."

Even in the lampless gloom John saw the shine of Sneezer's teeth. "Gonna be fun, alrighty goddam!"

"Don't hurt them," John nearly shouted after Sneezer's departing form, then lay back and smiled until he went to sleep.

CHAPTER 8

Morning was high when John walked his horse to the edge of Eskiminzin's rancheria and dismounted. The chief met him there and
shook hands, taking the reins in one hand and John's arm in the other,
and led them to his own wickiup. John took in the village and its
activity. "I didn't realize your camp was so large."

Eskiminzin gestured around. "Not all my people. Lots of Diablo's
people here to visit."

"Diablo? Here?" John's heart raced at the prospect of meeting the
great chieftain at last.

"No. Diablo and some men go to mountains, hunt, watch over
women while they get pine nuts. Rest stay here to visit."

The rancheria straggled up the side of a hillock above the creek flat,
the wickiups blending almost preternaturally into the brush and boulders. John pointed behind him. "Wouldn't it be easier to live down there
where it's level?"

"Maybe. Long time ago, I not chief yet, Diablo give me lots of advice.
One time he tell me, 'Never live in open place. Always live in rocks on
hillside.' Then we go to Camp Grant, Whitman say, 'You pretty safe
here, camp anywhere.' We camp on flat place by creek; white men from
Tucson bring up Mexicans and Papagos, kill all the families. Now we
camp on hillsides." Eskiminzin's wickiup was situated near the top of
the rancheria, on a little prominence overlooking but not removed from
a number of others.

"That my woman," he went on, indicating a tall, rotund woman,
bigger than he was, with ample, straight black hair that was parted in
the middle and, curiously, gathered and wrapped in a tail behind each
ear. John smiled at her, and her smooth bronze face suddenly crinkled
deeply as she smiled back. She had good teeth, worn down evenly from
working the buckskins for tanning.

She took John's hand in her own, larger than his and gritty with
cornmeal not carefully wiped away. "How," she said.

He looked at Eskiminzin. "What's her name?" In reply the chief spat out a succession of friendly-sounding consonants that levitated John's hands helplessly. "Oh, my word, I'll never learn all that! I know, I'll call you Ethel. That's a good American name, and it sounds sort of like your real name."

Eskiminzin explained the proceedings in their own language; when he was through she laughed and said, "Eth-el!" and returned to patting out and frying tortillas.

The chief indicated a blanket under the ramada. "We sit here. Pretty soon eat." When they were comfortable he continued, "My name too long? Maybe you gotta give me American name."

John thought for a moment, his eyes responding to the challenge. "I think I'll call you Skimmy," he said at last.

Eskiminzin's face clouded. "Skimmy. Never hear Skimmy. What is Skimmy?"

"Well, I guess you could say it means, always takes from the top."

He nodded. "Takes From Top. Good!"

The conversation faltered, and John pointed to Ethel. "Your wife works very hard."

"She good woman."

"I remember reading that your first two wives were killed at Camp Grant. I want you to know—"

The chief flashed up a hand for silence. " 'Paches not ever talk about dead people. Ghosts hear names and come. Not ever talk about dead people."

"Sorry." Keenly he was aware that he would be allowed one such mistake and be corrected before he got into serious trouble, but there was so much to learn.

Eskiminzin too was anxious to get the moment behind them. "You got a woman?"

John shook his head. "I'm not married yet. I have a girlfriend; I will marry her one of these days."

"What name?"

"Mary."

A look of profound impression swept over Eskiminzin's face, like the shadow of a thunderhead passing over a well-sculpted peak. "Maria?"

"Yes."

"Mexicans pray to Maria!"

"Oh, no, no. It's a different Mary entirely."

Eskiminzin shook his head with a grunt. "White people silly, maybe. 'Paches got everybody have different name. Much better."

"Yes, well, I'm inclined to agree with you." He couldn't wait to write Mary about this, that the next time he asked her a favor, she should consider it with some gravity.

"You done anything with her?" Eskiminzin looked at him with an innocent evenness, unwavered by John's flash of blasted surprise.

"What? Why, I should say not! No!"

"Good." Eskiminzin drew up his legs and rested his arms on his knees. "Lots white men go with different women. That no good."

"Not all white men are like that at all, Skimmy."

Eskiminzin smiled a little at hearing his new name in usage. "Well, we got a story about that, back in Old Time, when coyotes look like people."

"Oh, come on, now. Coyotes never looked like men."

John hadn't meant anything by it, but Eskiminzin took it up. "How you know that? You there? You see Old Time people?"

"No, of course not, but the Bible says, God created Man."

"Bible says, Bible says. You talk like other agents. Bible says, Old Time men look same as men now?"

"Well, no, not in so many words."

"So some men look like coyotes, maybe."

"There is no reason to think that."

"But *maybe* some men look like coyotes."

"I guess it's possible."

"All right. Don't go telling Injun how Old Time people look when you don't know."

"Skimmy, Skimmy, let's not fight. I made a mistake and you called me on it. I am sorry."

"All right."

John gazed across the rancheria. The day was growing warm, and a number of old people reclined listlessly in the shade of their ramadas, while the women went about their chores and the children their games. At the wickiup nearest Eskiminzin's own two very disagreeable-looking young fellows squatted on their haunches, sipping occasionally from two battered tin cups. Just as John caught sight of them, one who had been apparently listening to the brief quarrel lolled his head back to stare dully out across the valley. It was hard to pick what observations he could make innocently, and what would be interpreted as arrogant and superior. "Well," he smiled lamely, "I guess we both know some men who still look like coyotes."

Eskiminzin nodded, his eyes having regained some of their luster. "Act like it, too."

"Anyway, what is the story?"

"What story?"

"About the coyote."

Eskiminzin shook his head. "Can't tell you."

John laughed out loud. "What do you mean you can't tell me?"

"Tell stories in hot weather, coyotes get mad. Injuns tell coyote stories only when Ghost Face Moon come."

John looked around the camp, suddenly curious. "Where is the rug I gave you? The Navajo rug."

Eskiminzin rose squatly to his feet, smiling. "You come see." He pulled aside the canvas-swatch door of the wickiup and held it back for John to duck inside, then followed him through. He gestured to the wicker bed frame that stood about a foot off the ground, the sleeping area spread with straw and a whole cowhide. John saw his rug with its red and yellow blazes spread on top as smooth as a hotel coverlet, perfectly centered, not quite reaching the edges of the frame.

"Well, I have to admit it looks more at home here. I'm glad I gave it to you."

Eskiminzin patted him on the shoulder. "Me too. We eat now," and nudged him back out the opening.

They resumed their places beneath the ramada and Ethel served them a thick soup of venison and a starchy vegetable John couldn't name, the tortillas she had been frying, and hunks of glazed mescal that tasted something like burned squash. Ethel made strong black coffee that she boiled in a small pot; John looked on agape as Eskiminzin spooned into his cup two then three and four large measures of sugar, which he neglected to stir. "It's no wonder your sugar rations run short," said John. "Why don't you just put in one or two spoons of sugar, and stir it up?"

"Stirring no good." Eskiminzin held out his cup to offer a sample. "This way, sugar sink, go to bottom. Make bottom coffee real good."

"Gentlemen, halloo!"

"Sweeney, what are you doing out here?" John and Eskiminzin got to their feet.

"Hi, Old Soldier." Eskiminzin extended his hand and shook Sweeney's.

"Hello, chief. Got a couple of businessmen, boss, came callin', asked me to come out special and get you, as they can only stay a short time."

"You better go," said Eskiminzin. "Maybe he come talk about cattle. Maybe give you good deal." He winked. He started walking with them back toward their horses. "Listen. My people say, time maybe right we move up to mountains awhile. Got datil fruits and tornillo beans up there, maybe ready to pick, then go to White Mountain and get pine nuts. Diablo's people already there. You give permission?"

"How long will you be gone?"

"We gone a month, maybe. Gotta get food for winter. Come back here for winter, dig good ditches like you want."

"Are there any white people out there to bother you?"

"No."

John nodded. "All right. You have my permission."

From within his shirt Eskiminzin produced a pencil and a swatch of brown wrapping paper. "You write permission on paper, maybe?"

John glanced down briefly at the stubby little hands holding out the greasy, bitten-off pencil and the wrinkled paper that the wind lifted and rattled. He wrote out the authorization, grieving for the bitter experiences these Indians had undergone to make such precaution their second nature. He handed them back to Eskiminzin and looked him in the eyes. "I hope you find lots of food out there."

Eskiminzin nodded. "We get pine nuts, not need American flour. Save Washington some money, maybe." He shook hands with John and then with Sweeney. "Better go now."

Eskiminzin turned away; John and Sweeney mounted and turned their horses back to San Carlos, John lulling himself with the rhythmic crunch of the desert pebbles under the animals' feet, and breathing in a little harder when his nose caught the scent of a creosote bush. He was startled by the sound of Sweeney's voice when he said, "I'm sorry to tell you this, son. Eskiminzin was lyin'. Diablo's folks ain't out gatherin' pine nuts any more than we are. They're out on a raid."

"Lying? He wouldn't lie to me!"

"Well, he lied this time."

"Is that why you came out here?"

"Nope. I just happened to notice their garbage heaps. At some of the huts the bones were all in one place in little piles. The Apaches believe that when a raidin' party is out, their families have to save the bones of the food they eat. If the bones get scattered, they're afraid the men'll get scattered as well. Somebody's out to mischief, all right, been gone some days, by the look o' things."

"You haven't had any reports of a raid?"

"Not yet."

They continued on in heavy silence. John was trying hard to tamp down the anger welling up within him, but it was like tamping on wet sand; the more you press it down, the more water you suck up when you lift off. Sweeney held his peace until they were unsaddling their horses in the stable. "What are you going to do about it?"

"Nothing."

"Aw, you can't just pretend not to see things like that. They'll run all over you if you do that; you'll lose their respect."

"Skimmy and his folks will be back in a few weeks. I want to give them a chance to tell me about it themselves. If they don't, I'll worry about it then."

Eskiminzin was right. When Sweeney and John cantered up to the office a single messenger handed John an envelope. He looked at the return address of Reeble & Toomey, Commodities, and opened it—

CANNOT POSSIBLY REPLACE STOLEN CATTLE WITHIN MONTH FOR LESS THAN 16 CENTS PER POUND. CAN DELIVER 150 HEAD THIS PRICE. PLEASE ADVISE YOUR INTENTIONS.

"Thank you, wait here," John said, dismounting, and he and Sweeney went inside. Sweeney read it over quickly.

"A hundred and fifty." John shook his head. "They only stole a hundred."

"Oh, my, they're playin' you for a champion sucker, they are."

"Well, we can't have a beef issue without cattle. Tell him to send 'em on up."

John used the intervening week to develop a program of hygiene for the scattered Apache camps. Most of the Indians washed in the river daily and were cleaner than the people in Tucson, but they had not yet hit on such ideas as communal dumps for their trash. The only resistance he encountered was the digging of a latrine. He found his Indians so timid about their bodily functions that they were too embarrassed to use the same place for the same reason. John compromised, convincing them at least to bury what they left behind when they went off by themselves. There was grumbling also about his rule of sobriety, but that subsided when he increased their sugar and coffee rations, and told them of other interesting things to drink, like tea and sarsaparilla, that he would procure for them.

On the eighth day after the messenger's visit Grijalba called John out front as Reeble and six hands arrived with the cattle. John shaded his eyes, squinting at the sinewy longhorns, their knobby knees and wall-eyed brows heavily wrinkled above and below, stretching their necks to avoid one another's horns, herded bawling into the corral.

They fetched Sweeney and all strode over, seeing as they approached what they needed to see. They barely greeted Reeble before John waved impatiently over the lowing animals. "Many of these cattle have the same markings as the ones that were stolen. Do you know anything about that?"

Reeble flustered a bit under the veiled accusation. "Why, no! Of course, many of the cattle for each delivery come from the same ranches, so their brands obviously would be the same."

"Brands?" John shot back. "I don't mean brands. After your last visit we half-bobbed the tails of all the cattle then in our corral, and every last one of them is in this bunch here. They were taken down the San Pedro Valley and then back up to your stockyard in Tucson, which is about the oddest coincidence I ever heard of."

"That's ridiculous."

"I had trailers on them every step of the way."

Reeble looked around as if he wanted to hide someplace. "I don't know what you're talking about."

John went on. "Now look, we're reasonable up here. You finding yourself in possession of our stolen cattle, it was kind of you to return them to us, without even asking a reward. Of course, we don't need the extra fifty head now, as they weren't allowed for in the budget, but since you have been so gentlemanly with us, we'd be willing to take them off your hands for oh, say, ten cents a pound."

"What!"

"Well, naturally you don't have to. You could try to drive them back through—all that hostile Indian country if you want. But since the incident seems to have come full circle, if you sell us the extra fifty I think the Agency could omit any mention of the whole affair in any of its reports."

Reeble positively shook with rage, but with Sweeney and Grijalba standing right there, and not accidentally, Sneezer as well, looking very fierce, he made no threats. As he handed John the consignment sheet, though, he leaned forward and hissed like a viper right in his ear, "How long do you think you can hold out here, city boy?"

He shook his head calmly. "I'm not going anywhere." He saw no need to weigh the cattle again, as the contractors had counted on the higher price.

"Just you remember, cleverer men than you have gone down out here, and you're hardly worth a decent man's challenge."

John signed the receipt and a bank draft and handed them over. "Always a pleasure doing business with you, Reeble." He patted him on the back, steering him toward his horse. "You come back and visit us anytime."

John glimpsed Reeble as they galloped away, his weak little chin and tightly clamped mouth shaping his face like a hateful "V"—vengeance, spelled as plain as cold type.

Eskiminzin's people were gone six weeks; by the time they returned the first cool breaths of October had swept out the hot, stale air left from summer. The nights were becoming chill, and John was glad they had finished remodeling the office before cold weather set in for good. The stove had been moved to the back room, and a large adobe fireplace added to the office, opposite the hall door. Best of all, the four rooms and hall had all been fitted with plank floors.

When Eskiminzin strode in wearing a new white cotton shirt over his Mexican pantaloons he stopped and caught his breath, looking around. *"Yei, ei!* You people have been working around here."

"Skimmy, hello." John crossed the room and shook hands with him. "Did you have a good trip?"

"Yes, plenty food for winter now."

"Are you thirsty? Here, drink this." John poured a light-colored liquid from a pitcher on a side table. "It's called lemonade."

"Make me foolish?"

"No, it's not whiskey. It's good; try it."

Eskiminzin took a draft, and his cheeks ballooned out as his nose wrinkled and his eyes squinted tighter than a newborn bobcat's. He stamped one foot and shook his head, but managed to swallow it, unwilling to spit on the new floor. "Eee, eee-ee! Why you give me this to drink?" he demanded. "You not glad to see me, maybe. Give Skimmy green persimmon juice to drink!"

"No, no, it's good. Watch." John poured himself a glass and drained it, making finial gestures with his hands like a circus performer.

Eskiminzin looked on, horrified, his mouth open and his tongue protruding a little beyond his teeth. "You got green persimmon for a tongue, maybe. Agh!"

"Well, I'm sorry you don't like it." He set the glasses back on the table. "But I am glad to see you. Did all your people get back safely?"

"Got two new babies. Left one old woman in the mountains. She pretty soon die, maybe."

John hung his head abruptly. "Skimmy, you know I don't like for you to do that."

"Enju. It was her time. Old people think, better die alone than everybody stand around and watch. She say herself, 'You other people go on. Spirits come for me pretty soon.' "

John crossed his arms and looked at him sternly, not yielding the point but electing not to spoil their reunion.

Eskiminzin was ready to go. "Listen. Old man gonna tell stories tonight. You come out tonight after supper, hear some pretty good stories, I'll bet."

"Yes." He brightened. "Yes, I'd like that very much. I will come. Are you back in your old camp?"

"Yes. Bring Old Soldier, too."

By the time John and Sweeney saddled their horses for the ride to Eskiminzin's camp the sun had set, and the sky was already past the massive blazing embrace of yellow-orange and mauve that John had come to see less with awe, and more with a grateful familiarity, conscious of the change and wondering at the same time how far the change went to explain the difference between the way white people beheld the world and the way Indians attuned themselves to be part of it all. Not dark, the sky had turned deep purple, the long straight clouds smoldering dark orange like bars of steel cooling from the furnace.

They set off to Eskiminzin's rancheria with a switch of their horses' tails, three miles—not far—and the trail was well worn and not treacherous by night. "Did he mention it?" asked Sweeney.

"What? The raid?"

"Aye."

John sighed. "No."

"You can't go on ignorin' it forever without bringin' Crook down on your head."

"I know, I know. I won't spoil the party tonight, but next time I see him after that, I'll ask him what happened."

The night had grown quite dark by the time they reached the camp, guided the last hundred yards or so by the flicker of cooking fires. Eskiminzin met them, turning their horses over to a couple of boys to care for. He shook hands with them, saying only, "Gonna hear some stories now, you bet." He led them through his rancheria and along a trail in the brush to the neighboring one.

The man who would tell the stories was very, very old. He was missing most of his teeth on the upper left and lower right, so that when he chewed his corn mush he looked rather like a cow chewing its cud. His name was Angry Carries His Deer Meat; Eskiminzin introduced John to him and they shook hands. The old man indicated a spot on the inmost of several ill-defined circles, a few spaces removed from his own and near a huge pile of corn cakes stacked on a buckskin, and several *tsas* baskets of roasted piñon nuts. Eskiminzin sat next to him so he could whisper translations of the stories into his ear, and Sweeney sat behind and between them to listen in.

The old man waved his hands in front of him once. "Before I begin, I want everybody to see there is one here who has never been with us before." Those large, watery old eyes held that twinkle of merriment that is peculiar to old people, people who have seen much, and seen much at which to be amused.

"Now, I've heard about this young white fellow," Angry Carries His Deer Meat went on, and Eskiminzin whispered. "He says he can't remember our names, so he makes us new names to help him remember. I don't know how such a forgetful man got to be agent, but here he is." The crowd chuckled; it was growing larger, over a hundred by now.

"Some of us think he can't remember his own name, maybe, so we better help him out. From now on we're going to call him Nantan Batunni-ka-yeh: Chief High Forehead."

Sweeney leaned forward. "Baldy would be more like it." He reclined and laughed in his basso gravel.

"Eskiminzin, you ask that young white man how he likes his name."

John nodded and grinned, seeing he'd been had. "It is true. It is good. I like it." He looked up. *"Enju."*

Among the crowd there was a spattering of hands slapped on thighs and satisfied sighs of *"Ao, ao!"*

Suddenly a young man John couldn't see spoke up. "Never mind about that. We came here for you to tell some funny stories."

"All right, hold up there," said Angry Carries His Deer Meat, cocking his head to one side. "Don't get all worked up like a young pony. You might get too excited and run into the fire." Another chuckle rippled through the crowd. "Is everybody here who is going to come?

All right, some of you young fellows here pass around these nuts. You women pour up some of this good acorn coffee."

A cool breath of wind swept through the rancheria, and John was glad to be seated near the fire. This was going to be the first really cold night of the year.

Angry Carries His Deer Meat gestured to the center of the circle. "Some of you men throw more sticks on the fire. Make it good and warm for when that young fellow jumps in." They did it, smiling. John looked over his shoulder and saw the youth squirm as his companions poked him in the ribs, laughing.

"Not long ago, up Arivaipa Canyon above the spring, I saw tracks of four white men, on foot, going in circles like they were crazy." He pushed out with his fist. "I know how those tracks got there.

"It happened when Coyote was going on his journey. He was poor and hungry, looking for food. He looked back over his shoulder and saw four white men coming along behind him. They were those who cut Yellow Metal out of the Earth Mother and sell it for money. Because they did this, they were no good at all, but they had fine horses, and pack mules full of goods and food.

"That Coyote said, 'I am hungrier than they are. I think I'll just get me that food.'

"He went to the side of the road and made dung, then covered it with his hat. He held it there, waiting.

"Pretty soon those white men came up and saw him. They said, 'Ho, what are you doing there, looking so silly? What have you got under that hat?'

"That Coyote said, 'We are resting. I have my little bird under this hat.'

"Those white men said, 'What kind of bird is it? Let us see him.'

"That Coyote said, 'No, you cannot see him. He is the wisest bird in all the world. He knows everything there is. Anything I want to know, I just ask him.'

"Now, those white men were all thinking the same thing, and talked among themselves. Finally one of them spoke up. 'Does he tell you how to get money?'

"That Coyote said, 'Yes, he tells me that all the time.'

"Those white men got all excited. That's the way white people are. They said, 'Sell him to us. We'll give you a pack mule for him.'

"That Coyote said, 'No, I don't want to sell him. He's worth a lot.'

"Those white men talked among themselves. They were greedy. Finally they said, 'Look, we'll pay you everything we have. Our horses, pack mules, goods, food, everything.'

"That Coyote held back like he didn't want to do it, but at last he said, 'All right, I will sell you the bird for everything you have. But you better listen to me. This bird and I have been together a long time, and he likes me a lot. You better let me get away from here before you take that hat off, because if he gets away and follows after me, you'll never see him again.'

"Those white men said, 'All right.' They got down off their horses.

"That Coyote tied all those horses and pack mules into a string, and got on one of the horses. He said, 'You see those four mountains over there? When you see me go over the last one, then you can take the hat off. It should be pretty safe. But listen to me, you better grab pretty hard under there, because that bird is fast.'

"Those white men said, 'All right.' That Coyote rode off, leading their horses and pack mules. When they saw him about to go over the fourth mountain they all said, 'All right, get ready.'

"When that Coyote went over the last mountain they pulled off that hat"—Angry Carries His Deer Meat leaned out and made two fists in front of him—"and they grabbed real hard in that stuff and it came out between their fingers.

"Ah, they surely were angry. They said all those nasty things that white people do, but there was nothing they could do about it. So they just walked around there and went crazy. I don't know where they went." Angry Carries His Deer Meat held up a hand suddenly. "Hold up here. That young Batunni-ka-yeh is white. Maybe he knows what happened to them."

When John heard the whispered translation he nodded sagely, saying slowly, "They went to Washington."

When Eskiminzin told them what he had said, the assembled Apaches whooped and laughed; a couple of strange hands pounded him on the shoulder. John reclined back on one elbow and dropped into his mouth a few of the toasted piñon nuts on which they had all been snacking. He leaned back, taking in the whole sight and its ambience, the cold wind warmed by passing over the fire and by the press of dark, lithe bodies in close familiarity. He was aware that at home in New York he might be spending this evening at some tepid church social or political lecture. But here—ah, here! Had he been feasting among Bedouin in the middle of Arabia he could not have felt more alive, felt a keener sense of adventure, not just of the body but of the spirit.

As the night wore on, the assemblage ate their way through several *tsas* baskets of toasted piñon nuts, and drank gallons of coffee, dark, bitterly nutty coffee made of *chechil* acorns and Gambel Oak bark. Dawn could not have been more than a couple of hours away when Angry Carries His Deer Meat slapped his hands down on his thighs. "Well, look at me, how I have kept you all awake. I have robbed you of your sleep, and you won't want to work tomorrow. I better give you some things to eat so you won't be mad at me. Get up in a line over here and we will give you the rest of these corn cakes."

First light had already come upon them when John and Sweeney flopped into their bedrolls and slept heavily.

CHAPTER 9

It was about a week after he attended the storytelling that John saw Eskiminzin ride up to the commissary building where he and Sweeney and Grijalba were poring over sketches for a new roof and a second room off to the side. A number of Apache boys crawled nimbly around the roof tying up new thatching, and a few men crouched with picks, clinking metallically at the side wall for a new doorway. A second crew down by the river were slopping clay and straw into molds for adobe. Eskiminzin was walking his horse and leading a string of six others. Riding beside him were three young Apache boys, teenagers by the looks of them, seeming very downcast and subdued. John handed the sketches over to Sweeney and dusted off his hands as Eskiminzin handed him the leader to the string of horses.

"These horses belong white people. Don't know who," he said. "These young men go hunting with Diablo, split off by selves and make raid. Not big. Nobody killed or nothing. Diablo give me boys, says, 'Take 'em to new agent, see if he speak true about makin' 'Pache court for 'Pache people.'"

John put his hands on his hips. "Well, Sweeney, what do you say about that?"

"I'd say I owe your Diablo an apology. Looks like he means to try you out."

John walked up close beside Eskiminzin and shook hands. "Yes, I told you the truth about having an Apache court. You bring them back on issue day and we will have it. I think you and Casador and Sanchez should be judges, but you talk it over among yourselves." Partly as an afterthought and partly as bait he added, "If Diablo comes down for rations he should be a judge, too."

Eskiminzin inclined his head toward the three youths. "You gonna put 'em in guardhouse till issue day?"

John shook his head. "No. Diablo trusted you with them. So do I."

"Good."

Eskiminzin started to turn his horse to leave, but John reached up and caught the bridle. "Skimmy, I—" He started to thank him for the display of confidence, but remembered the Apache reserve about expressing gratitude too liberally. "I really do think this will be what is best for your people from now on. Don't you?"

Eskiminzin nodded thoughtfully.

"It won't be too much trouble to watch over them till issue day?"

"No. Boys not bad enough for guardhouse. Gets hot in there."

John patted the horse on the withers and backed off. "Good day to you then." Eskiminzin nodded and left with the three boys in tow, and John turned to Sweeney. "We better get a letter off to Crook right away and let him know we've got the horses when somebody files a claim."

"Aye, and tell him who it was that brought him in. My, won't he be tiffed?"

"No, no, I don't think so anymore. I think he does want to be fair now. He was just lacking in confidence that the Indians would go along. Why don't you take the horses over to the barn and sketch out the brands. Mary Hilda," John got his attention, "we've got to go to the office for a bit. Keep the boys busy, and remember to brag on them a little."

The food issue was always on the first and third Fridays of a month, and as the crowd gathered for the next one they found arranged before the commissary a table with four chairs, and off to its side, another, more stout table, with one chair. When Eskiminzin came in with the three boys Nosy, Sneezer, Tauclee, and Goody-Goody tied their hands before them and marched them to the heavier table, up the chair and onto the table, and stood guard as the three boys stood shackled as on a pillory. Eskiminzin took in the scene darkly but said nothing, understanding John's motive already, that if the chiefs disappointed him and failed to punish the boys they would have at least suffered a few minutes' humiliation.

"Did Diablo come down?" John asked him.

"No."

"Very well. You three judges sit there," and he took the fourth chair away. John interrogated them through Grijalba, and asked whether they had anything to say for themselves. They did not.

"Which one of you was the leader?"

The three boys looked at one another uncomfortably until the one in the middle tossed his head with something like hauteur. "I was."

"What is his name?" John asked Eskiminzin.

"Bacon."

"How old is he?"

Eskiminzin's face scowled as he tried to figure the English number. *"Diez y ocho,"* he said at last.

Eighteen, mused John. He was a strong-looking fellow of medium size for an Apache, built lithe and slender like a runner. He had a curiously asymmetrical face that seemed to have been pieced together by different hands—one eye and brow higher than the other, a mouth that crossed his face at an angle like a new moon, turned up at the corners. It made him look predisposed to insolence or amused disdain, an impression that his attitude did nothing to correct.

"Why did he do it?"

"Family pretty poor," said Eskiminzin. "Need some things. Em—" He was trying to broach the subject delicately. "Bacon got a sweetheart. My cousin's daughter. Name Consuela. Maybe need some horses for presents."

"I may be getting married, too, but I wouldn't want my bride to think she was getting a thief."

"Been different out here." Eskiminzin's tone grew suddenly cool.

John knew he'd better not fight him. "All right, here's the way this has to work. I am the agent, and I have to be able to justify to Washington anything that happens out here. So, you judges decide, and if I can approve of it, that is what we will do."

Casador and Sanchez and Eskiminzin all studied each other searchingly, without verbalization, a communication that John still found unnerving but knew better now than to show it. After a few minutes Eskiminzin stood. "We are agreed," he said.

"Prisoners will rise," John ordered grandly, and when nothing happened he motioned to Tauclee. "Stand them up."

"All right, Skimmy, how will it be?"

"In this raid, if somebody killed, we say, treat them rough. Punish them. Put them in guardhouse; whip them, maybe. But that not so. Nobody hurt. Stolen horses going back to white people. Young boys like fast, wild horses. You tame them, they do good work. You break spirits, they no good to nobody. So we say, let them go this time. But we tell them, you boys listen; you raid again, you go to guardhouse, maybe get whipped, maybe get heads cut off." Up to now John had seen Eskiminzin talk and banter with his people like a respected leader, but he had never heard him speak with authority. It was a different tone of voice altogether, earnest and not to be trifled with. "Nantan Batunni-ka-yeh, do you agree to this?"

"Frankly, I had rather you punish them. When Washington hears about this, they may say, see, you gave the Apaches their own court and they refuse to control their raiders. They may use it as an excuse to send the soldiers back. Did you think of that?"

"Yes."

"You know that if they act up again, we may all be held responsible, even me."

"Yes."

John nodded solemnly, realizing it was not Washington's reaction that was at this moment in the balance, but the strength of his own word. "Very well. I said that from now on, you will have your own court. If this is what you decide, then that is how it will be. But I want you to take those boys off and warn them so that they don't forget what will happen if they mess up again. Will you do that?"

"Yes."

"All right." John waved to his police. "Let them go." Two of the boys took their freedom quietly and blended into the crowd, but Bacon hissed a vulgarity to Tauclee as the latter slipped the bonds off his wrists.

Tauclee, instead of bridling, looked profoundly sad, but John didn't have time to discover the issue before Eskiminzin was at his side. "Injun worried there for a minute—thought you were gonna say, no good." He seemed his old self again.

John laid a hand on the chief's shoulder. "I almost did. But they are your boys, and I trust you to know best for them."

"You do right." From Eskiminzin's voice John knew he was getting a lesson in that Apache telepathy, gleaning from the chief's eyes that much more had been at stake here than John was aware of. "Doing right like planting fruit," Eskiminzin said at last. "Do it now, fruit come later."

"Which reminds me," John said loudly, raising his hands for quiet. "Before you all go on about your chores, we have one more little business item." He stood on a chair, pulling a small leather sack from his pants pocket. "All you people have been working very hard all winter, digging ditches to water your crops this year. Now, we haven't told you about this, but we have been watching to see who works the hardest, and now they are going to get a reward. I want the chief Zele to come up here."

The Indians in the commissary yard cast their gazes around until all settled on a tall old man in white Mexican breeches and a breechcloth of spare green floral print. He was obviously surprised by the call, but after looking about strode forward, leaning heavily on a slender cane of mountain mahogany to ease the arthritis in his hips. He did not look pleased, and John knew of his earlier reputation as a raider and recalcitrant, but the chief stood in front of him, his long hair almost evenly divided black and white, the skin of his face as furrowed as an old orange peel. "What do you want?" He asked it in Apache, but Grijalba was there to interpret.

"The people from your camp dug more length of irrigation ditch than anybody else. I have here some pumpkin seeds that I brought all the way from New York. They are the best seeds that can be had, and I give them to your people to thank them for their hard work."

Zele grasped the sack of seeds in a gnarled hand. "I was a warrior. I did not work on the ditch."

"No, but you are the head of the camp that did the most work, and so I'm giving the seeds to you. If you need any help with these pumpkins, just ask me."

"What do you know about it?" John didn't need to understand the Apache to hear the offense Zele had taken.

"Why, when I was a boy, I got a prize for growing the best pumpkins in my county."

As Grijalba interpreted, the wizened chief raised his brows, an unmistakably equal mixture of nonplus and contempt. He spat out a few words of Apache as he opened Grijalba's hand and slapped the little sack of seeds into it. He harrumphed straight at John and left, digging his cane furiously into the ground to ease his limp. Grijalba burst into a baritone roar, his chert-like teeth showing pearl gray within the black wool of his beard.

"All right, Mary Hilda, you want to tell me what's so funny?"

"He tells me to tell you, he gonna learn to plant pumpkins, all right, when he get to be an old man!"

"Well, I guess he's got me there." John took the sack.

"When you gonna learn, hombre? You still a boy to him."

The Apaches began dispersing as John kicked the toe of his boot into the gravel and walked away, and Grijalba ambled off to his casita. In the office John told Sweeney about the incident as he tossed the sack of pumpkin seeds onto a shelf. "My mind'll be much eased," declared Sweeney, "when you get it through that thick skull of yours that to the Apaches, young men don't instruct older men. They make suggestions, respectfully. So you haul off and tell a great war leader that he knows

less now than you did when you were a child. And what's more, most of
them still believe gardening is an insult to a warrior. When you tell
them you did it as a boy, they just wonder why you didn't grow out of
it."

John plopped like a sack of potatoes into the chair behind his desk.
"Then may I suggest—respectfully—that you put some water on the
stove? I want some coffee."

"That's better." Sweeney nodded like a schoolmarm. "And aye, you
may."

"What do I do now?"

Sweeney threw a stick in the belly of the stove and set the pot on one
of the lids. "Admit the mistake. Send him the seeds as a gift; tell him he
may want them when he gets older. Make a joke out of it. Mary Hilda
knows how; let him do it."

It was after Chow Soon had brought them lunch when Eskiminzin
came into the office, grinning quirkily. "Injun hear, you pretty big
farmer."

"Now, don't you start in."

"Hi, Old Soldier."

"Hello, chief."

"Listen," Eskiminzin went on. "My wife's cousin has daughter.
Pretty girl. Bacon's sweetheart. You remember?"

"Yes."

"Pretty soon now Consuela gonna be a woman. 'Paches got custom—
have big ceremony when girl become a woman. Three days, holy time,
big religion. Fourth day, have big time—big party, fiesta. You come on
fourth day, bring present?"

"Wait a minute, chief." Sweeney ran a hand down the back of his
head. "No white man has ever been allowed to go to one of those
religious shindigs. What are you getting us into? Are you sure it's all
right with the girl's parents?"

Eskiminzin bit his lip, stalling, wanting to be honest but needing to
put a good face on it. "Injun tell 'em, times changing. Getting different
now. Need to let white people see how we live. They say all right, but
you only come when holy part is over. Fourth day all for fun. Okay you
come for that."

John pushed out of his chair. "Now, Skimmy, I realize you are trying
to help your people into the future, and I am grateful for that, but I
don't know the etiquette for such an appearance."

"What?"

"I might say the wrong thing and get into trouble."

Eskiminzin shrugged. "Don't say nothing."

A smile spread over John's face, slowly, the way first light comes in the morning, at the ready practicality of these people that he could never quite catch on to. "All right, but I want you to stay with me and not let me do anything stupid."

"Sure. Injun do that all the time, anyway." He laughed suddenly when he saw John had not taken it as a joke.

"When's the happy day?"

"Not sure. Consuela tell her mother when first blood come, then have ceremony pretty quick. Injun come tell you in time."

John blushed like a tomato in the sun. He'd had no idea that Eskiminzin's phrase about becoming a woman was tied literally to the onset of her first monthly course. He nodded lamely.

"Oh." Eskiminzin raised a hand into the air. "Injun remember. That old man with the cane say, you give him pumpkin seeds now, maybe. He got a grandson want to plant them."

Sweeney threw his head back and roared, spinning into the back room as he did.

John swiped the sack off the shelf. "Take them. Tell Zele I didn't mean any disrespect."

Eskiminzin took them and headed for the door. "Did that already."

When the mail came that afternoon Sweeney went through it, handing one letter to John. "Here's somethin' interesting. A citizens' group in Tucson is offering to buy uniforms—real matching uniforms—for your Apache police."

"Oh Lord, what are they up to now?" He took it and read it over, thinking hard and fast. He was quiet for several seconds.

"What are you makin' of it?" Sweeney broke in.

It came to him in a quietly sure way, the way a bear turns into the wind and knows exactly what he smells, and John was pleased that at last he was beginning to tune himself to the realities out here. "I'd say it looks like they want to outfit my cops in identifiable clothes so later on they can accuse some of them of something or another and swear they recognized them by their uniforms. Something like that happened at the Camp Grant trial, didn't it?"

"Aye, that it did." Sweeney thought back. "The fellow with the missing tooth."

"That's it."

John leaned back and scratched at an impish feeling that had crawled up his neck and lodged behind his ear. "Gee, free clothes are hard to turn down, but with only four cops it hardly seems worth the bother. Now, if we had a force, say, the size of an infantry company, maybe forty or fifty, now that would be a meaningful gift."

Sweeney raised an arm and pointed southward, his own enthusiasm becoming apparent. "Then march 'em down to Tucson to be in the Fourth of July parade, to show how friendly they are."

"We'll march them under an American flag."

"Ah, my, but won't that be a lovely sight."

John banged his bootheels onto the floor, delighting in the resonant knock of wood at last under his feet. "Get right on it. Let's not give them time to change their minds."

"Aye, now, if you're goin' to have your own army, you'll be needin' somebody to command it—drillin' and trainin' the new fellows. Can you hire somebody?"

"Well, I guess we can find the money."

"I've got just the lad—name's Beauford, just mustered out like me. He's a-coolin' his heels over in Globe tryin' to think what to do with himself."

"You know him?"

"Aye. He's good, an' reliable. He commanded Apache scouts for Crook in '72, an' he speaks the lingo better than I do."

"Get him out here, then." John looked around and took a deep breath. "Is that all today? Nothing from Crook?"

"Just the usual." Sweeney moled through his papers until he found the right one. "Seems that Chiricahua chief, Geronimo, has been at it again. Killed a bunch of people down near the Dragoons. Took one farm woman out to her own smokehouse and hung her up on a meathook. She was still alive when the soldiers found her but she died soon after."

Like a slide in a stereopticon John imagined the scene, and it took shape for him down to the buzzing of the flies and how the woman's shoulders must have sagged forward as she hung twisting on the sharp metal hook. Sickly he pondered how a people as capable of reason and humor and decency and modesty, as he knew his Apaches to be, could also be capable of such unspeakable barbarity.

Sweeney's voice brought him back. "Anyway, Crook says, Geronimo's probably headin' north, and we should keep an eye out for him."

"What does he expect us to do with him?"

"Send for the troopers, I suppose. But I'll be doubtin' they come up near this far. These Apaches up here got less use for them than those buzzards in Tucson. At least the Ring found a way to make money off'n him. These folks up here just think Geronimo gives them all a bad name. They'd kill him if they got their hands on him."

"You think Apaches would fight other Apaches?"

"Aye, for a certainty. Don't you go thinkin' for a minute that just because these people here call you Nantan an' dig ditches for you that they're any less capable on the warpath. When they fight, they're every bit as cunning, and brutal as well. I've seen 'em."

John sat vaguely troubled for several seconds, until, like the motives of the Ring in offering clothes for the police, this issue too clarified for him. "So that if," he doodled in circles with a pencil, speaking slowly, "we do increase the police force, it is possible that one day we might have to take on Geronimo."

"Aye, that's possible."

"And if we do, even Crook believes that Apaches are better at fighting their own kind than white soldiers. Isn't that true?"

"Aye, that's why he recruited scouts from Diablo."

"So that, if our Apaches got forced into a fight with Geronimo, they'd be proving their loyalty to the government; they'd be doing the army a favor by fighting their battle for them, and they'd have a better chance of winning, not to mention rid us all of this evil man." John's voice trailed off, and he looked up at Sweeney.

"Aye, and have a chance to blow off some steam as well."

John leaned back quietly, not thinking thoughts, but as he was learning to do, like an Indian leaving his consciousness open to whatever possibilities came to him.

It was shortly before planting time that Clay Beauford arrived, a big, imposing, iron-jawed bear of a man, a former infantry sergeant with piercing, slightly maniacal eyes. John was sure the man could wither a Joshua tree dead over its roots if he looked at it hard.

On the day of the planting there was a ceremony over the sluice gates before they were opened. There had been good snow up in the mountains, and the river was strong. As the gate was raised and part of the Gila swirled into the ditches, an elderly medicine man in a leather and feather cap, tied with thongs under his chin, chanted and cast pinches of corn pollen into the water. John, too, offered a prayer of thanks, and conducted a short course on modern agriculture. The Apaches heard

him out respectfully before setting to work, planting fields in their traditional manner—the corn set out in rows, beans scattered among them
to vine through the cornstalks, a hill of squash where any natural little
rise presented itself, and a patch of pumpkins wherever the spirit moved
them. John declined to correct them, partly wanting not to spoil the
mood of the moment, but partly too in deference to the possibility that,
in their own desert, their traditional methods might actually work better.

It was at this ceremony that he presented Beauford as Captain of the
Apache Police. He didn't know what to anticipate in reaction, but certainly had no idea—that after his introduction, a number of strapping
young Apache men went up to Beauford and shook hands and chatted
with him as they might an old friend.

"Listen." Eskiminzin held John's bridle as he mounted to leave. "Injun been askin' around about more police. Tell young men, be a policeman, get new clothes, get pay."

"How has the response been?"

"Didn't get forty. Got a hundred, maybe."

John looked down, his mouth open. "Oh my. I'm afraid there will
only be money for forty." He thought fast, not wanting to lose the
opportunity. "I tell you what. You pick the forty best. Tell the others
there isn't money for them all the time yet. But tell them, be ready to
help out if the others need them. That is what we call an auxiliary force.
I will pay them when I need them to work."

"All right."

"Can you find forty who are reliable?"

"What?"

"Can we trust them?"

"Yes, but better maybe you make first four chiefs over police—give
each one ten, maybe—keep an eye on them."

"Good idea. I'll tell Beauford."

"One more—my wife's cousin's daughter. I told you. She becoming a
woman now. You come out in four days, bring presents—maybe coffee
and tobacco?"

"All right, but remember what I asked. Stay by me."

"I hear you," he said. "You know, spring good time. Everything new.
Everything good." Eskiminzin backed off and smiled, slapping John's
horse on the rump as he trotted away.

He found Eskiminzin's camp all but deserted, but the chief was already mounted and met him at the edge.

"Where is everybody, Skimmy?"

"Out there, having big time. We go, too." They rode upstream a few miles to a place where an enclosed little valley opened out into the flat. From several hundred yards out John could see the games and races; they tethered their horses at a communal stake rope and walked into the valley as Eskiminzin hailed a young relative over. "You give boy presents. He take them on ahead to girl's family."

John gave the boy a can of coffee and five small tins of tobacco, and they went on in, soon coming to a large clearing dominated by a huge log construction of some kind.

The sight of this ceremonial lodge surprised him, first because it was shaped like the frame of a teepee, and in the whole of Arizona he had seen nothing that even remotely resembled a teepee, but more because of its size. The four principal logs fitted into holes in the ground aligned with the directions of the compass; joined together at the top were whole, thirty-foot pine trees with the lower limbs cut away, and the uppermost boughs left intact to form a high canopy. The Apaches must have dragged them for miles down from the mountains. Smaller logs rested on the four big ones to form a round perimeter. The green-needled boughs that had been cut from the trunks were woven through the lower part of the framework, making a fragrant, softly impenetrable green wall to a height of about eight feet. John shaded his eyes with a hand to see the very top of the structure, where wafted streamers of eagle feathers and grama grass, talismans he didn't understand but resolved to ask about later. "That's quite a house, Skimmy."

"Girl becoming a woman in there," he answered proudly.

John could hear, coming from inside, drumming and singing, the soft, repetitive nasal chanting whose succession of words held such meaning for these people. John started into the clearing but Eskiminzin touched his shoulder. "Better walk around. Come from east, like sun."

They walked around the plot of ground that had been chopped free of brush. "Can I ask what they are singing about?"

Eskiminzin mulled heavily for a minute, apparently weighing how much of the ceremony it was safe for any white man, even John, to know. "Girl's family," he said at last, "hire old woman that everybody respect. Big job. Pay her a horse, maybe. Girl live in big lodge four days, old woman take care of her. Dress her, comb hair. Tell her how to be a woman—be wise and good. Not have men till she get married.

Make good home for her husband. Help out old people and poor people. Raise children right. Be grateful for what she got. All that in the songs there."

John was struck by how much more profound all this was than anything that was done for white girls at that age. They received the usual Sunday school stuff and morality at home, but no recognition that came from the whole community, no gateway into the adult circle that made her feel part of anything more than the immediate family she had always known. "That's lovely," he said, and wished that Mary were here to see it.

"Yes."

On the east side of the big, pine-boughed teepee John saw its opening, the only one, and extending out from it on the ground a lane or runway about ten paces wide and fifty yards long, kicked free of rocks and marked off by willow saplings stuck in the ground. Family groups and their lean-tos were scattered about on the east side of the clearing, irregularly, like a poorly organized fair. Just off the end of this runway the girl's family had set up shop—a long line of lean-to shelters with cookfires going in front of them, and even a couple of wagons loaded with sacks of glazed mescal and corn cakes and fry bread. Several women, of different ages, were spreading buckskins on the ground and piling up food for everybody to eat during the day.

All at once an elderly woman came out of the lodge and gave a ululant cry or yodel, her tongue wagging back and forth to the sides of her mouth. The sound was taken up by all the women in the camp, the games stopped, and the whole crowd began to gather about the runway.

After several minutes the girl appeared, about fourteen and small for her age, dressed in the most magnificent buckskin dress John could have imagined, heavily trimmed with fringes that tied at the ends to tiny tin cone tinklers, both skirt and blouse gorgeously dyed with crosses, crescent moons, and other designs in red and yellow. Rank on rank of bead necklaces piled about her neck; even her moccasins, also of buckskin, just visible through the fringes of the dress that fell nearly to her ankles, were beaded and decorated.

The girl's hair, long and thick and straight, was dusted solid with the clinging, golden yellow corn pollen, and her face was rubbed with it, but that didn't hide the fact that she was strikingly handsome. Her smile was gentle, beatific in a studied but genuine way; none of the Indians present, least of all herself, had any doubt that she could collect the forces of good luck from out of the ether, and dispense them through her pollen-rubbed hands.

The old woman led the girl to a big flat rock about a foot high that had been spread over with a buckskin, then stood by the girl's side with a tray basket of pollen. The people began forming into a line, and Eskiminzin steered John to the end of it. As they looked forward they saw her repeatedly pinch into the basket and sprinkle grains of pollen over each person who came to her, and converse with them briefly in the most charming and regal manner. After each blessing the person moved onto the long line of food that her parents had put out and helped himself. When John's turn finally came, Consuela held out her powdery yellow hands to him, palms down, and he took them. Looking down at him, she said something after several seconds to Eskiminzin.

"She says, 'This man has his eye on a sweetheart.' "

John felt his lower jaw go slack before he raked up a smile to cover it, but she knew she had found him out. She dipped into her tray basket and sprinkled pollen over John's bald head, one of the very few times any of the Indians ever saw him hatless. "May you have good luck with her," she said.

Eskiminzin interpreted and returned John's thanks, when she nodded to him in dismissal, and they walked away. "Don't rub that off." Eskiminzin pointed at John's head. "Luck go bad."

They followed in the line over to the food, and Eskiminzin introduced him to Consuela's parents, who received him with a frost that told him instantly that none of this met with their approval. For the first time John saw in Eskiminzin's eyes a look almost of helplessness, or at least, insecurity that he had done the right thing.

"Skimmy, I want you to tell them exactly what I say."

"All right."

"Tell them I am glad they have let me come. Call them by their names, and thank them. Tell them I want to shake hands with them."

When Eskiminzin was through the girl's father, a large man with features at once round and angular, glared stonily at Eskiminzin before extending his hand. John shook it, then the woman's.

"Tell them, some men in Washington say that Apache religion is a bad thing and ought to be forbidden. But I see that this is a good ceremony, and because you have let me come, I can tell them the Apaches are doing right and ought to be left alone."

Eskiminzin spoke slowly and carefully, and Consuela's father said back through him, "This is how our chief said it would be. We are not sure about it, but he is our chief. Go over there and eat some of our food."

Eskiminzin nudged him on. "That pretty close," he whispered. "You sure say the right thing."

"I meant it." They helped themselves to some glazed mescal and fry bread, and a hunk of roast venison, mingling and making talk as friendly as John could with the crowd, most of whose behavior was guarded in a way that he had been spoiled away from. At one point he touched Eskiminzin's arm and pointed out the insolent young Bacon and the companions he remembered from the trial. "Are he and the girl still engaged?"

"Sweethearts? Yup. They get married pretty soon now you bet."

"Maybe I should go over and wish him well."

"That maybe not too good thing. Injun think, he maybe not want to talk to you. I tell him for you later."

John nodded. "When we get back I'll give you a couple of little presents to pass on to them. Would that be all right?"

"Yes." After a while Eskiminzin whispered, "Better go now. Mountain Spirits not come if you here."

They walked back around the clearing the way they had come in, John glimpsing as the front of the big lodge passed from view the crowd gathered to cheer Consuela as she ran a course out the runway, fetching a bundle of food from a basket at the end of it.

"Injun stay here. You go on." Eskiminzin seemed troubled. As John mounted, the chief looked up at him. "You think Skimmy mess up? Let you come?"

John laid a hand on his shoulder. "No. Surely not."

The summer was peaceful, and the crops grew well. At the Fourth of July parade in Tucson, John and Eskiminzin rode at the head of their forty uniformed police. Nosy, Sneezer, Goody-Goody, and Tauclee had sergeants' stripes on their sleeves, each marching with his platoon. Captain Beauford was at their head, stopping at the reviewing stand in the brilliant sunshine to pace them through a rifle drill. Oury and the others in the reviewing stand smiled and applauded, and John knew they were loathing every minute of it.

He had paved the way. The Apache court met every issue day, and every time there was a conviction, John wrote an account of it to the Tucson newspaper. At first they were not printed, but when handbills began appearing on porch posts and barbershop poles, subscribed, "For the information of the people of Tucson, John Philip Clum, Agent," the paper relented and began publishing his reports, sometimes even with favorable, if grudging, editorial endorsements.

By the time of the parade, John had chosen a new look for himself. The brown duck suits were gone, replaced by white cotton breeches, Mexican serapes, and one item he bought during the parade, a huge straw sombrero. He grew a mustache as long and full as Mary Hilda's, but decided not to compete for the beard. Even before the parade, he and Sweeney had received word that an inspection of their Agency would be conducted in mid-July by elders of the Dutch Reformed Church, who maintained a peripheral role in its management. About a week after the parade, letters from Tucson began arriving at the Agency, some timid, some from housewives expressing their good will toward the San Carlos Apaches, some even enclosing small gifts or trinkets.

They spent a part of each morning, even the morning when the delegation was to arrive, in answering every letter, fully and kindly.

CHAPTER 10

When John heard the carriage pull up he rose from his desk and settled the great sombrero on his head. He pulled his serape from its peg in the hall and peered into the bit of mirror on the wall. He wrapped the garment first across his chest, under his arms, and up behind his left shoulder to hang down in front. Too Roman, he thought, pulling it off and draping it over his shoulders like a cape, and he bunched it under his chin. He could not have looked more in place. He waited until he was sure the wheels had stopped before he swung open the front door and stepped out onto the porch.

"Oh my God," he hushed to himself. He felt his starch drain down from his knees and flow through his boots out onto the porch. He paused for a second to plug the leak and regenerate some poise. He heard his spurs jingle distantly below him as he jumped down to the ground and strode over to the carriage. "Miss Ware." He had recovered his swagger. "It cannot be you. It is impossible."

"It is possible, Mr. Clum," she measured the return, "because I am impossible. You have said so many times, and I should very much favor a drink of water."

John stretched up his arms as she leaned out and put her hands on his shoulders and hopped to the ground. He caught her by the body, his hands just beneath her shoulders. He let them linger there for just a second, as close as he had ever dared approach physical intimacy. "Mary, dearest," he whispered.

"Johnny." Her eyes sparked to life for a bright instant. They were wonderful, dark eyes, set in a cream-colored, aristocratic face. Her dress and its gathered bustle were of the darkest red velvet, bordered at the long sleeves and high throat with a narrow band of black satin and trimmed with white lace. Her hair, which he knew fell in rich black tresses, was pinned up beneath a hat of the same red velvet, with a fall of lace. The touch of rouge on her high, curving cheeks matched her clothes so convincingly that when she spoke it was like a doll come to life—a beautiful face and dress, but nothing of warmth or substance beneath. Yet, he knew better. "You do have water here." She eyed him suspiciously.

"Oh yes."

"I believe we would like some, too." John had lost notice of the two somberly dressed, middle-aged gentlemen who had been riding in the carriage opposite Mary Ware.

"John, you remember these two fine elders, Mr. Hayman and Mr. Josephs."

"Yes, gentlemen, please come down and be comfortable." He shook hands with them as they descended. Josephs was stockier and more swarthy, but beyond that they were like two peas in a pod, both stout, round-faced, with red spots on the upper sides of their noses from spectacles being put on and taken off.

John conducted them into the office and excused himself. He poured a pitcher of cool water from the evaporator under the back lean-to and returned and poured their refreshment. "I am delighted to see Miss Ware, of course, but I don't understand how—I mean, how it happens."

Josephs nodded. "There were of course to have been three of us making this trip. Brother Desmond, whom you also know, fell ill at the last moment, and Miss Ware insisted on accompanying us, as our correspondent."

"Whatever for?" asked John loftily, but silently pleading in the other direction, that she would blurt out her love for him and throw herself into his arms.

"I always liked to travel," she answered in surprise. "You know that."

The banter between them was evident, and Hayman, who appeared to be much the less convivial of the two clerics, was beginning to show some strain in his indulgence. "Tell us, Mr. Clum," he broke in, "what have you arranged for us?"

"I thought you would prefer to rest this afternoon, after such a trip."

"Not at all." He thumped his glass down with decisiveness. "The sooner to work the better."

"Well then, presently my assistant, Mr. Sweeney, and I will take you on a tour of the Agency, pointing out improvements made during the year, and show you around the irrigation project. My interpreter, Mr. Grijalba, has gone out to bring in a few of the Apache chiefs who asked to see you as soon as you arrived."

Josephs looked up with some alarm. "Is that all we will see of your Indians?"

"Oh no, no. There is a full council on for tomorrow night. The ones over today are just a few intimate friends of the family, so to speak."

They heard the kitchen door open and shut, and Sweeney entered the office. "Well, speak of the devil," said John.

"I hope not," Hayman rejoined with some disapproval, as he and Josephs rose and were introduced.

Sweeney put out both his rough old hands to greet Mary, one under hers and one over it, patting incessantly. When he spoke there was a quality in his voice that was new to John's hearing. "Ah, now, 'tis a high pleasure to be meetin' you, miss. If you could hear how this young fellow talks about you days in and out, you'd know what a rare person he thinks you are." In embarrassment Mary's eyes flickered under the praise, like candles in a draft, and suddenly John realized what people meant when they talked about Irish charm.

"Well, Sweeney, let's go out and show these people around. Are we ready?"

"This tour sounds a little industrial for me," said Mary with a faint laugh. "You menfolk go on ahead; I'll stay here and catch my breath."

"Then I'll keep you company. Sweeney here can answer any questions you gentlemen may have about our programs."

Hayman's lips tightened as he left, followed by Josephs and Sweeney. When they were gone through the front door Mary stood up quickly. "I lied. I'm not the least bit tired. Let's take a walk."

John escorted her through the kitchen and out the back door. "You haven't changed. You're still the managing kind of woman, aren't you?"

"You seem to be managing pretty well yourself. You must have made quite some progress with the Apaches to be referring to them as intimate friends of the family."

"Ha! I couldn't very well tell them that the tamer chiefs wanted a chance to come in and eyeball them before trusting them with the wilder chiefs tomorrow."

Mary stopped dead in her tracks. "Oh dear!"

"You don't need to tell them I said so."

She walked again, still serious. "No. Do you live in danger out here, Johnny?"

"Nah." He waved it off. "The biggest danger to me is being pen-poisoned by somebody—you remember I wrote you about them, the warmongers and profiteers."

"You called them the Ring."

"They are smart and they are powerful, and my success here is a thorn in their side." They walked on in silence until they reached the river, lower in its banks now with the progress of summer, with larger rocks breaking the surface with low, hissing gurgles as the water flowed past. "Up or down?"

"Away from the others," she said.

"That'll be down." They covered much distance both in yards and small talk, before he got the courage to reach down and touch her hand, and she stopped. He cleared his throat. "You remember when I asked you to marry me?"

She smiled. "Which time?"

As usual when he tried to talk serious, it seemed the safest course was to join her game. "Pick one."

"All right, I've got one."

"I've never forgiven you for turning me down."

Mary laughed out loud. "You were only twelve!"

"Of course that is the time you would have to pick." He looked up across the river. "Well, we would have managed."

"Oh yes. I remember that was the year of the mighty pumpkin crop."

He put his arm around her and led her on. "If you had married me I would have diversified."

"Oh, Johnny, it's just—" She freed his hand from her shoulder and pulled his arm tighter around her neck. "It's always seemed like my life should stand for more than just being somebody's wife. I've needed time to discover what I need for myself."

"Will you let me know when you find it?"

She smiled wryly. "I'm thinking of another time you proposed."

"No, never mind." Their walk downriver had taken them beyond a thicket of carrizo that put them out of sight of the Agency buildings. "You've had an excuse every time." He picked up a smooth, flat pebble and threw it low across the water; it skipped twice before smacking a rock on the opposite bank. "But you'll run out of them one of these days."

Wistfully she nodded. "Very likely." She seated herself on a low boulder and took in the valley. "Not exactly the mighty Mississip, is it?"

"We're lucky it's lasted this long. It'll be gone in a few weeks. Then hopefully we'll get some rain in August or September to boost the crops into harvest. The Apaches have worked so hard; this would be a terrible year for the rain to fail."

"It must get lonely for you here sometimes."

He scraped the sole of his boot across a sharp-edged rock, leaving a thin curl of yellow-brown clay, and walked over to her. "Once a week for nearly a year I've written you how terribly I miss you, and you come out here and ask me if I'm lonely. It is cruel to tease me so."

His back was to the sun, and she squinted when she looked up at him. "I'm not teasing you, Johnny."

He looked at her for a few seconds in a kind of dumb appreciation, wondering at but not calculating the weight and meaning of this last assertion. "Well, we'd better get back so we can meet the chiefs when they come in."

The two approached the compound and knew they were late. Sweeney, Grijalba, and the two churchmen stood among a group of Apache men wearing an assortment of pantaloons and breechcloths, some with shirts and some without; a huddle of women and children hovered in the background. John was aware of a quickening of Mary's senses for her first meeting of Indians, and just as intuitively felt her attention being drawn to the women and bashful, dirty-looking children. "Well, I see you've already gotten acquainted," he said when they were near enough to speak, and he shook hands all around with the Apache men.

"Aye." Sweeney gestured over the group. "All workin' in the fields they were, even the women and wee folk."

"Wonderful!" Mary had held back as John greeted the chiefs, and he retreated a few steps to fetch her. "Just the impression I wanted to make," he whispered. "Just perfect." He turned and cleared his throat. "Now, you chiefs and headmen of the Apaches," he was going to make quite some little production of this, "I want you to meet my very special friend, Miss Mary Ware, of Ohio."

Eskiminzin hissed an urgent command, and in front of her the Indian men formed up in a line at the back of which he stationed himself. John introduced her to the chiefs individually, in unexpressed alarm at the way her delicate lily of a hand was taken and squeezed by other hands as dark and hard as walnut burls. She received them all graciously, with a smile and a nod, and a personal question expressive of the common touch, inclining her head to Grijalba to translate but never breaking her kindly gaze into their eyes. John was afraid Zele and some of the other older chiefs would think her too forward, too much at ease in a situation where, like their women, she should be a quiet spectator. But then it struck him, unexpectedly, the similarity between this scene and Consuela's Blessing Ceremony a few weeks previous. These old men were behaving exactly the same, accepting her modesty and favor with a meekness that could not have been more decorous. Only Hayman and Josephs remained guarded, silently alert for some treachery or disrespect. John was so proud of her he could have popped.

When Eskiminzin was finally presented to her he removed his hat, a black hat with a low domed crown and wide flat brim, like a schoolboy's or a bishop's. He took her hand and said, *"Bienvenidos, señorita."*

"Gracias."

"Agent Batunni-ka-yeh talks all the time Mary, Mary. Now you here." He leaned forward and made a furtive gesture at John. "Be careful. He not let you leave again, maybe."

"John has written me much about you. Thank you for being his friend."

Eskiminzin stood back, rimming his hatbrim with his fingers as he cleared his throat lowly for John to move in closer. "My woman," he mumbled. "My woman want to meet your woman."

"Mr. Grijalba," Mary spoke up. "Please thank Eskiminzin for his esteem, but kindly explain to him that I am not 'his woman.' " If annoyance could be pleased, hers was, and it showed, but as Grijalba explained the lack of betrothal Eskiminzin's face fell.

"Soon, maybe," said John, and Eskiminzin broke into a hearty laugh. John took Ethel by the arm and pulled her forward, her big body shyly resisting the shine of expectation in her face. "Mary, may I present Ethel Eskiminzin?"

At the mention of her name Ethel thrust her big brown hand forward. "How!" she said with gusto, smiling so broadly that her eyes became quite small, like tiny black buttons in Morocco leather, and Mary noticed her yellow, even teeth.

Mary extended her hand and saw it consumed by the thick, meaty, dark fingers, pumped four times vigorously, and then released. "Mrs. Eskiminzin, I am so delighted to meet you at last."

Ethel looked with confusion at Grijalba, who framed the words into the proper Apache. She smiled, satisfied, and stepped back a few feet, her face gradually assuming an expression of pure appraisal. Other conversation lulled as Ethel nodded sagaciously. Mary looked queasily at John but had no chance to speak before Ethel began slowly to pace a circle around her, looking her down and up and down again. "No got much bottom," she said at last. "No much good make 'em big little agent baby."

Mary gasped. "What!"

John turned away suddenly and lowered his head, unwilling to provoke Mary's displeasure with a show of mirth. Mary's face blanched white and then blushed so heavily that her rouge nearly disappeared. "Mr. Grijalba, please tell Mrs. Eskiminzin I agree that motherhood is a blessing, but surely a woman can be good for more than just bearing children."

As Grijalba spoke Ethel nodded, shifting her weight to her left leg and putting her left hand on the hip. When Grijalba was through she said, "You cook?"

John buried his face in his hand and shook all over. He always believed that Mary's most expressive features were her wonderful eyes. They were so elegantly defined that when she widened them in surprise the resulting expression was one less of query than of profound insult. It was a look that conveyed sufficient disdain to drop a bull buffalo stone-dead.

"Yes," frosted Mary, "me much good cook."

Ethel, however, failed to take her meaning. "You make 'em good 'pache fry bread?"

"No, I have never been taught to make fried bread."

Ethel gave a satisfied harrumph. "You come. I show." She reached out to Mary's hand and tugged her with such energy that Mary lurched forward out of balance.

The elder named Hayman waded forward. "Now just a minute." He broke Ethel's grip and pitched her hand down to her side. Before he could say more they were all stricken by a look in Ethel's face of the most wretched pain and remorse. Her eyes dampened, and with her mouth partly opened she looked first at her husband and then at John. She looked pleadingly at Mary and shook her head in ignorance of what she had done wrong.

Like a bolt Mary realized that Ethel's husky familiarity was totally unaffected, brittle as glass with insecurity and an almost pathetic desire to please. John suddenly believed that he saw the entire Apache experience in that flash of shame and anguish and embarrassment. "Go on, Mary," he said softly. "It would mean a lot. You'll be safe."

Hayman started to protest, but Josephs touched his arm. "Perhaps we should allow it. It's why she came."

John had no time to puzzle over this before Mary reached down, took Ethel's hands in her own, and smiled. "Okay, Ethel," she said. "You show."

Ethel understood only that the confusion, whatever it was, had passed, her meaning finally perceived. "Good," she said, and the two women disappeared in the direction of Eskiminzin's camp.

When they were gone Eskiminzin stood by John's side. "You got good woman. Not 'fraid."

"I think so, too. Can you see she gets back by dinnertime?"

"Got to," he answered placidly. "She bringin' you bread."

Sweeney, Grijalba, and the workers ate and retired to their evening diversions, leaving plentiful remnants to simmer while John and his guests waited. They talked pleasantly if warily until nearly sundown, when they heard the sound of horses outside.

John crossed to the window to see Mary sliding as best she could down off an unsaddled horse. On the other horse Ethel loomed above her, her long, side-flowing ponytails cascading about her shoulders. She was balancing on her lap a tray basket whose contents were lumpily covered with a swatch of trade cloth. She lowered the basket down to Mary, then reached down for another emphatic handshake. "Good bread," she said. "You eat 'em all up. Get big, strong like Ethel."

Mary balanced the basket against her waist. "You surely showed me something new today. Thank you."

Ethel nodded, took the reins of the second horse, and led him away.

"Well, look at you." John chuckled when Mary made her dusty way into the office.

She crossed the room and set the basket on John's desk, and whisked the cloth away to reveal a mound of golden fried hunks of bread. "I did it," she said proudly, and alternated between gusts of laughter and embarrassed stifles. "Oh mercy, I look like I've been in a war," she said at last. "My good dress, I didn't have a chance to change." Two brown smudges showed where she had spent most of the afternoon on her knees.

"We placed your baggage in the front room across the hall," gestured Josephs. "You'll find water and towels. You must want to rest before supper."

Mary's hands flew up to her cheeks. "Oh no, you waited for me? You should have gone ahead and eaten. I won't be a minute." She rushed across the room with a weary kind of energy, still resisting the press of unescaped peals of laughter.

Chow Soon had made a rabbit stew, with dumplings in the absence of potatoes, and pungent new turnips from the early planting in the garden. Canned peaches were the dessert, and Chow Soon had even whipped some cream, a talent retained from his San Francisco days. There was also jam to dollop on Mary's fry bread. In the front room after the meal, Mary settled herself with feminine exhaustion on the parson's bench. "My word, what a day," she sighed.

Josephs took a chair, crossing his legs and leaning forward, situating himself in a curl for all the world like an old tomcat. "Well now, Mr. Clum, this seems an opportune time to discuss something on our agenda that we have neglected."

John had been lighting the lamps on his desk, and turned and looked at him expectantly.

"The Indian Bureau has noted what appears to be an unusual degree of cooperation between yourself and the army in Arizona." John's eyes widened, but Josephs held up a hand and continued, "Now, they regard this as a very good thing, of course."

"Of course."

"But, well, frankly they are worried at what the cost might have been."

"The cost?"

"The Bureau in Washington wants us to return with your assurance that in order to win this . . . relationship, with the army, that you have not surrendered to them any prerogatives of the Indian Bureau."

"How can they think that? I've put this Agency back under Bureau jurisdiction after nearly three years of army control."

"It is their view that titular control of the Agency has little meaning if the source of power still lies with the army."

John began to feel the discomfiture of smelling a rat without being able to call it a rat. "I'm sorry. You'll have to be more specific."

"We did see prisoners in your guardhouse today. That traditionally has been a function of the military."

"Oh, is that all," breathed John. "Those fellows were sentenced to the calaboose by Apache judges on their own court. They—"

Josephs and Hayman exchanged confounded stares.

"Didn't they tell you in Washington the Apaches have their own courts and police force now? Surely they must have."

"No." Josephs shook his head. "I don't recall mention of that at all."

The insulting question strained to leap from John's mouth whether it hadn't occurred to them that they might have been told only what some one particular rat in Washington wanted them to know. Indeed the angle was new to him, a potentially useful resource to be husbanded with care. "Who briefed you before your trip?"

"The Assistant Commissioner."

John nodded. He should have known.

"I'm sure it was just an oversight." Josephs waved off the point. "They approve of this program?"

"Naturally. An enlightened judiciary is an essential element to their advancement, in my view."

"Then there are no military guards."

"There are no guards at all, for the moment. All the Apaches know who is locked up and why. If one escapes there is no place to go but home, and then the Apache court will send them back for a double term, as punishment for skipping out."

"No guards," glowered Hayman.

"All prisoners currently confined are held for petty crimes. None of them are really dangerous or I would have a couple of guards on duty."

"There haven't been any serious crimes."

"Nope." The truth was that John had heard of a couple of killings, but in both instances the victims' families hunted down and dispatched the murderers with such swiftness that they never came before the court. It was an aspect of Apache justice that John thought it best not to relate. If it ever worked less well than its American counterpart, he could change it then.

"I think we may say that your explanation on this point is satisfactory," said Hayman without a trace of expression. "But now then, Mr. Clum, as regards your more ecclesiastical duties, apart from your official position as agent. A few things have reached our ears concerning your obligations as a missionary that have caused no little distress among the leadership of our Church."

John smiled uneasily. "Well, as you might gather from your tour, we have been so taken up here with meeting everyday necessities to be very effective in that work."

"Yes, that is understandable, but please, if we may?" He extracted some notes from an inner coat pocket.

"Yes, by all means."

"We have heard in this connection that you once told an Indian, not that God created man, but that . . . early men looked like coyotes? Whatever could you have meant by that?"

"What!" John flushed with anger and pointed at the papers. "Who told you that?"

"We have numerous sources of information."

"No doubt."

"Did you say this, Mr. Clum?"

"Not with anything like that meaning, no. This is taken entirely out of context and I demand to know who reported it."

"We cannot tell you."

"Then how do you dare to present me with this kind of hearsay? Don't you know there are elements in Washington, as well as Arizona, that have an important financial and political interest in seeing this Agency fail? Their influence reaches to the highest levels of the government. They stoke you full of hints and innuendos, and you come flapping out here like Chicken Little to see what I am doing to make the sky fall. Any disruption on the reservation serves their purpose, and you play right into their hand when you believe everything they tell you."

"Mr. Clum." Hayman's visage assumed the frosty, formal rigidity that nature was kind enough to reserve for joyless churchmen. "We cannot think that you exculpate your own misdeeds by scattering about such wild and vague charges."

John threw up his hands. "What misdeeds? What have I done now?"

"We have a reference that as recently as last month you attended pagan rites known as"—he glanced down at the paper, wrinkling his nose through his pince-nez—"a Puberty Celebration. Can this be true?" John saw Mary sink back in the parson's bench, her mouth open.

"I was only being polite!"

Hayman removed the spectacles from his nose and shook his head. "I must say we are deeply shocked. What could you have meant to accomplish by such a thing?"

John's demeanor passed from protest into a low but deliberate smolder. "I believe you will find an answer in your Bible."

The fear in Mary's eyes was apparent. "Steady, Johnny."

"No, Mary, this is an old fight—the same one that Saint Paul went through with the Corinthians." He glared straight at Hayman. " 'And unto the Jews I became as a Jew, that I might gain the Jews . . . I am made all things to all men, that I might by all means save some.' You do remember reading that somewhere down the line, don't you?"

Josephs pinched his chin between his thumb and first finger, nodding slowly. "I can agree that you must have been well intentioned. However, we cannot think it a wise policy to in any way lend your approval to such barbaric perversions as primitive sexual rites."

"For your information there is nothing sexual about it."

"Bah," Hayman scoffed. "How could there not be? A festival cele-

brating the"—he waved his hands in search of a delicate phrase—"onset of fertility?"

"Because," John started to shout, then gave it up and sighed, and got
to his feet. "Gentlemen, this Agency has never been in better shape. The
Indians here have never been so well disposed, industrious, and cooper-
ative. We are making progress, but if you are dissatisfied with my work
here, you have only to replace me. Today you inspected the building
and irrigation programs; in the morning I shall lay out all my books and
records for you. Most of the chiefs and headmen will be in for a conference tomorrow evening so you can meet them and ask them anything
you want. You may then reach any decision you please. Good night."

John strode quickly into the hall and out the back door, hearing
before it banged shut behind him the scuff-scuff of moccasined feet
running off into the gloom. He sat in the open tail of the buckboard that
had brought the three to San Carlos, not caring for the moment what
Indian the spying feet carried away or whose side he was on. Yet, the
realization that the Ring had an informant even in Eskiminzin's camp
was hard to bear. He stretched his legs across the back of the bed and
folded his arms across his chest, not moving until at the sound of other
footsteps he turned his head and saw Mary walking slowly toward him.

She said nothing, but leaned against the back of the wagon. When she
wrapped her arms around his neck he uncrossed his arms and held her
for several minutes, not daring to relinquish the comfort he had longed
for ever since he came here. When at last she pulled back a little he
released her, and saw that all the while she had been quietly crying,
without even a quiver in her breathing. He smiled and brushed her
cheeks. "You'd better go back inside before those old goats think I'm
having my primitive way with you."

She ran her fingers through his hair. "Be sure and say your prayers
tonight." Mary left as quietly as she had come, and John remained in
the bed of the buckboard until he saw the lights go out in the headquarters building. Then he went to bed down in the commissary.

The morning was refreshingly cool, and John was up before any of
the rest. Only Chow Soon had been about, for there were coffee, biscuits, and jerky gravy waiting on the stove in the kitchen. John ventured briefly into the office before returning, chucking onto the breakfast table a stack of papers to sort through. He poured himself a cup of
coffee and sat down, then looked up as he heard a rustle of cloth at the
door. "Mary, my goodness, you're up early." He was surprised and

comforted to see her looking so well rested and, to his eyes, radiant in such a forlorn place. Little did he suspect that she had hardly slept at all.

As he got up and poured her a cup of coffee she looked over the papers, progress reports on the building and irrigation works. "What are you doing?"

"Biscuits?"

She shook her head.

"I've got four hundred men who volunteered to work today. I have to find jobs for everybody or they find less constructive ways to spend their time."

When she sat next to him he ignored the papers to gaze at her, but she sat still and quiet, unsmiling, one hand on her coffee cup and one in her lap. "You are still angry about last night, aren't you?"

He held her free hand. "Not at you, Mary. It's just that I can't see how grown and intelligent men could come all this way to throw such ridiculous twaddle up at me."

"They're not bad men. Surely you don't think they are involved in this conspiracy that you talk about."

"No, no, but what's just as bad, they absolutely refuse to see that it exists. And I am doing the best possible job under the circumstances."

"They know." She squeezed his hand. "Believe me, everybody knows you are doing a marvelous job at running the Agency. But look at it from their side. They're not bureaucrats, they're churchmen. The government says it wants their influence on the Indians but doesn't give them a bit of power over policy. Their only concern is for the Indians' souls, and it's not your ability as an administrator that concerns them, but your energy as a missionary. And, Johnny, they're not wrong; you must also be spending time at that."

He looked into her eyes and knew she was right. "What do they want me to tell them? Believe in Jesus or I'll shoot you? That's what the Spanish did; it didn't work. Believe in Jesus or I won't feed you? They don't need us to feed them. They managed perfectly well before we ever came along. It's not as simple as saying go out and convert Indians." He knew that she was not chastising him but trying to make peace between him and the Church hierarchy. He gave an amused snort. "The irony of it is that these people are already closer to God than most preachers I know."

"Well, you've gotten them to trust you. That's a good start. Now, I want you to fix me a biscuit and take me for another walk."

John opened two of Chow Soon's biscuits, spooned on some jerky gravy, and closed them. He handed one to Mary as he held the back door open for her. They walked upstream beyond the irrigation ditches, through the low flats by the river, taking in the curious, paint-store pungency of the creosote bushes in the bright yellow flush of the morning.

"One thing I am curious about," she said. "That ceremony, or whatever it was, that you went to, what was it really?"

"Oh, the Apaches believe that when a girl becomes a woman, it's such a blessed time in her life that she has the power to spread good luck to her family and neighbors. So her folks throw a big shindig for her to bless the people, and they hire an older woman to lecture her on adult responsibilities."

"Oh, is that all?"

"Basically. It sort of combines confirmation with a sweet-sixteen party." John wished the moment would last forever, the crunch of gravel under their feet muffled by the lightest fall of dew. "Is that so awful?"

"No, I think it's lovely." Small Apache rancherias were spaced through the brush, moved down to be near the shallow hiss of the river while it lasted. The smoke from their breakfast fires rose thinly from the wickiups of the early risen. Some of the Indians looked up as John and Mary passed within sight but did not wave or offer any greeting. "They don't seem very friendly," she said softly. "I thought you were so popular."

"They don't just halloo out at someone. Bad manners."

Mary nodded.

"Of course, now that we've been seen taking a walk together the gossip is going to spin for days."

She half scowled. "Which you knew perfectly well when you brought me out here."

"Well, let's give them something to talk about." He pulled her hand up to his lips and kissed it.

She struck a pose. "Oh, my reputation is forfeit."

"Look over there, Mary. Don't stare, just look out of the corner of your eye." Through a clearing in the greasewood they saw a young Apache woman sitting on the ground, beneath the ramada outside her wickiup. Bare-breasted, her image softened by thin mist, her hair cascaded unrestrained about her shoulders. She was bathing her baby, laid before her on a soft buckskin, rinsing him off with a sponge of ball moss. The cradleboard stood unlaced against the side of the wickiup; she began to sing quietly as she picked the infant up and nursed him.

They watched her for several seconds, then walked slowly off, holding hands. "Mary, this is the closest thing to Eden left on earth."

"What is she singing?"

"It's a lullaby about how to become a chief. To be kind and gentle and generous. To fight only in defense; to be fair with everyone." John turned her toward him and put his hands on her shoulders. "I could get her to teach it to you—to sing to our children."

Mary's dark eyes looked away, half afraid. "Don't be silly. I can't sing a note and you know it."

John touched his fingertips to her chin and turned her head back. "Marry me. Marry me, my dearest heart."

Her back shivered. "All right."

"All right?" Every ounce of him wanted to leap up and whoop until the whole valley echoed. "Did you say all right?"

"Yes, you've caught me in a weak moment. I shall marry you."

Absently he led her on. "Well, well, we better set a date—to give me something to look forward to." Their walking had brought them to a sandbar close to a willow thicket, and Mary edged toward the trees. "When's a good time?"

"In Ohio, next spring." She withdrew her hand from his and looked out across the river. "Reverend Jeffries has us down for April 15."

John's face went utterly slack until the truth hit home. "Why, you, you came out here with every intention—"

She backed away, giggling, daring him to chase her. When he lunged for her she dodged and dashed into the willows; when they were out of sight she let him catch her. They crashed to the sand with a rustling whump of her petticoats and she rolled onto her back, beaming. He pinned her with his hands on her shoulders, and waited a minute, catching his breath. "My God," he whispered. "My God, I do love you so." He lowered his head and kissed her.

She closed her eyes to savor the moment as well, until she felt a wet drop on her cheek. She opened her eyes and saw his close, closed lashes holding their moisture like a thistle arrests the fall of rain. She had never thought it possible to love someone so much.

It was midmorning when they finally headed back to the Agency, arm in arm. "One thing about all this still has me buffaloed," he said.

"How in the world did you talk your way into a ticket out here? Didn't your papa fight you?"

"No. I told him that you had several times proposed marriage, that I was disposed to accept, but I didn't think it wise to undertake the life of a missionary's wife without seeing firsthand what it would be like. I had met Mr. Josephs before, so I wrote to him for permission to tag along on this much of the tour."

"And if I hadn't proposed again?"

"I would have had to take matters into my own hands."

Yes, he thought, she would have.

When they regained the headquarters they found Josephs and Hayman quietly leafing through account books he had set out for them. Josephs looked up at Mary. "Now?"

"Now."

He rose and extended his hand, approaching John. "May I be the first to offer my congratulations?"

"Well, you certainly are that." John took it. "I am supposed to be in charge here, and I seem to be the last to find out anything."

Hayman shook his hand as well. "We've just made a start on the Agency records. They are quite meticulous, and we must certainly commend your thrift. How, for my curiosity, did you come by cattle at ten dollars a head?"

"Shrewdness is an important virtue out here."

"Last night." Hayman shifted his weight, stalling. "Last night I spoke hastily."

"No, please." John cut him off. "Mary and I talked it out this morning. You were right. Now that the Agency is on its feet I think we can make much better progress in the missionary field."

"I'm sure you will. Now, Mr. Josephs and I are going to release you and your intended to your duties, while we prepare our report. When will the chiefs be in?"

"For dinner. I'll have Chow Soon kill a steer and we'll tie the feed bag on 'em before they talk."

John and his guests feasted that evening—on steak, with beans and fresh greens and corn bread. For the Indians, Chow Soon had roasted chunks of the rest of the steer, and in front of the commissary he cooked a huge kettle of beans, and placed more bins of corn bread. The Apaches began to drift in about dusk, and after the chiefs and warriors had eaten their fill they filed into the building, leaving their families to finish up and pack what they could not eat.

A table with chairs were set up inside the building, and the several kerosene lanterns that hung from the walls were lit, lending their peculiar, close-hanging illumination. All the chiefs knew by now that John and the men from Washington had quarreled, and they eyed the two strangers with a kind of narrow worry tinged with dread, the way you look at a dog when you first suspect it might be going mad. Hayman and Josephs, returning their looks with what had mellowed into a somber curiosity, took seats at the end of the long table, next to Mary, then John, and Sweeney at the end. Grijalba stood next to Sweeney.

Josephs opened the meeting mildly, asserting that they wanted more to listen just now than talk, to hear from the Apaches how they thought they were progressing, and wanted to ask some questions of each. Casador, as the eldest chief, spoke first, then Eskiminzin. They spoke concisely, intelligently, on the conditions before and after John's arrival, not using any of the ridiculous "heap big" and "many moons" images which, from Josephs' and Hayman's own remarks, they clearly came prepared for. The two churchmen, once it became obvious how conspicuously silly they themselves sounded using them, dropped them out of their agenda of prepared questions.

The lesser chief named Sanchez had just started his talk when a ripple of murmurs riffled through the seated Indians as the brief gust of wind sifts through the meadow grass with news that rain is coming. All eyes turned to see a smallish elderly Indian standing regally in the commissary doorway. He wore beautifully decorated toetab moccasins that reached up past his knees, and a long white cotton breechcloth that hung down below his knees front and back, just giving sight of bare flanks once well muscled, but showing now some of the slow emaciation of age. His fringed buckskin shirt was superbly made, his hair well combed and held in place by a wide white headband. A red-and-yellow-striped blanket was draped over his right shoulder.

Sanchez turned and saw him, and sat down. "Lord have mercy," Sweeney leaned over and whispered to John. "That's Diablo."

Casador rose and made a hurried series of introductions which Diablo took quietly in, nodding to each as they were introduced but not going forward or offering his hand to any. When Casador had finished, Diablo said softly in Apache, "I heard these men came from Washington. I wish to speak briefly to them, if they will permit it."

John started to thank him for coming but stopped, remembering that in the Apache scheme of things this might not be a solemn enough occasion. "Ask him to come forward," John told Grijalba. "We will be glad to hear whatever he has to say."

Diablo went to the spot where Sanchez had been standing. "I want these men from Washington to know, that I was the first of the chiefs out here to make peace with the white people. That was eight years ago." He nodded to Grijalba, who added on his own, "That's true. He never fight against the army or anybody."

Diablo went on, gesturing infrequently with his left hand. "Up to now, the agents you have sent us have been thieves. You know this is true, that is why Gray Fox ran the last of them off. Now you have sent this Batunni-ka-yeh out here, and he has shown us what good white people can be like."

He paused for Grijalba to catch up. Mary held John's hand under the table, and he thought he might melt away like butter on warm toast.

"All about us," Diablo continued, "white people eat good food off plates and things. Sun did this. He made things the way they are and He made us the way we are. Sun feeds us just like the birds. I Diablo say this."

When Grijalba was through he went on. "We eat the seeds out of the bushes. I wonder how Sun feels about us when we eat. Like lizards we run about this country. Sun should not have done this. I Diablo say this."

There was another exchange. "You white-eyes in the black coats come here from Washington and say this agent is bad and does not do right by us. I say you live far away and don't know anything. We can live like white people if he will show us how. We look to him and not you. Because he is the way he is, I am bringing my people down from the mountains before winter. I Diablo have spoken."

The slow flicker of the kerosene lanterns made the shadows weave back and forth on the high adobe walls of the great room, not quickly like a candle's flicker, but ponderously, eerily. John saw the lamplight reflected like pinpoints in Diablo's wide, indifferent eyes, eyes that conveyed, more than did his words, that he was a man of authority and did not overmuch care whether anyone took offense at what he had to say. The chief thumped his left hand on the center of his chest. "Me, Diablo," he said. *"Enju!"*

Josephs leaned and cupped one hand over Hayman's ear. "And that, as the man said, is the name of that tune."

When the council broke up, John tried to mask how small and awed he felt at finally meeting Diablo. They shook hands, and John saw he was short and slight, and getting quite old. "From today," the chief said, "we are friends. Give us time to gather in the tornillo beans and piñon nuts, and we will be in before the snow is on the mountain."

It was two weeks later when John finally had an afternoon free to himself. He had kissed Mary good-bye, and was sustained by the electricity of such an accomplishment, and dispatched Nosy and Goody-Goody to escort the buggy back to Tucson. But on this first free afternoon he put his feet up on his desk to think, of how to make the strictures of his white man's religion comprehensible to the Apaches, and yet present it in a style sufficiently uncompromising to suit his Church.

It occurred to him how an Apache medicine man, when he sang a ceremony over the sick, was believed to have the ability to take the sickness upon himself and disperse or nullify it. Somewhat like Jesus, he thought, but then dismissed the line of thinking. Even to concentrate on the sacrificial nature of the act would not offset the odium, in the Church's mind, of comparing Jesus to a tribal sorcerer. He knew that much now, at least.

He wished he knew more of the Apache religion but none of them, not even Eskiminzin, could be induced to explain more or let him see more than had already happened. Dimly he heard comings and goings, but apparently nobody needed his personal attention, for he was not disturbed until late afternoon when Sweeney brought in the day's mail to answer, which took well into the evening.

CHAPTER 11

They were still writing letters when they heard several horses come cantering up to the hitching rail, followed by footsteps and a sharp knock at the front door. They exchanged confounded stares as Sweeney pushed himself out of his chair and stalked across the room. "Who the devil could it be at this hour?" Involuntarily John glanced down to his desk drawer to make sure his revolver was still there.

Sweeney returned in a second with a corporal of cavalry, saluting with a dust-covered glove. "General Crook's compliments, sir, and will you please return to Fort Whipple with us?"

John leaned forward. "What's wrong? What's the matter?"

The corporal beat the dust off his hat onto the side of his leg. "I don't know, sir, I just have orders to request you to come with us."

"What do you make of this, Sweeney?"

"I haven't the faintest, but it sounds like you'd better go."

John's brow knitted at the puzzle of it, but failed to uncover a meaning. "How many men are with you?"

"Seven."

"Very well, Corporal. You and your men can bed down in the commissary tonight, and we'll get started in the morning."

"Begging your pardon, sir, we must start back immediately."

"Tonight?"

"Yes sir. The general asks that your visit be held in strictest confidence. He doesn't want anyone to know you're gone. We'd like to be well out of the area by daylight."

Sweeney poured a cup of still-warm coffee and handed it to John. "Why don't you just take your bedroll; I'll send Tauclee and Sneezer out in the morning with the rest of your things. They'll catch up with you."

"There will be Indians riding with us, sir?"

John couldn't quite tell if his voice was apprehensive or about to make an objection. "It's all right, Corporal. They're quite harmless, as long as I am unharmed."

"I was thinking of the secrecy, sir."

John chuckled. "Corporal, don't you suppose you've been under close observation for maybe the last thirty miles? But don't worry. My police are completely reliable. Now, if you will be so kind as to wait outside with your men I'll be along in a couple of minutes."

Sweeney took a lamp and made his way over to the barn to saddle a horse. He led it back to the office, stopping for a minute by the commissary. It was Goody-Goody standing watch; quietly Sweeney dispatched him to roust out Tauclee and Sneezer. Goody-Goody saluted and left, and Sweeney watched him disappear beyond the illumination of the lantern, fading like an apparition into the gloomy mystery of which he was part and parcel. As he led the horse to the headquarters he mused absently at the childish joy the police seemed to take in military formalities—saluting, marching in formation, drilling. Perhaps it was the rigorous, precisely ordained formalities of their own religion that predisposed them to it. In their religion, if they didn't observe all the steps, the ceremony wouldn't work. So too, perhaps, they felt about being soldiers. Sweeney smiled. He remembered training a regiment of Illinois infantry who would have done well to have such a frame of mind.

He found John quietly talking with his escort by the headquarters porch and handed over the reins. John swung up into the saddle. "Hold down the fort, Sweeney. I'll be back quick as I can."

"We'll be here."

They rode about eight miles north toward the Rim before pulling into a draw in some low hills for a few hours' sleep. The soldiers awoke with some consternation to find John poking at the remains of the campfire, whispering with Tauclee and Sneezer. Not one of them had heard the Apaches come into the camp.

All during that day and most of the next the troopers eyed the two Apaches with a constant, low wariness, like the last ember of a fire that won't go out. They weren't afraid, but not trusting, either, an uneasiness fed by the Indians' habit of not riding with the troops. They followed anywhere from fifty to a hundred yards behind. After they picked their way up the Mogollon Rim and headed west on Crook's Trail through the level pine forests, Tauclee late in the afternoon trotted up alongside the column, a few yards off to the side, until John pulled over to confer with him. They spoke in Apache.

John cantered back up to the corporal and slowed to a walk. The soldier didn't take his eyes off the trail to ask, "You really do understand that gibberish?"

"Bit by bit, Corporal, but it might interest you to know that he asked me that very question the last time I spoke with you."

His gaze remained fixed ahead, but now with a hint of a smile. "What did he want?"

"He was curious where you intend to make camp. There's a place up ahead where lightning has hit a bunch of trees. They'd like to stop and gather some bits of wood, but they don't want us to camp near there. I hope you can oblige; it has to do with their religion."

John half expected the usual chin dribble about Indians having no religion, but the corporal surprised him. "Happy to. We'll go on as far as the next springs before making camp. Anything else?"

"Oh yes. He said, you people ride pretty good, for white boys."

The corporal looked over at him, eyes wide, before bursting out laughing. "Go on!"

They raised Fort Whipple on the afternoon of the fourth day, but made camp in cover well behind the timberline until after nightfall. The moon was up early, and they approached the dark hulk with its pinpoints of lantern light across the grassy meadow where they were easily seen. The gates opened just a few yards ahead of them and closed immediately behind them. Tauclee and Sneezer flanked John on both sides, entering with him, silent, but their eyes wide as full moons at their first sight of such a thing.

Whipple buzzed with activity—wagons being moved, supplies loaded, inventories taken. General Crook's office was brightly lit, animated with the scurry of adjutants filing and storing papers. John dismounted at the hitching rail and handed his reins to Sneezer. "You boys better wait here."

Alone he entered the office he had visited with Casador, and saw at the desk the same dark, handsome young lieutenant he had met, only when he looked up at John it froze him in his tracks. He wore a patch over his right eye; the right side of his face was a mass of scars, the hair over his ear just growing back in patches. "What—" John tried but couldn't get the words out.

"Led a patrol down Date Creek three months ago. Turned out to be an ambush; just caught the edge of a twelve-gauge spread. Gave me quite a new look, don't you think?"

John averted his eyes, ashamed and embarrassed, thankful he had left Tauclee and Sneezer outside.

"The general's in his office. Go on in."

John pushed through the low door of the anteroom in the same act as knocking on it, and caught Crook in midstride. He was pacing the length of the room like a caged animal, but stopped when John entered.

"General, what in the world is going on?"

"I'm glad you could come. Sit down." He indicated the ladder-back on the side wall and leaned back, half sitting on his desk, still restless, drumming his fingers on the wood. "I've had my eye on you, and I have to admit it, you have done much better with those Indians than I ever thought you would. And that business with the cattle was a neat piece of work." He nodded in a way that was angular and distracted. "You've been holding your own."

John insisted, "General—" but Crook's hand flashed up and waved it off. John sensed that whatever he had to say was terribly difficult, and Crook would have to find his way as he went.

"I have wondered from time to time when the Ring was going to really go after you. I wondered how long you'd last. After that business with the cattle, and with all the smoke and fire the last few weeks I thought for sure they'd started on you. They got the commissioner down on you and then had some of your own church people come out and make trouble. Well, I was wrong. They were too smart for us, Mr. Clum."

"I don't understand."

"It's been a diversion. What they were really hoping was that I would be the one to force you out, but while I've had one eye open to keep you out of trouble, they came after me from the other side." Crook worked his tight little mouth. "I'm being transferred. Me and my whole damn regiment."

"What? Where?"

"Dakota Territory. I'm going to lead an expedition against some hostile Sioux. It seems that somebody in Washington finds more value in me as an Indian killer than an administrator."

John was surprised to feel himself fighting down more fear than he had known since coming to Arizona, surprised at how much he had come to rely on Crook's rough honesty—the same reliance, it suddenly struck him, that the Apaches had come to feel for him. "But who will they replace you with?"

"August Kautz."

"I don't know anything about him."

Crook resumed his pacing, his arms folded across his chest. "Well, I have to tell you he hates Indians, and he hates Indian agents."

"Is he fair?"

"Now, Clum, General Kautz is an officer in the United States Army, as am I. I am not at liberty to impugn his character or his motives."

"You mean you have your suspicions."

"I am saying your honeymoon out here is over. The time won't be long before you're really into it with him, and you'd better know now, I won't be able to help you. I won't even be able to speak out for you."

John folded his hands under his chin, letting the development sink in. "Well, at least if they send you to Dakota you'll be closer to Mrs. Crook. Maybe she can come out to see you."

"Yes, we've thought of that. We hope we can work it that way." Crook was leaning on his desk again. "I hear you will be tying the knot yourself one of these days."

"Yes, but I have to go back to Ohio for it; put on the big show for her relatives."

Crook smiled, the first time he had done so without John thinking it seemed tight or strained. "What's her name?"

"Mary."

"Well, if you're going to marry your Mary I suggest you take your leave of absence and get right to it, because once Kautz gets out here you'd better not turn your back for a minute."

John's fingers straightened and his arms fell into his lap. "Why Kautz? Is he in with the Ring?"

"I don't think so. But the Ring knows I've been helping you and they know he won't."

The worst part was to feel so blindfolded. "I just wish I knew what they are up to."

"I don't envy you. I just felt it proper that I should warn you. Now, I don't want to run you off, but we've got work to do. Your detail will see you safely home."

"Thank you, no. I've got a couple of my Apache Police with me. We'll be fine." He stood to go, offering Crook his hand. "Thank you for sending for me."

Crook took it. "I am sorry for it to end this way, but I want you to know, I think you are onto something with your Indians. You're a good man, young Mr. Clum, and I wish you well."

"Good-bye." John headed into the outer office and strode across it without looking back. "Good-bye, Lieutenant. Good luck to you."

The words "You, too" followed him out the door.

Outside, Tauclee and Sneezer exchanged probing looks as John swung onto his horse and cantered toward the gate ahead of them.

When they were well down the trail Tauclee pulled up even with him. "Gonna be trouble?"

"I don't know."

Tauclee didn't press him further, knowing that John had acquired the Apache habit of communicating all he intended with one answer, but after they made camp John added, "Don't tell anyone where we've been. If you're asked, just say we went out scouting around."

The whole thing took close to two months, from the day he shook Sweeney's hand and rolled out of San Carlos. Eskiminzin had met him at the edge of the compound. "That Bible says, people bring peace have beautiful feet."

"That's right."

From a string tied to his belt Eskiminzin produced a pair of breathtaking moccasins of the softest buckskin, gorgeously beaded, and handed them over. John knew they would fit Mary perfectly. "My woman says, 'Let your woman come in beautiful feet.' "

John could have wept. He and the chief grasped each other hand to shoulder for several seconds. "I'll see you again soon."

"You be careful. 'Paches don't want to start somebody new."

As John expected, his future parents-in-law offered some resistance to the change in wedding day. But Mary brought it off by explaining to them that, while his title might only be Indian Agent, his actual position was more like an ambassador or a British kind of Governor General. For reasons of state, she said, they should give in, and they did.

October had almost gone when from the roll of the buckboard they saw the adobe buildings of San Carlos rise lumpily from the gravel and sagebrush. Of course, they had been observed for miles, and Sweeney and Grijalba were standing in front of the headquarters to greet them. John shook hands vigorously all around, then pointed to a small new building about halfway out to Grijalba's casita. "What's that?"

Sweeney growled and pulled his chin. "Oh, that's just a little something."

"What do you mean?"

"Well, some of the native boys and, uh, I, thought you lovebirds might like a place to stay with a little privacy, so they just built you a little house."

"A house!" Mary was too feminine to shout, but not too adult to bounce up and down. "Oh, Johnny, a house. You sweet man." She planted a smack on Sweeney's cheek and thought it, suddenly, rather like kissing a saddle.

"Aye; that isn't all. We got something else, inside."

From the office they passed into what had been the kitchen, and saw a table with a fully wired telegraph set. Through the back door they saw a generous, three-sided adobe lean-to with the stove and chopping block, and tinware pegged to the walls. John looked around. "Where's Chow Soon?"

"Gone down to Tucson to pick you up some welcome-back fixin's; he didn't think you'd beat him back up here."

"What's the news? Army been treating us right?"

"Why don't we give your missus a look at her house, first?"

Mary's attention flickered at the evasion, but she didn't suspect that it was intended to exclude her. She held John's hand as they walked across the yard. "Where's Eskiminzin?" She looked around. "I'd have thought he would be here to meet us."

"Apache custom," said John. "Never call on newlyweds until they call on you. Otherwise you can't know when they'll, uh, be ready for company."

"Oh dear. Practical people, aren't they?"

"Every inch." The house was a simple, two-room adobe with a packed-earth floor, but Mary was beside herself. *"Voilà, le Château Saint-Jean Philippe."* She swept through the parlor-dining room, and peeked into the bedroom. "Oh, we can really fix this place up."

"Not exactly," John confided to Sweeney. "She spent all my money in San Francisco."

"Aye, well, that's what comes with women. Stores and shoppin', shoppin' and stores."

Mary scowled and fished with purpose in her handbag. "In that case I probably shouldn't give you this." She handed Sweeney a silver pocket watch and matching chain.

"Why, I'll be blessed!" Sweeney's face went totally slack.

"Mary, Mary, look quick. You'll never see him like that again." The two men carried several large boxes in from the wagon and Mary shooed them off to begin unpacking.

Back at the office John fingered the telegraph lightly. "There's no wire going out of here. Who do we talk to?"

"Nearest station is down at Fort Grant. The wire is on its way from San Francisco. The Apaches will put it up themselves."

"What?" John sat down at his desk, getting the feel of it again.

"They're terrified of contraptions. How did you get them to agree to that?"

"I just told 'em Gray Fox was leavin', and the army was goin' t'start up tellin' lies about them like they used to. I showed 'em a little swatch of telegraph wire and called it the truth-string, and once it was hooked up, we could make sure people really knew what was goin' on out here."

John studied Sweeney's lined face for the source of the inspiration, relieved that San Carlos could be left in such capable hands.

"O' course, the chief won't even go in that room, now. Says if a machine talks, there must be a witch in it."

John chuckled. "How about the real witches, over at Fort Whipple."

"Crook's gone." Sweeney took a deep breath. "Kautz is a hard-bitten old son of a bristlecone. Here." He handed John a folded sheet of paper. "He's startin' off with his heavy guns. You got instructions to go up to Camp Apache and force all Diablo's people down here—just before winter's startin', too."

John studied it. "They were planning on moving down, anyway."

"Aye, but Diablo don't take kindly to bein' told what to do."

"Still, he'll help us out when he knows the situation."

"Well, that isn't all the situation. Kautz has got his own man in charge of the garrison there. He's tied those Indians to the post, countin' 'em every week to make sure they ain't out raidin'. You'll have to cooperate with him, and ye can't tell me they ain't aimin' to cut the ground out from under you once you get there."

"So, they're going to start off playing dirty."

"Aye."

"Well." John leaned back. "Suppose Diablo was to get all his people together and out of there, and never even go into the garrison. If— what's his name, the commanding officer?"

"Ogilby."

"If Ogilby was to disappear long enough not to be able to give any orders to cause trouble, we could get them down here under the protection of our cops before anybody knew they were gone. The army wouldn't dare attack them here."

"It might work, but it's a dangerous play."

"Well, the old game plans probably aren't going to work anymore. How many of Diablo's people are still up there?"

"Six hundred, give or take."

John slapped his hands on his knees. "Well, brother Sweeney, I'm going to leave you out of planning this escapade, just in case somebody stakes you over an anthill and asks questions. But have a campsite ready for them to relocate to."

"Will do."

"I'll go see how Mary's making out in her château." He stood to go. "Thank you, for the house. That really was splendid of you."

November had just dusted the first snow on White Mountain, and the army had just sent a new inquiry to San Carlos, asking when the agent intended for the Camp Apache removal to take place. Sweeney read it, and laid it with some ceremony on John's desk, patting it down atop the other mail awaiting disposition.

It was in the dead of night when a short figure, wrapped warmly in a striped serape and topped by a huge sombrero, knocked heavily on the door of the garrison commander's residence at Camp Apache.

When it opened, a rough-looking, middle-aged man appeared in an open-throated officer's tunic. He had gray eyes and a neatly trimmed iron-gray beard. "What do you want?"

"I'm John Clum, San Carlos Agent." He extended his hand, which Ogilby had to take. "Just came by to pay my respects."

"The hour is very late."

John tried to look pathetic. "Sure is cold out here."

Ogilby held back. "All right, come in." They passed into a parlor, and Major Ogilby in passing a sideboard quickly poured John a glass of whiskey, before sitting at a paper-covered writing table. "Come now, what is it you want?" He looked up, and John's features were more revealed in the lamplight. "They sure hire 'em young in your business, don't they?"

"I think they try to get hold of us before we get corrupted."

"Noble idea. Pity it doesn't work."

"The fact is, Major, I came up to place you under arrest."

Ogilby leaned back in his chair, his eyes wide and mouth open, and guffawed. "Oh, you did, did you? On what authority?" At the open throat of the tunic John saw the line where Ogilby's sun-leathered neck bordered suddenly on tender white wrinkles.

"By law an Indian agent is deemed an acting United States Marshal on his designated reservations, and Camp Apache has been put under my jurisdiction."

Ogilby laughed again. "Say, that's pretty good, sonny. What's the charge?"

"When you arrived here you removed my subagent, without proper authority. I am arresting you for illegally opening his mail."

"Is that so?"

John raised his eyebrows candidly as he lifted his hand up and pushed the brim of his sombrero. "Yup." At the signal, two Apache police appeared at the back window, leveling their needle guns on the sill. Two more kicked open the front door and flanked John, their rifles crooked in their arms. "Be a good gentleman and come along quietly. You won't be hurt."

Ogilby's eyes narrowed. "I could have you hung for this."

"For what? All anybody will know is you got drunk and slept in for a couple of days. We'll make sure you have a good time." John inclined his head toward the door. "Walk normally and don't try anything. If you don't do as I say, I'm not sure I'll be able to control my savage charges, if you take my meaning."

"Don't be a fool. You can't get those Indians out of here without my cooperation. My men have orders to attack them if they leave without permission."

"You never had any intention of letting them go until the civil government kissed your army's boots, and you can't have it your way this time. Get on this horse, please."

The group arrived at a clearing in a pine forest where Grijalba was waiting for them. John watched as Ogilby and the Apache police dismounted. "All right, you boys get him good and drunk; when he passes out, take him home and put him to bed."

John and Grijalba left again, and soon arrived at an anxious canter in Diablo's camp in the foothills. "Chief says, he sure hope you know what you doing."

"So do I. Are they all ready to move out?"

John looked about and saw a couple of San Carlos chiefs, including Eskiminzin, who greeted him. "You come on. Diablo gonna talk to the people before they go."

John followed him to a firelit camp circle with several hundred of Diablo's White Mountain Apaches seated in a natural amphitheater, guarded by a tall crest of lodgepole pines. As they entered Diablo took the central place. He was wrapped in a large blanket, more against the cold than as an emblem of office, and for several seconds he set his face straight into the wind, the way an elk does to divine the strength of the coming snows.

As Grijalba whispered into John's ear, Diablo said, "It has come to be as the young bobcat agent said it would be. The soldiers have come up here to set us against him, make trouble. This very night, we are going to pack up our things and go to San Carlos for a while. This will be a new thing for us and a hard time. We must be careful not to have any trouble.

"I called all you people here to say some things. We didn't used to all live together. We won't be used to it. We used to live in different places. We got along all right and sometimes we fought. That is why we may fight there. Fighting is no good and we have to do better.

"When we get to San Carlos, if a hungry man comes to see you, it isn't because you look pretty! Give him something to eat, even if he is not in your clan. This is how we will all stay alive. Don't make him sit around and have to ask for it. That is how white people do. Remember we are all Apaches.

"If a man comes to you barefooted, give him your moccasins. Your wife can make you others. He may not have a wife. Maybe the white soldiers killed her. Then he will tell everybody about you and say how good you are. This is how Apaches should do. This is how we used to do, before there were so many of us that we started fighting. If we have to live all in one place, then we have to be like relatives. That is how I want us to do. That is what I wanted to say. Some of you other men can talk now, if you want."

As Diablo sat down a murmur of *"enjus"* rolled among the seated men. With Grijalba whispering rapidly in his ear as he picked up most of it himself, John heard several of the other headmen echo what Diablo had said.

After Eskiminzin had spoken and seated himself John recognized, for he had learned what to look for, the moment when the men began exchanging looks to see whether anyone else wished to speak. The eye-flickering vigil ceased abruptly when a slender young man at the back of the group jumped to his feet. "I have something to say. I have waited my turn. Now you are all done and I want you to hear me."

"Who's that?" whispered John.

"They call him Bacon," Grijalba answered lowly. "You remember him, from the trial, then Consuela's ceremony. He's a young hothead, belongs to Diablo's camp. He's Tauclee's brother."

"What?" John looked at him in surprise. "Tauclee never said he had a brother."

"Maybe you never ask."

When they looked back up the young man had made his way to the front of the gathering. "All you old men sit here and say we have to all do what the white-eyes tell us. When you were young you were men. You went down to Mexico scouting around, looking for things, and you came back with horses and foolish water and other good things. For the women you even came back with pots and cloth and beads for them. You provided for your families. That is how you did when you were young.

"Now you tell us young men we must not do that. You want us to ask the white-eyes for everything. You don't want us to have any life at all. Well, some of us are going to be men whether you like it or not. What do you say to this?"

Diablo rose to his feet; as he took the center of the clearing Bacon retreated a couple of rows into the crowd, but did not sit down. Diablo looked to various places in the group, his oddly whimsical mouth seeming to heighten what was probably only mild amusement. "I remember when Bacon was just a boy," he said. "I made play arrows for him. I did it because his father never did. His father wasn't much good, but he was my own clan so I didn't run him off. I think maybe Bacon still has those little arrows. I want him to go get his quiver and let us see whether he does or not. He might as well. He can't kill white-eyes with them." Most of the seated men smiled; a few chuckled.

Bacon clenched his fists in anger, but dared not shout back at a chief. "Diablo never did much for us! We were poor and had a hard time. I remember him from when I was little. He was old even then. I think my father remembered him from when he was little, too. I think strong young men should lead now. Diablo is getting too old and going down. I want to know how old he is."

Diablo nodded slyly. "It is true that I am getting older, but my power is still good. People still follow me. I think maybe they know that when a devil gets older, he gets real tricky. Old Bacon," he paused and shook his head, "just turns green."

There was an explosion of laughter; John saw Bacon's face turn positively livid before the young Indian turned on his heel and stormed away. Grijalba's whisper was hoarse in his ear. "That take care of him for a while, but you keep the eye on him. Could be trouble later."

"What about Tauclee? Do you think I can still trust him?"

"I don't know. I think so, probably. But don't set yourself between them and make Tauclee choose."

John nodded. "They look like they're done now. Do you think I should say anything to them?"

"No. Is their show. Wait till they break up, then thank Diablo for letting you come."

CHAPTER 12

The escape from Camp Apache was flawless. The Indians were sixty miles from the post when Ogilby awakened and sounded an alarm. By the time Diablo's trail was discovered, the White Mountain women were already cutting green willow saplings to bend into wickiup frames only a couple of miles above Eskiminzin's own rancheria. John composed the briefest of reports that Diablo's people had arrived and been provided for, and when the fusillade of recriminations and demands came from the army, he merely referred them to his report, and played dumb.

It had not taken long before further orders came to go down to Apache Pass in southern Arizona, take over the Chiricahua Reservation, and remove those Indians to San Carlos. Tom Jeffords had been agent to those Apaches ever since before Cochise had died. He was a good man, and for him to be fired and his books seized for audit let John know that the Ring was still plowing its nefarious course. That had been a difficult undertaking. There had been violence this time, and a few Chiricahuas killed for fighting the removal, but two scenes from it still stood out in his mind these several months after.

One incident involved the chief, Cochise's son Taza, who suddenly materialized in John's camp one day to plead his cause against removal from their ancestral home. Taza had stood there, remarkably tall, silently statuesque and bronze, having apparently agreed to let Eskiminzin do the talking. "Chiricahuas not wanna go to San Carlos."

John waved it off wearily. "Skimmy, we've been through all this before."

"Yes, but you not understand," Eskiminzin nearly shouted. John looked up in surprise and saw the chief in a lecturing stance, his feet planted wide apart, one hand on his hip and the other gesticulating angrily.

John had never seen this before, and raised his hand in appeasement. "You're all Apaches; you should be able to get along."

"But we not alike! Say you live on some place. Your home there. Your ancestors there. You like it. Then all niggers move in, tell you, you not allowed to live there anymore. They say, you go that place, live with Chinamen. You gonna live with Chinamen because all niggers tell you to? Hell no."

"If the move were for my own good, and it was in the best interest of my people, I would move."

Eskiminzin slapped his hip and spun away, looking up and then down in disgust. Suddenly he faced John again. "You a Christian. You say God is Jesus."

"That's right."

"What Church you go?"

"Reformed. You know that very well."

"You a Mormon?"

"I should say not!"

"All same. Believe Jesus, all Christian."

"We most surely are not the same!"

" 'Paches different just like that." Eskiminzin tossed his hands in the air and folded his arms across his chest, his head cocked to one side with his jaw set, waiting for John to admit defeat.

The other scene that stayed in his mind was in Tucson, where a grand jury had indicted several of Taza's lesser chiefs for theft and murder, and the sheriff had issued warrants for their arrest. To build good will and show his willingness to cooperate with local civilian authorities, John and Sweeney and a guard of policemen rolled up to the sheriff's office with the wanted men tied together in the back of a wagon. The strange Mr. Oury was absent from the town, and for a quarter hour of bitter arguing in the middle of the street, the sheriff refused to accept the prisoners, citing army jurisdiction, danger to the town, and everything but the phase of the moon. He jailed them only when the district judge volunteered the opinion that, since the sheriff had issued the warrants, he had to take them.

John and the balance of the Chiricahuas were back at San Carlos less than a week when word came that the wanted leaders had escaped from jail and returned south, linked with Geronimo, and gone into New Mexico for new raids. He was sure the Ring was behind it, but there was no proof.

All this had been months since, and his daily attention was taken with running his overcrowded reservation. The Chiricahuas were not particularly welcomed by the San Carlos Indians. Bickering over fields and campsites was common. Supplies were constantly running low, and

John's creativity was constantly strained just to keep them all fed and occupied. Through it all Mary had been gloriously good, but he no longer allowed her to visit Apache camps—except Ethel's—without a police escort.

And now there were new orders, these to go to New Mexico, capture Geronimo, and move those people in as well. He had kept the telegram open on his desk for weeks, hoping in his Apache consciousness that it would speak to him of how to do it, but it had revealed nothing.

John was shaken from his reverie by a commotion in the yard, the loud babble of Apache sounding not at all unlike a ruckus in a henhouse. He rushed outside and froze in his tracks. "Here, what in the world, Mary Hilda? My God!" Grijalba was supporting Bacon's wife, Consuela, who shuffled along in a stoop, clutching her sides, her hair falling around her face in a dust-matted mass that did not conceal her blackened eyes and the blood clotted around her nose and mouth. "My God, Mary, what happened?"

"Bacon beat her."

"What! Did he! Bring her inside."

Grijalba helped her into the office while explaining, "She go back to her folks, but they throw her out. They say, everything been bad with her ever since you go to her ceremony. Say, she better come here to you since you go to her ceremony."

They got her in and sat her down, and John dipped his handkerchief in a pitcher of water and began washing her face. "Mary Hilda, go get my cops. Bring them here, with Bacon, at the double."

Sweeney came in from the telegraph room, his face falling as he caught sight of Consuela. "Aw, no, what is this?" He asked the question but his experience told him everything he needed to know.

They cleaned her up as best they could, John dabbing at her cuts even after they were washed, to reassure her. It took only ten minutes for Grijalba to return with Nosy and Sneezer, who had Bacon by either arm. The instant they entered the room John approached the restrained young Indian and slapped him hard across the face.

Consuela lurched from her chair, shouting, "No!" but Sweeney held her back.

"Is this how you treat your wife? You want to know how it feels?" He slapped him twice more, palm and backhand. "This woman is not your wife anymore. If you ever go near her again, I will have you locked up so hard you will never get out. Do you understand? Never even speak to this girl again. Now get out. You men let him go." Nosy and Sneezer turned him loose.

Grijalba interpreted in an equivalent tone of voice, and Bacon's eyes got as big as coffee saucers, as he worked his mouth open and shut, shaking his head in disbelieving rage. *"Ahagahe!"* he wheezed at last, shaking his head again violently. *"Ahagahe!"* He turned and stormed toward the door, slashing as he went at a chair that spun across the room and crashed into the wall.

"Whew, that ought to hold him for a while," breathed John when he had gone. "What was that word?"

Grijalba nodded. "Pretty bad. Kind of like, 'Now you did it, look out.' He sure gonna make trouble now. You not ever tell Apache how to treat his wife. Nothing worse than that. Even another Apache get killed for that."

Sweeney grunted. "I'll be sure to tell the police about it so they'll keep an eye on him."

"Well, I did what I had to do. This kind of thing can't go on."

Sweeney gestured to Consuela. "What'll we do with her, now? Think you and your wife can take her in for a spell?"

"We could, but I don't think it would be best for her. We can't go setting up a refugee camp for collaborators without playing into the hands of diehards like Bacon. Mary Hilda, tell her we'll put some medicine on those cuts. She'll be safe if she wants to stay here a few days, but if she wants I'll ask Eskiminzin if he'll take her in for a while."

Grijalba spoke to the woman for a few seconds and she answered. "She says her husband isn't bad. He was just drunk."

"Drunk?" John's attention sharpened like a fox who hears the brush rustle. Consuela knew she had said something she shouldn't have. "Where did he get it? Did you fix him a batch of tiswin?"

Grijalba asked her and she shook her head. "No."

John was getting angry. "Do you like for him to get drunk and beat you up?"

"No," she blurted it out herself without Grijalba translating the question. John knew she couldn't have understood him; she was just going to deny everything.

Sweeney was distracted by the clicking of the telegraph and returned to the other room.

"Mary Hilda, tell her, I came out here to help her people. When they get drunk they do bad things like this. That is why I have forbidden drinking. She and other women like her are the ones who suffer when the men drink. Why won't she help me?"

As Grijalba lectured her, Consuela shrugged uncomfortably and muttered a few downcast syllables. "She says she doesn't know where he got drunk. Maybe he found a little spring of whiskey."

"Uh-huh." John brushed the blood and dirt from under Consuela's eyes. "Why don't you take her out to the pump and clean her up." He handed him the handkerchief. "Make her as comfortable as you can."

Grijalba led her toward the door, when suddenly she turned and fixed John with an agony in her eyes that told him she wanted to talk but was frightened, that she was searching for a way to tell him without telling him. Suddenly she blurted a torrent of Apache, as Grijalba struggled to keep up. "She says she thinks maybe there really is a stream. On the north side of the river beyond the fields, in a little canyon where a tall rock juts out of a prickly pear thicket. She doesn't really know about it; the men don't allow the women to go there." Consuela cowered and disappeared into the hall. "You know what she sayin', boss?"

John nodded. "I have a pretty good idea."

When Grijalba had followed her out John sank heavily into his chair, molding his body into it like a half-empty feed sack. "Oh, Sweeney, I don't know," he said when Sweeney came back into the office. "Sometimes I just don't know."

Sweeney gave him a curiously calm smile. "I got you a little something."

"What?"

"When we came through Tucson and tried to turn those Chiricahua troublemakers over to the sheriff, I slipped over to the store and bought you a little present. 'Tisn't much, but I've been savin' it for the right time."

"Why, Sweeney."

The old man reached into his shirt pocket, pulled out a red, flaccid rubber object, and held it out across the desk.

"A balloon?"

Sweeney shook it in his hand. "Go on, blow it up."

John laughed in bafflement and took it. He put it to his lips and blew hard, but it took several seconds for the rubber to give way and expand. He blew it up all the way, pinched the nozzle, held the balloon out, and regarded it. "Well," he shrugged with a smile.

"Keep on blowin'."

"I can't. It'll burst."

"No, it won't. That's the surprise. It's a new kind of rubber they got now. It don't break, it just keeps on expandin'." He smiled broadly. "Go on, blow it up some more."

John put the nozzle back in his mouth and blew hard against the resistance. The red balloon gave about another quarter inch before shattering with a concussive bang; John jumped back in his chair until it almost turned over, his fingers flung out in thin air. A flush of absolute rage flashed down his face. "You son of a bitch! What do you mean by that?"

Sweeney leaned across the desk, his smile gone, his eyes like steel bearings, and his features like speaking granite. "Mean? I'll say what I mean. Hearken ye to me, boy. That balloon was your reservation. My tellin' you to keep blowin' was the big boys in Washington tellin' you to keep bringin' in more Indians—keep blowin', keep addin', keep pushin' —and if you don't see it and stop it," Sweeney snatched a rubber shred off the desk and shook it in John's face, "then this is what is goin' to happen."

He threw the rubber onto John's chest and raised up straight. "Now they want more." Sternly he held out the telegram he had been taking. "The details of your tea party with Geronimo. He's still hangin' around the Warm Springs Agency in New Mexico. Colonel Hatch will meet you there with two companies of cavalry on May 21 next to assist in Geronimo's capture, and the removal of his people to here. More flamin' mouths to feed. And what's more, if they've been out raidin', those people will come in here decked out like the princes of England, showin' off all the goods they stole. Eskiminzin will never keep the young bucks in the camp after that."

Of all the ears John now had planted around the territory, there were none at Fort Whipple to hear Colonel Hatch get his orders from General Kautz about the impending Geronimo capture. It happened over a map table and glasses of whiskey.

"Now I want you to clearly understand that your orders officially are to cooperate with Clum on this." The coyness in Kautz's voice was heavy to the point of sarcasm.

"Officially?"

"You are to rendezvous with him at Warm Springs on May 21, and aid him in the capture of Geronimo and his renegades."

"What if he meets Geronimo before I can get there?"

Kautz nodded. "Well, I'd guess you'd find a dead agent and a bloody little disaster for the army to have to clean up."

Hatch smiled. "Yes sir."

"Now if Geronimo and his bunch should kill Clum and his bunch, you are authorized to use every method at your disposal to exterminate him and his whole band. That would probably be better for the country, anyway"—Kautz lowered his head—"if you take my meaning."

"Yes sir."

"Geronimo dead, I mean."

"Yes sir."

CHAPTER 13

Over the months John took an increasing interest in the Book of Proverbs. The Apaches seemed to set great store in their own maxims and sayings, and he found it handy to show them with an appropriate observation from the Bible that their native wisdom really was not far from God's intent. The Church, of course, had kept insisting that he show them how far they had to go, not how far they had come, but John classed this element among those about which it was not necessary for the Church to know everything.

It was the first flowering of his third spring in Arizona, during the planting of extensive new irrigation fields, that Eskiminzin came up to him late one morning. "You say, God good."

"Yes, just look around."

"Those 'Pache Pass people, got good fields now, like us real 'Paches."

John saw the bait, but didn't rise to it. "That's right."

Eskiminzin gestured upriver, beyond his own fields. "God so good, why he let those coyotes pee in the river, make our crops come up taste funny?"

"Why would they do that?"

"Geronimo one of them. We goin' out after Geronimo tomorrow. They don't like it. So, they gettin' even a little, maybe."

John pointed out a distant thunderhead, from which the blue-gray smudge of a shower depended to the horizon. "Our Bible says, God makes the rain to fall on the just and the unjust—good and bad alike. He won't come down from heaven to punish every little thing. When the world is over He will settle all the scores. Until then, He showed people how to do what is right, and it is up to them to keep order. That is why we are going out for Geronimo—to make him stop killing people now. We don't have to wait for God to punish him after he dies."

"Other 'Paches help Geronimo die, God punish him a little sooner, maybe."

"Maybe. Tell you what, Taza's people probably think more of Mary

Hilda than they do me. I'll go up to the office right now and write him a note. He will go out and ask them to use latrines, like everybody else."

"All right. We come in the morning, go get Geronimo."

John walked lazily down the stream to the compound, enjoying the advent of the season with its new smells and colors—enjoying it, too, that he could now look at most of the new-appearing desert plants and know what his people used them for.

At his desk, John pulled a sheet of cream-colored octavo notepaper toward him and wrote the order. He had just signed it when he jumped at the splitting bang of a pistol shot and saw tiny chips of adobe fly into the air from the opposite wall. He dove behind his desk and counted out five more shots in rapid succession, two of which zipped through the canvas door to the telegraph room, and one of which cut the bottom from the globe of his desk lamp—unlit, he noted thankfully—and sent the rest crashing to the floor.

After a few seconds' silence he heard an explosion of profanity from Sweeney and the bang of the back door, followed by more shots, from a different gun, and the cracking spit of a carbine. Snatching his gun belt from atop the desk, John bolted in a crouch out the front door. Outside, he heard Sweeney shout to Captain Beauford whether he was all right, and followed the sound of the voices.

When John rounded the back corner of the commissary he saw Sweeney and Beauford standing just outside the shed, their guns drawn, and Tauclee, nearest him, who spun around to face him with a stricken look in his tear-filled eyes that froze John in his tracks. Tauclee's hands, limp and numb, barely grasped his Winchester, a curl of smoke wreathing up from its muzzle and hanging still, with no wind to dissipate it. Beyond Tauclee, his brother Bacon lay stretched on his back on the ground, the bright red stain of his blood inching out from the center of his chest into the white linen of his blouse. His pistol lay beside him, half buried in sand and sawdust, the cylinder open and a few bullets scattered close about. Bacon's knife, partly drawn, was still inserted in his sash. His writhing was almost finished—with one final twist from the waist he drew one leg up under him and lay still, his dark, widely opened eyes glazed unseeing up at the sky.

"Oh no," John moaned gently as he put out a hand to Tauclee's shoulder, but the policeman turned away and shuffled off, his gun muzzle down at his side, leaving John's hand in midair.

Sweeney took it instead and squeezed it. "Leave him be," he said. "Leave him be. He'll be back when he sorts through it."

"What happened?"

"Almost got the drop on us," said Beauford. "Came ridin' into the barn, calm as you please. He walked right by me while I was workin' in the shop; I didn't think nothin' of it. Then he got over near the headquarters and started actin' real crazy. Pulled the damn gun out of his shirt and started shootin' in the back door."

"Yes." John raised a brow. "I was in on that part."

"Then he come a-runnin' back toward the shop, gibberin' in Spanish he'd killed Sweeney and now he was gonna kill me and then he was gonna kill you. I figured he meant business since he was puttin' bullets in his gun, so I pulled out my pistol and shot him but he kept comin'. Then Tauclee, I don't know where he came from, was there behind me and plugged him with the Winchester. Damnedest thing I ever saw. Shot his own brother to save our hides."

Sweeney nodded. "He knew Tauclee was on duty and figured he wouldn't have the guts to shoot."

All three men tensed at the rushing scuff of footsteps approaching around the corner of the commissary, but straightened and relaxed when Mary appeared, her hair down and a worried, apprehensive look in her eyes. "What is it? What's happened—Tauclee brushed right past me like he didn't even see me." Suddenly she caught sight of Bacon's body and covered her mouth with her hands. She didn't scream or cringe or do any of the womanly things John imagined she might if she were ever confronted by such a sight. Instead, Mary edged through the sawdust of the shop until she stood next to John and wrapped her hands around his arm. "Is there anything we can do for him?"

"No, no, I'm afraid he's gone on to his happy hunting ground, as they say."

"That's Tauclee's brother, isn't it?"

"Yup."

"No wonder he was so upset. How did it happen?"

"Bacon got it in his mind to assassinate all of us. Opened fire on Sweeney there but missed. Tauclee had to shoot him."

Mary's eyes drifted painfully back in the direction where Tauclee had passed her. John holstered his pistol and wrapped his arm around her neck, leaning her head over onto his shoulder. "Why don't you go on back to the house? We're all okay."

Quietly she spoke into the collar of his shirt. "Do you need me for anything?"

"No. I'll call you if we do."

Mary pulled away and returned, not back through the shop by the body but down the near side of the commissary. When she was out of hearing John gestured downward. "What do we do with him?"

Sweeney pulled at his big chin. "Well, wrap him up, I guess, and leave him in the shop. His folks will be comin' down for him when they hear about it."

"All right. Beauford, I want you to call in a few more of our cops so Sweeney can put them to work around the commissary or somewhere. I want them handy just in case his family makes trouble. Then find Mary Hilda and send him over to me."

John walked back to the headquarters, feeling vaguely sicker with each step as he sucked in his stomach to unbuckle his gun belt. He chunked it onto the top of his desk and sat heavily in his chair, unable to concentrate on the work before him. His eyes wandered to the two neat little bullet holes in the canvas door to the back room. All he could think of was the look in Bacon's eyes as he died, the hatred, the defiance. "He never understood," he said to himself. "That's the worst part. He never understood what it is we're trying to do." And John could not wipe it from his mind that he was supposed to represent a Church of love and kindness, and yet such a thing had happened.

He sat that way for a quarter of an hour, motionless, his fingers knotted together under his chin, his mind sifting, sorting, weighing where he had gone wrong, trying to discover either the inevitability of it or else a way to prevent it from happening again. He looked up and saw Grijalba standing in front of him. "You heard what happened?"

"*Sí.*"

"I want you to stay around pretty close in case we have to explain things to his family."

"They know he gone crazy. One of his cousins come in right after breakfast to tell me he punish Consuela—"

John felt his neck extend outward a little, his eyes narrowing like a telescope coming into focus. "What?"

"Consuela." Grijalba looked down at the floor. "Bacon—"

"What is it? Bacon what?"

"Before he leave he catch her. He say, she had gone with you, and he cut her nose off."

John's gaze blurred, the way you lower a scope when you have sighted a target and lost the stomach to shoot. His mouth slackened and his lips parted.

"Apache men always punish, when they think—"

"I know." John waved it off faintly. "Go on now." Grijalba had almost got to the door when he heard John's sudden but barely audible voice. "Where is she now?"

"Her parents take her back in. They feel sorry for her now—maybe throw her out later." Grijalba left.

Alone, John sat quietly for several minutes, his head falling forward by slow degrees until his neck was completely loose and, for the first time he could ever remember, tears of grief and frustration rolled down his cheeks.

He didn't feel like going home for lunch; Chow Soon brought him some beans and stew which he ate slowly while trying to compose a report for the commissioner on the whole affair. It was still early afternoon when he looked up at the sound of the front door latch. "Hello, Skimmy."

"Nantan Batunni-ka-yeh, I hear you had some trouble here today."

"Yes, I'm afraid we did." He knew that any explanation he could make would add nothing to what the chief already knew. "How is Tauclee?"

Eskiminzin grimaced. "Feel pretty bad. Not angry, though. All right he come see you later?"

"Yes, of course. I want to see him, too. Are you thirsty? We got fresh lemons in from California this week."

Eskiminzin made a backhanded swipe toward the side table. "No horse pee. You got water, maybe got good coffee?"

John was grateful to laugh. "Coffee is in the telegraph room. Help yourself."

"Injun not goin' in there with talkin' machine. Maybe you get coffee for me?"

"Oh, all right, but I tell you it really is quite harmless." Eskiminzin seated himself on the parson's bench and John returned with a steaming tin cup.

As John resumed his seat Eskiminzin tilted the cup and peered as deep into the brew as he could. "You put good sugar in coffee?"

"Yes, just the way you like it."

"We still goin' tomorrow after Geronimo and his coyotes?"

"Yes, bright and early."

"Soldiers still gonna be there?"

"Yes."

Eskiminzin tapped his cup on the arm of the bench, shifting his weight the way you do if you sit on a burr in company too polite to pull it out in front of. "Injun thinkin', maybe better we just go ourselves. 'Paches good to catch 'Paches. Soldiers just mess it all up—maybe shoot us by mistake."

"Yeah, I know how you feel. But see, there's more to it than that. Ever since I came out here the army has opposed me. Crook was the only one that helped, and he's gone. But you and your people have been at peace, working hard. We've brought in the other Apache tribes, and things still seem to go pretty smooth. I admit it isn't the best arrangement, and I know you have to work at getting along. But you're doing it. Maybe if we work together with the soldiers a few times, they won't be so quick to work against us. Don't you think so?"

Eskiminzin shook his head, doubtful and sidelong like a mule that doesn't want to be coaxed. "Sound pretty good, all right. But—something there just not true."

"What?"

"Don't know." He stood up to go, slugging down the last of the coffee and licking the last of the syrupy residue from the inside of the rim. "Pretty good. Need more sugar, maybe. How many Injuns you takin' out to get Geronimo?"

"Oh, I guess two companies of police should do, since the cavalry will be there. Why don't you pick which ones and have them here in the morning?"

"Good. Tauclee come by pretty soon now, maybe."

It was as John figured, that Tauclee had been hanging around the edge of the compound, behind Grijalba's casita, waiting for Eskiminzin to return and assure him it was all right to come in.

When he entered the office it was almost timidly, downcast, fidgeting with the buttons of his blouse. Only when John went forward and embraced him did he see how swollen his eyes were. "Tauclee," he whispered. "I wish there were something I could say."

Tauclee shook his head, reaching up and stroking John's chest, touching his own and John's again, as though the repeated touching back and forth would help communicate what it was he needed to pass from himself to his agent. "No. Me, all right. You safe. Me policeman to Apaches. You, Nantan, came here to help us. Me do right thing. Policeman duty, protect people. You say so. Policeman duty, protect Nantan. Eskiminzin say so."

"Tauclee—"

"No. He who is gone was my brother. We grew up together. Hunt together, become men together. He gone now. But me do good thing."

These last words shook him. "Got no brother now." Tauclee's chest began to heave beyond control and John held him tight.

"No, you're wrong. I am your brother now. I will be the best brother you ever had. I promise you that." He who is gone, thought John. How strict, how ingrown. From the very moment of death an Apache would not speak the name of a deceased, no matter how dear. He held the sobbing Indian, reflecting on how much trash the newspapers had printed about the Apaches' monochromatic barbarity and inhumanity.

Tauclee regained himself and pulled back. "It over now. *Enju.* Me, all right."

"I tell you this also. The President himself is going to hear about what you have done, and he will be very grateful."

Tauclee shook his head sadly. "No good reward for kill. Don't want money. Don't want medal. Just forget. All right?"

"No, no, what I meant was, the President will hear about you, and he will know how hard your people are working to settle down. Maybe he'll increase our budget—more rations, better equipment. By what you did you could have helped all your people."

Tauclee considered this. "That true?"

"Yes, absolutely."

Tauclee seemed to draw more strength from the utility of his act than the pity or the pardon, and he straightened himself. "I go with you to Warm Springs after Geronimo?"

"You will ride beside Eskiminzin and myself."

"I go get ready. Get good sleep."

He turned to go but John caught him by the shoulders and fixed his gaze deep into Tauclee's eyes. "You saved our lives today. Thank you, Tauclee."

The policeman nodded solemnly and left.

John spent the remainder of the afternoon composing and polishing a report of the whole incident to the commissioner. He stopped only to eat the dinner Chow Soon brought him. When the report was done he signed it and folded it up, but having put it halfway into the envelope his hands stopped, the odd sensation coming over him that he was about to misstep, that he was somewhere uncovered. In a few minutes it became clear to him, that such a report, praising the Apaches for the bravery and dedication, might never make it out of the Indian Bureau— might be conveniently mislaid.

Sighing, partly from fatigue and partly in satisfaction at having stemmed a possible blunder, he drew up two identical copies. One he addressed to the Secretary of the Interior, and one to the President of the United States. It was well after dark when he set his lamp on the hall table and blew it out. Outside, the moon was not yet up and he could not discern the outline of his house, but the illumined small front window pulsed irregularly from the firelight within.

CHAPTER 14

Mary looked up from her mending; the combination of firelight and lamplight gave her features a golden glow that John thought made her look more beautiful than he had yet seen her. "I still don't like the idea of your going out after Geronimo," she said. "I've heard so much about him, all of it bad. What if he really is as evil and clever as people say?"

He crossed the room and put his hands on her shoulders, kneading tenderly. "People have been saying the same thing about me for nearly three years now. It ought to be an interesting confrontation."

"Oh, Johnny, be serious! You could get killed."

He knelt beside her chair, and she let her sewing fall into her lap as he enclosed her hands in his own. "I am clever, but I'm not stupid. I'll have my police with me, and there'll be two companies of cavalry right there to help if things get rough. It seems the army has finally agreed to cooperate with me. The government wants all the Apaches on one reservation, and these are the last bunch still out—except for Victorio, and nobody knows where he is. Once I bring in Geronimo things will be slick as a sleigh ride. You'll see."

Mary leaned back and smiled. "I could do with a sleigh ride. It's been so hot during the days."

"You know, I haven't taken a leave this year. If things go all right with Geronimo's people during the fall, we could go home for Christmas. Would you like that?"

"Oh, Johnny, do you mean it?" She read his answer in his eyes. "That would be just too wonderful." He pulled her to her feet and put his arms around her, resting his chin on her shoulder as he swayed her gently from side to side, timing with the loud tocking of the mantel clock but thinking nothing of time.

They each pulled back when they heard a horse canter up. John drew the curtains aside, then opened the front door. "Edwin, hello. Mary, it's my master spy reporting from Tucson."

Edwin entered, thin, blond, and more scraggly-looking than when

John had last seen him. Mary held out her hand. "I'm so pleased to meet you. John speaks very highly of you."

He took her hand bashfully. "Oh no, ma'am, not me."

Mary laid her other hand atop his. "Yes, he does."

"You look a sight and a half," said John. "What's going on?"

"I rode the whole way. Only stopped once."

"Here, drink this. It will refresh you." John handed him a glass of lemonade.

Edwin poured the whole glass into his mouth at once, the fashion of drinking reinforced by years of habit. His face puckered like a mummy's and John slapped him on the back to help him swallow. "Godammighty! Beggin' your pardon, ma'am."

John took the glass. "I'm sorry it's a little tart. The Apaches' sugar rations ran a little short this month, so we gave most of ours to them."

"That goes down harder'n a shot of snakehead."

"Except that this is good for you," said Mary.

"Yes, ma'am, so's castor oil, but I don't take trouble to drink it on social occasions."

"Is this a social visit?" asked John.

Edwin mumbled lowly, leaning his head toward the door, "Um, can we go over to the office?"

John and Mary exchanged looks. "Sure, I guess so. We'll be back in a minute."

Mary closed the door after them, worried afresh that something was transpiring to which she was not privy.

John clicked open the unlocked latch of the headquarters and they passed quietly inside. He lit a lamp in the hall, turning the kerosene flame as low as it would go, and held it before them into the office, motioning Edwin to a seat on the parson's bench. John set the lamp on the desk and sat down, not in his own chair, but on the bench next to Edwin. "What is it?"

Edwin wiped at his short, thin beard before knotting his long white fingers, burying his fists into his lap. "I was afraid I'd be too late."

"Tomorrow you would have been."

"I been hangin' around the saloons like you told me to—actin' drunk and sittin' on the sidewalks. The soldiers and the big shots talk and say anything, like I wasn't even there. They think I'm too far gone to make sense of anything. Sometimes one of 'em will toss a quarter at me and act like he's doin' me a big favor. But I been listening. I been hearing everything, just like you pay me for."

John patted him on the knee. "I know. I am so truly sorry they treat you like that."

"Two nights ago, some officers came in from Fort Lowell. I heard 'em say you got orders to go out and bring in Geronimo, and the cavalry would back you up."

"That's right."

"Don't go." Edwin seized John's hand almost fiercely. "You can't go. It's a trap. I heard the officers talking to Oury and the others about it." John felt his hackles rise at the mention of Oury's name. "When you get out to Warm Springs the troops won't be there. They're gonna let Geronimo take care of you, then the army will ride in and start a fight with him to get him back out on the warpath." Suddenly Edwin pounded a fist into the open palm of his other hand. "The lousy scum!"

John leaned back, aghast. "So they knock me out of the way and get a new war started, both. Two birds with one stone."

"What are you going to do? You can't go."

"I have to go." He held up one hand against a protest that would have been almost violent. "But now that you have warned me, I can make plans. I'll have the drop on them, you can be sure."

"Then let me come with you. Please."

"No, I can't risk you out there. You're too valuable where you are."

"I can't go back. If anyone figures this out they'll kill me if I go back."

John thought for a second, then got up and carried the lamp into the telegraph room, fishing the key ring out of his pants pocket. He unlocked the strongbox and counted out twenty dollars in silver, put the box away, and returned to the front room. He sat down again and pressed the coins into Edwin's hand. "This will get you to San Francisco. I know a man there who can give you a job. He runs a hotel. I'll write him a letter tonight and you can deliver it yourself when you get there. Is that all right?"

The kerosene flame made tiny bright pinpoints in Edwin's eyes as tears welled up and he fought them. "Ain't nobody ever been so good to me as you. I won't never forget that, long as I live."

"Nor I you. Now, I want you to go bed down your horse in the stable, and you can roll out in that room across the hall. Chow Soon will give you a good breakfast in the morning and plenty for the road."

When John reentered his house he found Mary again by the fire, not sewing but staring into the flames; he would have likened her to a seeress divining the future, only when she looked up her visage was one of knitted confusion. "What is it, Johnny? I want to know."

"Oh, Edwin ran into some trouble in Tucson. He's having to retire as my spy there. I'll be sending him to California—for his health, as they say. Nothing to worry you."

Like looking for a warm ember with a poker she studied his answer for some hint of a fib, but found none, and she seemed to relax.

"Go on to bed if you're tired. I have to write a letter or two, and I'll be along."

John and Mary awoke together, and held each other without speaking for at least twenty minutes. She would not protest further, and she would not again voice her fears, which she knew he understood, and which she knew, whether John admitted it or not, he shared. It was a time merely to be together, and convey her love in that quiet way women have, of holding, and smiling occasionally through her deeply understanding dark eyes.

When they had dressed and crossed over to the office, stopping by the barn to saddle John's horse, Chow Soon had breakfast ready for them. John had him prepare a third plate and cup, which he carried into the front storeroom, and found Edwin sleeping, his arms bent up at the elbows like a baby. "Wake up, Cinderella, your livery awaits."

"My liver?" Edwin mumbled. When his eyes were open John gave him an envelope with a name and address on the outside.

"This is the fellow for you to see in San Francisco. He'll take care of you. Here." John handed him the cup of coffee. "We'll be ready in a half hour or so. Chow Soon'll have your grub ready."

Sweeney had been up before any of them, working from his big mesquite chair, his barrel mug of coffee hoisted to his lips as slowly and rhythmically as though by a dock crane. "Telegram came from the army yesterday," he said, "confirmin' your rendezvous with them at Warm Springs on May 21."

"Did they? Good." John was looking out the window. With Mary present he would not tell Sweeney of their real plan, and thus did not need to consider whether if in private he would have done so. "Where is Captain Beauford?"

"Over at the commissary a-fittin' out your forty. They'll be linin' up here when they're ready for you."

John nodded and sat on the parson's bench next to Mary, holding her hands. Edwin joined them presently, having hitched his horse next to

John's. In a few minutes more Eskiminzin strode quietly in, announcing, "Scouts ready, Nantan."

It still jarred Mary's ears that Apaches never uttered greetings. Just information, economically passed. She and John rose, and Mary took Eskiminzin's hand. "You be careful. I want all of you to come back safely."

" 'Paches," Eskiminzin made a motion outward from his eyes, "see like nighthawk, quiet like mountain lion. We be okay"—he patted her hand—"your man, too."

Outside, Edwin and Eskiminzin mounted as, on the porch, John pulled Mary to him one more time. "I'm sorry this could take a while. Just keep thinking about that sleigh ride we're going to take."

He let her go, and shook hands with Sweeney. "Hold down the fort," he said. "Send out a messenger if you need to for anything."

John climbed into his saddle, and then with Edwin and Eskiminzin slowly reviewed the double line of pantalooned Apache Police. They stood rigidly all at attention, their cartridge belts full. None looked to the side as the three walked their horses by, until John stopped right beside one. "Goody-Goody, your wife is a Yavapai, is she not?"

"Yes, Nantan."

"This man beside me has saved my life. If he goes back to Tucson the bad men there will kill him. I want you to take him to your wife's people, and they must take him down to Yuma. Will you do that for me?"

"Yes, Nantan."

"After you get him off to your wife's people, you come back here and get a horse. Find out if Old Soldier has any messages to give you, and then come out and join us." The Indian nodded and stepped out of the line to stand by Edwin's horse, as John gave Edwin his hand. "That about does it," he said. "Good luck to you, and thank you for your work."

Edwin said nothing but John could tell he was uncomfortable with the thought of being entrusted alone into the company of Indians. "Don't worry," said John. "You'll be safer with them than ever living among white people. Trust me."

Edwin gulped a kind of "Thanks," and he and Goody-Goody struck off on their own. John and Eskiminzin completed their circle of the columns, stopping by the side of Tauclee, who was at his place at the head of his platoon but mounted, not on foot. Quietly John said, "Tauclee, will you ride at the front with us?" Without expression

Tauclee guided his horse out of the line and accompanied them to the front of the columns, where Captain Beauford was waiting for them.

"Well, Captain, you may take your men out." As Beauford gave the command John nudged his horse to a walk, tipping his hat to Mary as they headed out south. Still she feared for him, but was so proud to see him exactly in the place she could easily have imagined him even when they were children—in a remote place, riding at the head of a native constabulary who adored him. Her hardest task now in the coming days was not to think of all the things she had heard about Geronimo, his viciousness, his cunning, his hatred of white people.

Not until San Carlos had dropped beneath the horizon behind them did John begin to talk to Eskiminzin. "The ranks look a little thin today, Skimmy. Where is everybody?"

"Some sick. Some got relatives with Geronimo's people, can't go."

John could tell the chief was embarrassed over the absences. "Well, I tell you what. I think for this operation it might be a good idea to call in the reserves. Beauford and I will take these and get started; I want you to go back to your camp and round up the auxiliaries. You can catch up with us tonight or tomorrow."

"I talk to sick men, they feel better pretty quick, maybe."

"No, Skimmy, thank you." He looked him right in the eye. "I really think now that we'd better take everybody."

"I hear you. We catch up tonight." Eskiminzin turned his horse and trotted off, scowling.

They made camp that night about twenty miles out, and when Eskiminzin joined them John counted a hundred and two armed men, including himself, which seemed adequate for the job, if he could work out a suitable plan.

Once they left the road and kept to the foot of the mountains, it was as though the desert swallowed them up. The footsteps of the few horses sounded small in the wilderness; the moccasined march of the police could not be heard at all.

"You look worried, Skimmy. What's on your mind?"

"Tell you before. Gettin' too many Injuns at San Carlos. Now Geronimo . . ." He shook his head.

"Listen, when we get Geronimo there, the only place he is going is the guardhouse. Almost every day I get reports of another raid of his. He is going to stand trial for them, and if he is convicted he will be hanged."

"Geronimo got lots women, children, families, old people. Need hunt, need farms and good ditches like us. San Carlos too small."

"But you know, once we get all the Apaches there and prove that you can all get along, I think the government might give you more land—enlarge the reservation enough that you aren't all piled up on each other."

"You think maybe?"

"Yes, I think there's a good chance of it. And Geronimo is the last—except for Victorio. There's no telling if we will ever be sent out after him."

"My people say, Victorio at Warm Springs during winter. Maybe there now, with Geronimo."

"Do he and Geronimo get along?"

Eskiminzin shrugged. "Not fight, but not live together. Both Chiricahuas, but not relatives. You not understand, maybe."

"No, I think I see. What you mean is, Victorio tolerates Geronimo and his people when they are around."

"That mean tolerate? Just mean, you stay all right, you go all right?"

"Something like that, yes."

The trip took well over a week, south around the foot of the Dragoon Mountains, then northeast through the forested heights of the Rockies toward Warm Springs. John rode mostly in silence, composing like dramatical productions in his mind the different ways in which he might capture the elusive Geronimo. One by one he uncovered flaws in the plots and discarded them. His conversations with Eskiminzin were mostly limited to questions about the particulars of Geronimo's character, probing for some weakness by which to bring him down. Eskiminzin showed himself ill at ease during these sessions; his answers, even for an Apache, were truncated and volunteered nothing beyond what was required.

It was a reticence John finally understood when he coaxed it out of Eskiminzin that Geronimo was a religious shaman, a medicine man who obtained his power through the cooperation of wicked beings long dead. Geronimo held Ghost Power, and all the Apaches, even those in his own following, were scared to death of him, as indeed they would be of anyone who could call spirits up out of the ground to destroy his enemies.

"You know, Skimmy, I don't want to pick on a sore spot, but once your people understand more about our religion that kind of nonsense won't frighten you anymore."

Eskiminzin seized on this slowly, as if he had wanted to talk about something for some time, but was unsure just how to go about it. "You say," he said at last, "Christians live forever?"

"Yes."

"But Christians die like other people. Charlie have Bible out when I kill him. He not live forever."

"Oh well, of course. But everyone does have a soul that lives forever."

"Soul. Like spirit, maybe?"

"Yes, exactly."

"You mean, white people really believe people got spirits?"

"Certainly."

Eskiminzin's eyes got big. "Why, we know that. 'Paches always believe in spirits."

"Well, there you have it. Perhaps ours isn't such a hard religion, after all." Things were quiet just long enough for John to begin to puzzle how much, perhaps, God had planted of the essence of Truth among all peoples—even the primitive—tiny seeds wanting only nurture.

"Good people, bad people. Go to same place when die?"

"No, no. Good people go to heaven to be with God. That is a place of peace and joy and reward. Bad people go to hell—that is where they are punished for doing bad things."

"Bad people punished a little, then go to heaven, maybe?"

"No, people who live bad lives are punished forever."

Eskiminzin nodded. " 'Paches think, bad spirits go into bears. We afraid of them."

"Well, I don't know about that, but I can think of plenty of other reasons to stay away from bears."

Eskiminzin smiled, but it didn't last. "Bacon dead. Where he go?"

He should have known Eskiminzin was driving at something; in the whole time he had known him the chief had never indulged in idle conversation. John sighed. "I don't know. Fortunately, only God can judge that. No one man can judge another's life. No one is that wise."

"You put judges on 'Pache court. They judge all the time."

"Only little things, Skimmy. Little crimes like that, people have to judge themselves to keep everybody in line. But the whole length of a man's life—only God can judge that."

"But where you think Bacon go?"

"Skimmy, all I can say is that we know God is fair and merciful. He knows that sometimes people are hurt and confused and do things they don't really mean. That doesn't make them bad people. When it comes time for God to judge Bacon, I'm sure He will think about that."

Eskiminzin seemed satisfied, in that way you feel when you understand enough about something to put it to rest, without having to know every corner of it. *"Enju,"* he said quietly.

Once the facts about Geronimo were wrestled out of him Eskiminzin refused to discuss Geronimo further, and John did not press him, for finally he understood how he had to effect the capture. He could not merely try to catch Geronimo and then fight his warriors into submission. Rather, he must do it in such a way that Geronimo's power was shown to play him false. John knew Apaches well enough to know that if he could expose Geronimo as a fraud, the rest of the renegades would surrender as tamely as puppies.

Quietly they made camp in a secluded canyon about a half day's ride from Warm Springs, two days ahead of schedule. Only then did John reveal the army's true intention to Beauford, Eskiminzin, and Tauclee. They conferred in the dark, for they had not made campfires for two days; luck was with them, as the scouts sent out reported they were, as yet, undetected.

John explained his plan to them, and when he was done Eskiminzin shook his head in a sidelong, dubious sort of way. "Mighty big plan," he said. "Plan go wrong, you all dead men."

John considered this. "Well, can you think of another way that it might be possible to catch Geronimo without a lot of people getting killed?"

"No," he answered with his usual ready frankness.

"All right, then, that's what we'll do."

The Apache Police lay around camp all the next morning. At noon John mounted at the head of an escort of a dozen picked policemen. "Beauford," he said. "Come in timely or I'm a cooked goose."

"We'll be there."

Eskiminzin stepped forward and took a light hold of John's bridle. "When Geronimo come in, look for women," he said.

"How do you mean?"

"Geronimo bring only men, he ready to fight. Bring one or two women, he fight, but only if you start it. Bring women and families, nothing bad happen. Not then, anyway."

John and his escort rode brassily into the Warm Springs Agency complex about two hours before sunset. He scanned the grounds as they crossed them—a slightly different layout than San Carlos but similar in most respects. A number of Indians, Apaches by the look of them but unlike those at San Carlos in a way John couldn't quite pin down, lolled about.

It was Sneezer riding at John's side. He inclined his head ever so slightly in the direction of two burly, fierce-looking Indians at the door of a large building John took to be the commissary. "Geronimo people, you bet," he whispered.

John caught sight of them just as they skulked around the corner of the building and disappeared. "Well," he answered softly, "I guess we know where they're headed. Good. Very good."

There was no need to guess which of the buildings was the headquarters, as a tall, gangling old man appeared on the porch. "Are you Mr. Clum?" he called out in a high voice that sounded as though he had a pebble hung in his throat. John answered in the affirmative and the old man came down the steps and shook his hand. "I am Agent Lewis, and I have never been so glad to meet anyone in my life."

"Well, that's about the friendliest greeting I've had in a while."

"You won't think so when you find out what kind of a mess you've ridden into. I swear, if anyone ever told me the day would come when I'd be a prisoner in my own Agency, I'd have called him a liar, or else resigned on the spot. Are these your Apache Police?"

"Yup."

"Yes, I've heard of them."

John knew the particulars of Lewis' situation already, that Geronimo had moved in and set up a kind of free draw of rations for his people, bullying the local Mimbres Apaches out of their share and defying the agent to do anything about it. Still, John's curiosity was piqued about one thing. "Why haven't you sent for the army to restore order?"

"Oh, but I have." Agent Lewis ran a hand across the top of his pate, smoothing wisps of bright white hair. "I have requested troops in the most urgent terms I know, but nothing has happened. For weeks just silence, then a telegram that you would be here to close the Agency and transfer these Indians to San Carlos. I tell you, the army sure talks a pretty war, but when you get right down to it, they ain't nowhere to be seen."

John nodded, not so much in agreement as in sad disgust at how coordinated the army's plan really was. Caleb Lewis had a solid reputation in the Indian Service; it angered John to see a good man reduced to this.

"I tell you what." John swung down off his horse. "If Geronimo doesn't know I'm here yet, he will in the next ten minutes or so, but I don't really want him to come in until I've got a proper reception ready. Do you have a couple of friendly Indians you can send out and invite him in for a powwow in the morning?"

Lewis nodded, and beckoned to a couple of Indians leaning on the corral fence. "Just tell him," John continued, "that the agent from San Carlos is here, and would like to have a talk with him after breakfast, if it wouldn't inconvenience him."

"What do you intend to do?"

"Right now I think we are going to eat our dinner, and then I'd like for my police to bed down in your barn, if that's all right."

After the meal the policemen spent the evening in conversation with a number of local Indians who came over for a bite to eat—they exchanged news, no doubt, and, as Apaches always did in getting acquainted, compared genealogies to uncover which of them might be related through some distant marriage. But, John knew, his police were also gleaning little seeds of information that he might find useful.

John, however, kept to himself on this evening, worrying, calculating, preparing emergency alternatives in case something should go wrong. It was only a couple of hours before first light when he was finally convinced his plan would work, and was able to close his eyes at all.

It was Sneezer who stood the watch the two hours that John slept, and when he woke the men already had a plate of breakfast ready for him. When they were through they put the barn back in order, and shut but did not lock the big doors. The morning was bright and hazy, the kind of day you know will turn hot before noon; as John spaced his dozen police along the porch of the headquarters he hoped Geronimo would not delay long before coming in.

They waited only perhaps a half hour before two tautly wary Chiricahua men appeared in the Agency clearing, then a couple more. Before the headquarters porch they gathered like thoughts, converging, heavily armed, from all directions. They had scoured the countryside for some hint of ambush, and finding none were yet not satisfied; eerily alert, there were six, then ten, then two women, one old and one younger, short and very ugly with low-set eyes and massive jaws. Suddenly, from the quarter he least expected, along the side wall of the headquarters behind him and to his right, John heard the footfalls of a horse. When he turned to see, the steps grew louder, with no creaking of saddle leather, and then he appeared: Geronimo.

Their gazes met instantly and John felt transfixed, almost speared, by his intensity and charisma. He looked about sixty, but his squat face had seen much weathering—a good guess at his age was impossible. His eyes, fixed it seemed in a permanent squint, held the glint of perhaps magic, perhaps madness—the look you catch in the eye of few men. John had seen it only in a photograph of John Brown, and in the eye of William Oury. From the way Geronimo sat his horse John could tell he was short, his feet encased in buckskin moccasins that reached nearly up to his knees, the tops having been rolled back somewhat and slit to form knife scabbards. Inwardly John smiled: just as cowboys in the dime novels crouch and draw their six-shooters, Geronimo could crouch and draw a knife. He wore a long white breechcloth and blue army coat, decorated on either side of the chest with German silver conchas the size of coffee saucers.

John watched his dark narrow eyes scan the men on the porch, counting off the twelve he had come with, and old Agent Lewis, assuring himself that no Apache needle gun lurked behind a shutter in treachery. John thought he saw in those eyes a look almost of contempt that John had not attempted an ambush, as he himself would not have hesitated to do.

Geronimo slid off his horse with an almost pantherine grace, and swaggered over to the steps but did not mount them; his entourage followed him at a few paces' distance, fierce-looking but more timid. Geronimo stood truculently at the bottom of the steps, a Winchester resting in the crook of his right arm. "I heard that you sent for me. What do you want?"

"I want to talk to you."

"Talk."

John hooked his thumbs under his belt with as much confidence as he could muster. "Now, Geronimo, I don't want any trouble here. If you listen quietly and do as I say, everything will be all right."

The old shaman snorted. "If you talk with respect we will leave you here alive. Don't try to talk big with me, little Batunni-ka-yeh. If you do we will kill you all and leave your bodies here for coyote food."

"You don't need to talk so angry. The other Chiricahuas, Taza's people, have agreed to move to San Carlos. They are there now and they are happy. The government wants you and your people to live in San Carlos, too."

Geronimo shook his head, his graying hair that hung down to mid-back swishing from side to side. "I know better. A few sick ones maybe went to San Carlos, but Taza took most of them to Mexico. You haven't fooled me with your little boy's tricks."

"I am not trying to trick you. San Carlos is a good place to live. The other Apaches there are happy. Eskiminzin and the other chiefs there can tell you so."

"Don't tell me that," Geronimo spat back. "Eskiminzin and the others make San Carlos a bad place. You might even get me to live there if they were not there already."

John shot a glance at Sneezer and saw his face unblinking, absolutely rigid. John shifted his weight. "All right, Geronimo, I'll give it to you straight. The government thinks you have been out raiding. They think you have killed people and stolen property. You have to stand trial for it, and we are taking you to San Carlos whether you like it or not."

"Eskiminzin and Diablo have been telling lies about me. How can you think I will go live with them when they talk about me like that?"

"No, no, there is enough evidence about it that we didn't need them to say anything, so now you've got to come with us."

"I told you not to act big with me. You cannot take us without soldiers, and the soldiers you are expecting are two days away."

John could not conceal the slightest flicker of imbalance and astonishment before he regained his attitude. "How do you know that?"

"I have a power," said Geronimo, "and you'd better not mess with it."

"Ah, yes," John nodded. "I have heard about your power. I have heard that you talk to ghosts. Is that true?"

"Yes, owls too." Geronimo turned and gave a satisfied look over his warriors; John saw a couple of them fingering the buckskin medicine bundles hung around their necks and knew they were not comfortable to hear such a discussion.

"Geronimo, I really think you should come in. I have heard that many of your people don't want to follow you."

Geronimo sneered. "How do you know what is said in my camps?"

"How do you know where the soldiers are when you can't see them?"

"I told you, I have a power."

Low and hoarsely John said, "Geronimo, so have I. You say you control ghosts and owls and things, and that's all right. I have only one power, but it is more than anything you can imagine."

"What is this power?"

"The power of God."

Geronimo laughed out loud and then quieted. "I think you do not have such a big power."

"Well, believe what you like, Geronimo." John smiled with quiet bemusement, his left hand casually pushing the brim of his sombrero up from his eyes. "But my power has captured you."

At the touch of his hat the barn door banged open and Captain Beauford sprinted across the yard. He was followed by his forty Apache policemen, crouch-loping sideways in crablike unison, their needle guns at the ready, a white-pantalooned centipede that jogged left-right left-right across the yard, its eighty dark eyes glowering at Geronimo and his followers for the least excuse to start shooting.

Geronimo wheeled around at the crash of the barn door, then stood root still to watch the progression of tame pathetic Indians he detested cross the yard until they stopped, the closest pointing their rifles at him from only a few paces away. Slowly he turned in a crouch to face John again, with the look in his eyes that John thought the most malignant he had ever seen, a visage that only a demon foiled could generate. Almost imperceptibly the wrinkled brown hand with its long dirty fingernails crept up the rifle stock toward the trigger, the narrow hateful eyes drawing John's gaze deep into their own wicked vortex to hypnotize him away from looking down at the Winchester.

Suddenly Tauclee's platoon took one step forward, clicking the hammers of their needle guns in unison. Geronimo's hand froze where it was, less than an inch from the trigger guard.

John took a final measure of the situation and stepped forward. He put out his right hand to the rifle, one finger curling through the guard behind the trigger. "Now, Geronimo, you have to go to the guardhouse." As John tightened his grip the side of his hand just brushed Geronimo's; the old shaman swelled up and back like a rattler about to strike. With his left hand Geronimo could have whipped out his knife, slashed open John's stomach, and made a break for freedom, all in one motion. John knew it, and knew Geronimo was thinking about it, too, measuring the possibility of succeeding and getting out alive. He had done more remarkable things before.

Geronimo's eyes pierced as deep into John's as they could; John felt them, like cold surgical probes, searching out his confidence, his resolve, whether he was afraid. For a full twenty seconds John stared back at him, with Captain Beauford about to jump out of his skin, Geronimo's companions not moving until they received some sign of what they should do.

John pulled on the rifle, gently. "You must go to the guardhouse, now," and slowly Geronimo's hand slipped away.

"Enju," he said. "I will stay with you a little time."

John nodded to Beauford, who leaned his shotgun against the porch and positioned himself behind Geronimo, stringing out of a back pocket a length of leather thong. Roughly he pulled Geronimo's wizened hands behind him and bound them, the chief's eyes never leaving John's, never wavering in an insolent, maniacal mirth, conceding the skirmish but gloating in the surety that vengeance would be his.

Tauclee uttered a sharp command in Apache, and Geronimo's men stood their rifle stocks on the ground and let them fall in a tinkling clatter, followed by the thuds of heavy revolvers smacking the ground. Six of Sneezer's police leaned their needle guns into a neat stand and at his signal moved through Geronimo's warriors, plucking their weapons off the ground and stacking them by the porch. Then they swept through again, asking quietly for knives, offering reassurance that no one would be harmed.

As Beauford finished tying Geronimo's hands the younger of the two women abruptly raced forward, her face shaking back and forth in a livid shriek. Five feet from Beauford she flew into the air and landed perfectly astraddle his broad back, one hand holding on under his chin, the other pummeling his head and shoulders with all her might.

The burly officer released Geronimo and staggered a step under the force of her landing, but did not fall. Straightening himself, he reached over his head until he could grasp her shoulders, then bent violently and threw her as hard as he could. She was wearing a heavily pleated, multitiered Mexican skirt that swathed overhead arcs of red, green, and brown as she cartwheeled over his head, feet apart, landing in a grunting whump ten feet from him. Beauford pulled his revolver half out of its holster and the ugly young woman retreated among the others, cursing viciously. She spit repeatedly at the line of police, who made no reaction until she called one of them by name. She showed him a fist with her thumb protruding between her third and fourth fingers, then flung her fingers open at him. John understood her hissed words, "Smell mine!" The policeman lurched forward but was restrained across the chest by both men beside him.

"Tie them up," ordered Sneezer.

"Bring the old woman inside," John told him. "Captain, if you'll join me in here we'll decide what to do next. Sneezer, why don't you go out to fetch Skimmy and the rest."

Two of the policemen reached inside the headquarters door and lugged out the big trunk, unlatched it, and began unloading and caching the firearms taken from Geronimo's men. John looked down at the old shaman's Winchester in his hand, tightened his fingers around it, and carried it inside.

CHAPTER 15

"Well, Mr. Beauford, you certainly took your sweet time in getting here last night."

"Yeah, the moon didn't come up till nearly eleven. We were picking our way along and trying to be quiet and none of our boys knew the country very well. Frankly I'm surprised we did make it in before light."

John entrusted Geronimo and the rest to Tauclee, and spent the middle of the day logging inventory in the warehouses and loading up wagons to haul the supplies to San Carlos. When Sneezer returned with Eskiminzin the chief found John in the commissary. He shook his hand and looked him straight in the eye. "*Yei, ao,* you pretty brave son of a gun. Geronimo plenty mad—tellin' everybody what all he gonna do."

"I guess we'll just have to make sure he never gets the chance."

"Listen. Injun was right. Victorio's people up in the mountains right here. Victorio come into camp this morning and ask what you doing. Then Sneezer come."

"How did Victorio take the news about Geronimo?"

"Not bad. Lots his people been telling him, Geronimo no good. Better send him away."

"Why didn't he?"

Eskiminzin shrugged. "Not want trouble with Geronimo, not want trouble with white people. Victorio just staying out of trouble."

"Poor man probably never realized how hard it is to just stay out of everybody's way," sighed John, and he and Eskiminzin moved off toward the headquarters building. Eskiminzin's voice betrayed no little admiration when he asked, "You really tell Geronimo you gonna put him in guardhouse?"

"Yes, I did."

"You scared?"

John laughed. "Nah."

Eskiminzin's lips creased into a slow smile. "You make mighty big poker player. You got mighty big bluff."

"What makes you think I was bluffing?"

"Got no guardhouse here."

John couldn't help it; his eyes got big and he gasped. Geronimo must have known that, too.

Eskiminzin laughed and clapped him on the back. "Don't worry. We put 'em all in corral and guard 'em. Geronimo tied up, sitting in horse dung where he belong."

"Skimmy, did you tell Victorio I wanted to talk to him as soon as it could be arranged?"

"Yes, he come in tonight, maybe. But listen: Victorio not like San Carlos. You gotta make mighty big talk to make him go."

"Well, I'll do my best. Say, do you think one of your boys would mind going out to Geronimo's camp and tell them they need to get ready to move out? We've been working on the old lady he brought in—she can tell them nobody will be hurt and there'll be plenty of rations to go around."

"Injun think, better do that himself, maybe. Where old woman?"

"Inside the headquarters, talking to Sneezer."

"Okay Sneezer go, too?"

"Sure."

"See you tonight—come in with Victorio, maybe."

During the afternoon they found enough tobacco in the commissary to make presents to Victorio and as many of his headmen as he might bring in.

They rode in at dusk, boldly, without skulking as Geronimo's people had done. Eskiminzin rode at the side of a powerful-looking, middle-aged Indian, his iron-gray hair shoulder length and with a curious waviness that bobbed when he slid down from his horse. John had heard rumors, that the Apaches had denied, that Victorio was part Mexican; his well-managed, wavy hair must have contributed to the suspicion.

When Eskiminzin introduced them they shook hands firmly, looking each other straight in the eye. Victorio's posture was perfect, a man of medium height, and John was struck by his chest, not muscle-bound but well fleshed and strongly tapered in the "V" of a man who could ride or run for miles and not register any fatigue. "Eskiminzin has told us you want us to move to San Carlos. Why is that necessary?"

Victorio's question through Lewis' interpreter was frank and businesslike, not the least truculent, but John felt it must be significant that he opened the talk without introducing him to the men he had brought with him, as though he expected this might be a very short interview.

"For many reasons." John tried to look as confident as he could. "Mostly because there are so many white people moving into the country here that the government can protect you better if you are all in one place. Also, the issue of your rations and supplies will be steadier, because the government won't be trying to send a little here and a little there and a little some other place."

Victorio considered these things. "Years ago these mountains were given to us as a reservation. We were happy. We kept the law. Then they took it away, and said we must go elsewhere. We did not go, and after a while they gave us an Agency again. Why should we go now? If we stay, by and by another agent will come."

"No, I don't think so." John crossed his arms. "How many white people lived here then?"

"Not many."

"How many live here now? More and more move in every day. There has been too much fighting between you and them."

"They start it, not us."

"Yes, they start it. I know that." Such a frank admission provoked a subtle change in Victorio's bearing, as though for once the very lack of an accusation left him more willing to hear John out. "But they are ten to your one," John went on. "Next year, maybe twenty to one. You cannot fight them all."

"Yes, I can."

"You will lose."

"At least I will die at home, not in some hot place full of flies, like San Carlos. That place belongs to these policemen here. Not us. We would not live well there. We are different from them."

John shook his head. "Things aren't like that at San Carlos. Now, I admit I was concerned at first whether these different bands of Apaches would get along all right, but they are. Eskiminzin and Diablo and the other chiefs see to that. It has made them all more like brothers. It can be so for you, too. Besides, there is another reason your people will be happy there." Victorio looked at John with impassive expectation. "When bad Indians commit crimes, white people do not judge them anymore. There is an Apache court with Apache judges. Did you know that?"

"Yes."

"What do you think about it?"

Victorio gazed haughtily at the interpreter. "I think my Chiricahuas would as soon be judged by you white people as by the San Carlos or White Mountain Apaches. They do not know us that well."

"You don't understand yet. I want you to be a judge on this court, Victorio. Everybody knows you are fair and wise. None of your people will be punished for anything without your agreement, and you cannot punish any of their people unless the other judges approve."

Victorio registered some surprise, and turned to Eskiminzin. "You have agreed to this?"

He was surprised as well, but nodded.

"We will discuss this among ourselves. Have you anything else to say?"

"No, I am sure you will do what is right."

They shook hands, and Victorio mounted and led his men away. After they were gone John noticed with some mild alarm, "I forgot to give them their tobacco."

"Victorio don't take many presents," said Eskiminzin. "Don't believe in it. I think my people go back out and visit his people tonight. Work on 'em a little bit."

"Good. Excellent." John hadn't realized until the meeting broke up how very tired he was, with the strain of the events and only two hours' sleep the night before. The day had been too full to have a chance to write Mary what all had happened, but with official news to transmit he resolved to attend his paperwork in the morning and work until the army came—if indeed they showed up at all.

He rolled his bedding on the office floor and slept like a log. He hadn't bothered to post a guard in months. He knew one or another of the police would be at watch all night.

In the morning he wrote his reports and a letter to Mary, and worked busily to close up the books of the Agency, until about ten o'clock when Tauclee stole into the office with a wisely amused look on his face. "Soldiers coming now. Catch Geronimo, maybe, you think?"

By the time John got to the top steps of the porch the formation of cavalry was already clattering into the compound, two full companies in double column. The officer at their head pulled up at the hitching rail and saluted. "Colonel Hatch, United States Army. Are you John Clum?"

"Yup. Are you a dollar short or just a day late?"

"I apologize. The grazing between Fort Wingate and here was so poor we were detained a day to rest the horses. Has there been any sign of Geronimo?"

John could not suppress a frown. He had hoped to be worth a better excuse than that. "Yes, we've seen him."

"Have you any idea as to his present whereabouts?"

"One or two."

There was an anxious pause. "Well, where?"

"Get down off your high horse and I'll introduce you."

Hatch exchanged stares with a fair blond boy of a lieutenant mounted next to him. He motioned with his head to dismount and then himself swung down out of his saddle. John led the two officers over to the corral, where four of the policemen were perched on the corners of the fence.

"Sir, those Indians are armed," worried the blond boy.

"I see that."

Geronimo sat on the ground, his back to the fence. He sat cross-legged, his arms securely bound behind him, and sitting in a knot by him were half a dozen of his headmen, scowling like so many genies in a bottle. "There you are, Colonel, pigs in a poke. Now before you say anything, I want you to know I realize your orders probably didn't consider the possibility that I might live long enough to sack Geronimo without your help." Already he was steering them from the corral back to their troops. "I know you want him for a military trial, so just to clarify things, I don't have the authority to transfer these prisoners out of the custody of the Indian Office. However, if you have no other orders, I would be happy to have an escort back to San Carlos, to sort of keep a lid on the local ranchers who may not be satisfied to wait for the law to take its course." No officer in the army would be seen to set himself against the public that way, and John knew it.

They were back at the horses, and the officers mounted quickly. Hatch was beyond embarrassed; he was undone. "No, my orders are, if I am not needed here, to patrol the road down to Pinos Altos and sweep it of hostile activity."

Liar, thought John. You've got to fall on the nearest telegraph key and tell everybody it didn't work. Poor Kautz.

Hatch called out, "Companies, ho!" and disappeared, and their dust had barely settled when Eskiminzin padded across the yard.

"Soldier chief find out you still livin', he get plenty mad. Injun think, we better leave here pretty quick, maybe."

"I couldn't agree with you more, Skimmy. If we get everything wrapped up here we can pull out in the morning. What about Victorio? Did your boys make any impression on him last night?"

"We work on him real hard. Injun think, Victorio come along, maybe need little more talk. He comin' in again when soldiers out of valley."

John kept Caleb Lewis' interpreter close at hand, so that when Victorio came in, which he did about midday, they could get right to business. "We do not think you are a bad man," Victorio began at once. "Eskiminzin has told us you are a good agent to them. But long ago, maybe fifteen years, we had an agent who worked hard for us, and did right by us. When the army found out about it they sent him away. Will they do this to you?"

The question took John aback. He had known about Agent Greiner, but until this moment the similarity of their situations had not struck him. "The army was here today," said John finally. "Who was sent away?"

It was the kind of answer John had gotten away with before, but Victorio cut right through the sass of it. "That is today. It is tomorrow that worries us." The observation was rhetorical, and the chief waited for no reply before pressing on. "These Apaches of yours, they tell me you are a man of your word. Is that true?"

"I try never to make promises I cannot keep."

Victorio nodded, and gestured up into the high, green mountains nearby. "Not far away, there is a place where four meadows come together. This is where the world began, and where the Holy People went up into the sky. We get our life from this place, and we do not want to leave it. If we leave it for long, we will get sick and die off. Tell me this: if we come with you to prove our good faith, will you write to Washington and ask him to give us this land back for our reservation in the future?"

John nodded solemnly. "Yes, I will do that. But I cannot promise that Washington will agree."

"That is beyond your power. We understand that. What we ask is that you take up for us what you have for these people."

John walked up and shook Victorio's hand. "I will do my best for you, and I will try to have your mountains set apart as a reservation for you."

"*Enju,*" said Victorio with finality, the same utterance of agreement that seemed to be common to all Apache peoples. "We will be here in the morning for you to lead us away. Geronimo's people trust us more than your policemen, and they will travel with us."

As Victorio left John was supremely aware that this was a moment of unprecedented triumph, but what he felt was not remotely akin to gloating or even satisfaction in a job well done. What he felt was an affection for these people that transcended patronage; suddenly he was aware that from this moment, he was as much theirs as they were his, and the revelation shook him. Just as he had found himself promising Victorio to try to get him a separate reservation, or naming him to the Apache Court without consulting Eskiminzin—both correct moves that the Apaches would affirm—John realized that he had begun operating from the instinct of the moment, like an Apache, rather than from calculation as he had formerly done.

He was certain he could resolve it all, but it would take time, and it drained his concentration from the tasks of the moment.

The Apache Police worked long into the night lining up and loading the wagons with goods to be removed from Warm Springs. John was grateful to have so much work to do, without having to give thought to how Kautz and the army would take all this.

Their departure in the morning was delayed only by the discovery, though it was a disconcerting one, that one of Victorio's men who had been to Pinos Altos to trade with the miners had come down with smallpox. One of the wagons had to be unloaded and turned into a sick wagon. Victorio had seen the horror of an epidemic before, and almost pulled out, but fortunately for John he also knew of the white man's treatment called inoculation. When John dispatched a courier over a shortcut through the mountains to San Carlos, giving him both his official reports and his letter to Mary, John included a message to have a doctor waiting at San Carlos to vaccinate them all when they got there. If they moved quickly, perhaps few would succumb.

The march south to the pass where the wagons could turn north was peaceful, although John kept out a constant screen of scouts and flankers—being careful to include some of Victorio's warriors—to make sure the army kept their distance. Only once did John feel any alarm, when he heard an excited babble far back in the dusty, walking crowd of Victorio's people. He turned his head at the commotion and saw four women heading into a small, brush-filled arroyo. "Skimmy," he pointed, "where are those women going?"

Eskiminzin turned on his saddleless blanket to see them, then faced the front again. "That one woman pretty big. She have baby pretty soon now, maybe."

"What? Really?" The last of the women had disappeared into the bushes. "Hadn't we better make camp and wait for them?"

Eskiminzin shrugged. "No, plenty women have babies."

"But we can't just leave them out here!"

Eskiminzin was beginning to take some amusement in John's growing alarm. "Your woman make little agent baby, you gonna get all worked up about it?"

"You bet I will. Women have to be cared for at a time like that."

Eskiminzin laughed and shook his head. " 'Pache women not weak like white women. 'Pache women work, have baby, go back work. Some rest a little while, maybe. They not cowards about it. We go on, make camp tonight. They catch up before morning, you see."

John made no further argument, but Eskiminzin saw his restiveness cooking within him like beans coming to a slow boil. After a mile or so John couldn't stand it any longer. "Aw, nuts, I just can't go along with this. Skimmy, tell one of the wagons to go back and wait for those women. Have the men put plenty of blankets and pillows in it."

"Nantan Batunni-ka-yeh." Eskiminzin called him by his name and started to hold firm, but relented. "You the boss, I guess," and turned his horse around to tend to it.

Victorio was riding with them, and took in the whole discussion without saying anything. The tolerant amusement in his face, however, communicated that he felt there were, at least, possibilities for this agent who fretted so over a pregnant Chiricahua woman.

When they finally turned up the San Pedro Valley John knew they were an easy three days from San Carlos. The pace had been tiring, but of necessity; eight of Victorio's people had died of the smallpox, and it was imperative to get the others vaccinated. Three more babies had been born. The closer they got to home the greater John felt pulled to it, like a piece of iron to a magnet. He had missed Mary terribly.

He rode at the head of the column, flanked by the chiefs. When Victorio spoke it was in his own dialect to Eskiminzin, who relayed in English to John.

"This chief tells us," said Victorio, "that you had them dig ditches to the river to water their crops."

"Yes, and they have taken in good crops, too."

"We know this method. We did it for many years in our high meadows. Did you know this?"

"No!" John's surprise was genuine. "Did you get good crops?"

"Yes. After a time, some women, widows, do nothing else. Only grow food. We bring them meat and goods, get vegetables. Worked out good."

This struck John as though he was hearing of the very origin of the specialization of labor. "Why did you stop?"

"Crops take time. White people kept running us off. Burn fields."

"That won't happen at San Carlos."

Victorio huffed. "White people not want San Carlos." Remembering back, he added, "White pick-diggers come first, look for yellow metal. Then everybody else. You got pick-diggers at San Carlos?"

"No."

"What if they come?"

"I have a plan about that." John made the assertion blindly, knowing now that having said it, a plan would come to him. "I have some gold. Not much, but enough. If prospectors show up, I will give you my gold. Your people will scatter it in a river far away. We will let them find that, and the prospectors will forget all about us."

Victorio nodded gravely. "He who was chief before me. He did that. The pick-diggers tied him to a pole and whipped him. Then army come, cut off his head and boil it in a pot."

Eskiminzin translated that and added, "Need better plan, maybe."

Looking ahead, they saw a narrow cloud of dust, lengthening slowly, like a mole raises earth as it digs. "Somebody riding pretty fast," Eskiminzin said, pointing.

As it became apparent that the approaching rider was headed straight for them, John signaled up Captain Beauford. "Skimmy and I are going to ride on ahead a bit and see what this fellow wants. You keep an eye on things here." John and Eskiminzin spurred their horses forward, and Victorio followed instinctively. John pulled up and looked at him in surprise, but was met by the cool gaze of rank and the expectation that he meant to come along. There was risk that a messenger bearing bad news would upset him, but that was preferable to insulting him with a request to stay behind. John nodded with what he hoped seemed like ready trust, and gestured forward.

They slowed to a walk about a hundred yards ahead of the wagons and watched the rider come up. He was a young Apache, stripped to his G-string and moccasins, riding bareback, his bow and quiver hung across his chest from one shoulder, a small bundle of food from the other.

"My cousin's son," said Eskiminzin. John knew Skimmy would not register surprise in any case, but he sensed some apprehension. The youth was about sixteen, and when he reined to an abrupt stop he launched into a flood of Apache. Even after three years among them it was too fast for John to catch more than a few words, but he disliked the ones he did understand—San Carlos, soldiers, and trouble.

"What is it, Skimmy?"

Eskiminzin flashed up his hand to cut him off until the boy was through, then asked him a couple of taut questions. Looking at John squarely he said, "Many soldiers ride into San Carlos, stir everything up. Old Soldier and Mary Hilda got mad but they sent them away in a wagon."

"Sweeney!"

"Soldiers posted in storehouse, keep Injuns out of food. 'Paches all mad but not do anything till we get there. Soldiers acting all big, ordering them all over. Soldier chief take over your house."

"What!" Through the roll of bad news John was conscious of only one thought: Mary. Breathing hard, he said, "Skimmy, I've got to get up there at once."

"No." Eskiminzin's face was like wood. "Stay where we can see you. You go out alone, some Injun up there may get crazy and shoot you."

"Me? What do you mean? Mary's up there!"

"Your woman all right. Policemen take her to my camp, maybe."

"What policemen?" Then it dawned on him. "You mean the ones you said were sick?"

"Injun lied. Leave 'em behind with orders, watch over your woman."

John's thoughts had so fastened on Mary and the possibility of disaster that it took a sarcastic comment from Victorio to bring him back. He didn't need an interpreter. "No, Victorio, this is not what I brought you along for."

Victorio looked at him as though he was slapped in the face. Until that moment he had no idea that John spoke their language. But then he switched into English. "I don't need to tell you of all people that there are bad white men as well as bad Indians. I don't know what the trouble is in San Carlos, but when we get there we will set it right. In the last three years everything there has come out right because I mean to do good and these Indians mean to do good. If you mean to do good also, Victorio, it is even more certain that things will work out. Think about that."

John spurred his horse back toward the wagons, leaving Eskiminzin to frame his words into others that Victorio could comprehend.

The next three days were a nightmare for John; he worried every waking hour and then slept only fitfully. He endured it only because two other messengers brought news that the situation in San Carlos, though bad, was at least stable.

As they came up to the flat before the Agency, John and the chiefs rode on ahead with a dozen of the policemen; then came the wagon with Geronimo and the other prisoners, driven by one policeman with another sitting guard. The rest of the Apache Police followed behind, scattered among the several hundred of Victorio's people.

This was the moment when he had once thought he would turn in the saddle and take in the sight, and see whether he felt like Moses, but now his anxiety for Mary was such that all his attention was forward. He knew they had been seen when he made out a line of mounted men forming up, an officer sitting on his horse in front of them. John couldn't gallop out ahead, knowing how soldiers, like predators, sense fear and home in on it. They held their desert-wearied walking pace, and only when they were near enough to speak did John challenge, "What do you mean by this?"

The officer saluted. "Are you Mr. Clum?"

"I most assuredly am."

"Lieutenant Marshall, sir, United States Army. I have orders from Department Headquarters, Department of Arizona, instituting military authority over this reservation." He held out a crisp sheet of paper.

John snatched it from him and read it over. "General Kautz does not have authority to issue such an order."

"Maybe, sir, but that's between you and the general. I get my orders from him."

John looked up from the paper, to outward appearance surveying the Agency grounds; he alone knew how his eyes strained to make out his own house, scrutinizing it for any hint of change. He had just assessed that there was none when suddenly the door swung open, and Mary came out laden with a basket of laundry to hang, and John felt his heart lighten as though freed from a bear trap, and he turned his attention back to the lieutenant. "Where is my assistant, Mr. Sweeney?"

"Mr. Sweeney and your Agency interpreter were disruptively interfering with our carrying out of orders. I'm afraid we had to send them under guard to Fort Whipple."

"Did you?" John clenched his teeth. "Well, mister, you haven't seen the meaning of disruptive."

He spurred his horse in the direction of his house; Mary heard him trotting up and ran from the clothesline to meet him. John leaped from the horse and threw his arms around her. "Oh God, I've been so worried. Are you all right?"

"Yes." She stood him back to arm's length. "John, what's going on? The soldiers won't tell me anything."

"Offhand, I'd guess General Kautz is attempting a little revolution, and I'm afraid he's succeeding. Did any of the troops come into the house or try anything with you?"

"No, not at all. They won't let me into the office, though."

"Well, that must be it."

"What?"

"The Indian boy who brought out the news said the soldiers had taken over the house. Scared me to death. I guess he meant the headquarters."

"No, I'm fine. Those four fellows have me a little worried, though." She pointed to four Apache policemen sitting in a wagon just beyond the clothesline. "They haven't moved in three days. They sleep one at a time and some woman brings them food every morning."

"Have you tried to talk to them?"

"No, but I've given them coffee now and then."

John laughed. "Good. That's your bodyguard. Skimmy left them behind to keep an eye on you. If the soldiers had gotten rowdy they were going to spirit you away to Ethel's camp to ride out the storm."

"Oh gracious!"

John saluted to them and nodded, and the four policemen filed silently back to their camps. "I'm going over to the office and see what I can do. I want you to get things ready to pack, just in case."

"Is it that bad?"

"I don't know. If it's just Kautz I'm sure I can whip him. But if it goes any higher, I'd say we're done for out here."

Mary felt sick for him, but not sorry for the prospect of going home. "All right, go on. But be careful."

John just reached the edge of the veranda when a burly sergeant, only slightly smaller than the door, stood in front of it and crossed his arms. "What do you want?"

"I am the Indian agent for this reservation, and I mean to enter my office."

"Well, you can't come in without some authorization."

John looked over his shoulder. Most of the Apache Police were still watching over the wagons of prisoners, but as soon as John got one's attention they began to collect in the yard behind him—first five, then a dozen, finally forty. Sergeant Tauclee called them to attention and then to rest, their rifle butts smacking the ground in unison. "I have my authorization. Sergeant, stand yourself aside."

The plank door behind the sergeant clicked open just visibly, a voice ordering, "Let the gentleman come in."

John pushed by, confronting in the hall a cavalry lieutenant not much larger or older than he. "Are you supposed to be in charge here?"

"My detail is to take charge of these buildings, yes sir."

"M-hm. Well, I am Agent Clum, and I am going to send some telegrams and get to the bottom of this farce, so you and your men can go back where you came from and get a good night's sleep."

"I'm sorry, sir, but no civilians are to use the telegraph without permission. Lieutenant Marshall's orders." The officer passed into the office and seated himself at John's desk, with the look in his eyes that, as far as he was concerned, the interview was over.

John approached him, pulling off his dusty campaign gloves and tossing them into a chair. "Lieutenant, did you notice—I'm sure you did—how fast that company of Apache Police formed up behind me when I needed them?" He put his hands on the desk and leaned far across it. "I've got four thousand Indians on this reservation who are intensely loyal to me. It would just make a dull day enjoyable for them if I were to turn them loose on you. Don't think I can't do it. It's easy. Lieutenant, it's so easy to set them off you could even do it yourself. All you would have to do is make the least move to run me out. Now, unless you and all your soldier boys want to be crow bait by morning, you are going to let me in the telegraph room, and I mean right now."

The lieutenant looked jarred for just a second. "Well, you can't use it. Some of those treasured heathens of yours cut the line, and we don't know where it's down."

John was thinking fast how to prove him a liar when the sudden clicketing of the receiving key obviated the question. "Sounds like they found it in the nick of time."

The lieutenant scowled, then got up and opened the door to the telegraph room. "Let this gentleman exchange what messages he needs to."

A Signal Corps man did not look up from his writing. "Yes sir."

At what was once the kitchen table John drafted a telegram to the commissioner, telling as much of the situation as he could fit into a paragraph. Angrily he concluded it, "Authorize funds to double size of

Apache Police force, and army may be dismissed from this part of Arizona Territory."

The reply was only three hours in coming. The Corps man wrote intensely for a couple of minutes as the key clattered, then got up and handed the paper to John. "This is for you."

John looked down at it and knew the extent of the conspiracy: BY ORDER OF THE PRESIDENT, THE SECRETARY DIRECTS ME TO ACCEPT YOUR RESIGNATION, EFFECTIVE IMMEDIATELY.

"Thank you." John crushed the paper down into a pocket and pushed out the back door toward the house. Beauford caught up with him on the way. "We put Geronimo in the guardhouse along with his friends. The troopers went along in thinking that's where he belongs."

"Good. Carry on."

Mary jumped to her feet as he banged through the door. "Johnny, what—"

"Pack up. We're going home."

She could tell he was angry to the point of tears. "Right now? It's the middle of the afternoon. Shouldn't we get a start in the morning?"

"Nope. I don't want you out here when the Apaches find out what's going on. Just pack what we can take quickly. We can send for the rest later."

Mary opened the trunk at the foot of the bed as John pulled his old carpet satchels out from under it. He flung them onto the covers and yanked them open, then strode over to the chest of drawers with the grinding feeling in his stomach that now with every step, every footfall, the plans he had made with Victorio he was crushing underfoot like shattered glass into smaller and smaller pieces.

It didn't take long before he sat at Mary's small writing desk, drafting notes to Lieutenant Marshall and whatever acting agent would follow, instructing where to ship the remainder. Mary stood behind him, curling her arms about his shoulders and resting her chin on his head. "Are you going to say good-bye to Eskiminzin?"

"No."

"Johnny, why not? He's your friend."

"It's their way. If a man is beat down, you don't humiliate him by offering him comfort. He'd feel like he was humiliating me. Besides, if I go out there now it would make it harder for him to control his own warhawks. He'll understand."

When he had hitched two horses to the wagon and put their baggage in it, a queer sensation crept over him, like the first awareness of a tarantula crawling across your bedroll at night. He stood in the wagon seat and surveyed the agency grounds in all directions, and saw not a single Apache anywhere.

CHAPTER 16

For three days after John helped Mary up onto the wagon, whipped the horses, and pulled away in a circular dusty clatter of wooden spokes, the only activity at San Carlos was that of the soldiers. They administered an empty Agency, taking inventory in the commissary of stores to distribute to Indians who were nowhere to be seen. The wagon ruts on the road south from the Agency were not disturbed even by a wind.

At noon of the fourth day a sentry atop the commissary made out the rising dust of approaching horses. Over the farthest rise there appeared mounted men riding side by side, and then a buggy, black as a beetle, making its lumpy way across the desert. As it neared it proved to be a covered surrey carrying four men, two in the front seat wearing black suits, two in the rear dressed in dun work clothes.

As the conveyance pulled to a stop before the headquarters, Lieutenant Marshall stifled a comment on the ludicrousness of the swinging velvet tassels in such circumstances. "Agent Hart, I presume."

The driver of the surrey, a huge bear of a man with a full black beard and tiny dark squinting eyes, nodded. "I am, and you must be Lieutenant Marshall." He descended and they shook hands. "This is my secretary, Mr. Jenkins, my interpreter Pally John, and my employee Mr. Gurney." Agent Hart indicated in turn the other well-dressed man who had sat beside him, with prematurely thinning red hair and a curiously androgynous, worried-looking face, a Papago Indian in the backseat with no more expression in his visage than if he had stood rooted to a sidewalk in front of a cigar store, and a dull-looking, chunky youth next to him with short brown hair so dirty that it seemed from sheer grime to stand each hair straight out from his head. "Has the previous agent departed?"

Marshall nodded. "Four days ago. Right after he got the sack."

"Did you furnish him an escort?"

"He didn't need any escort."

"Well, I have to thank you for this one. It was spooky as hell gettin' here. Smoke signals everywhere and not even a rabbit movin' to be seen. Made my damn skin crawl."

Lieutenant Marshall scanned the Agency grounds. "I have to tell you I wished I hadn't spared them. That young blister Clum had his heathen police all lined up with their rifles like they intended to butcher us all on the spot. He threatened it, too, by God."

"Well, you needn't worry about him anymore. I'm sure by the time we audit his accounts we will find enough to keep his bondsmen after him for months."

"Is that so? The little brat was on the take?"

"We feel certain that is what the records will reflect."

"Well then," Marshall nodded. "It'll be good to have a reliable agent in charge here. Any way we can help, you let us know."

"I'd like to have a conference with the chiefs, first thing in the morning. Can you send out messengers to see they come in?"

"Yes sir." Marshall gave a lazy kind of salute and turned to leave.

"And I'll need you to release Geronimo in the morning as well."

Marshall halted and looked back. "Do you think that's advisable?"

Hart looked at him, surprised. "It's part of the deal. Didn't you know?"

"What deal is that, Mr. Hart?"

"Why, um—" Hart was nonplussed. "Peace with the Apaches, of course. Release their imprisoned chiefs in exchange for assurance of their good behavior. Showing our good faith, so to speak."

Marshall eyed him without nodding before walking away. When he was gone, the red-headed man climbed down from the surrey and stood next to Hart, squinting after the officer, his nose wrinkling like a rabbit's. "We better watch what we say around him, boss."

When Lieutenant Marshall approached the headquarters building the next morning he found the front door standing open, and entered without knocking. Through the office door he saw Hart and Jenkins sitting side by side at the oak desk with a sheaf of loose ledger sheets spread before them. They were talking low, pointing to figures, and making notes on a tablet; Hart suddenly made a sweeping motion with his hand. "This is no good. These are just copies. That damn weasel took the real books with him."

Jenkins twitched his pencil in the air while with his other hand he pushed his spectacles up to the bridge of his nose, from where they had been slipping. "Yes, yes, but look here. Maybe he's left enough for me to prepare a duplicate set—"

Marshall cleared his throat, and the two officials looked up. "The headmen are in the commissary yard. Except Victorio—patrol said his camp's deserted, even the old and sick. Campfires were still warm."

Hart nodded. "See how faithless these people are."

"Diablo, too," said Marshall. "I don't know where he is."

"Have you released Geronimo?"

"Yes sir."

Hart turned up the palms of his hands. "Where is he?"

"Why, he's gone on his way. Made a beeline back to his renegades, I suppose. You didn't really think he'd stick around here, did you?"

"Well." Hart surveyed the ledger sheets. "I don't guess we really need him to be here. Lieutenant, would you see to it that some of your men are standing by at the commissary?"

Marshall assented and left, and Hart stood; he donned his long black coat and placed a top hat on his head. From a coat pocket he pulled a comb and stroked it through his beard. "Let's go have a look at these people and see what we got. Is everything ready, Jenkins?"

"Just like you said."

"What about Diablo?"

"We took care of him."

The two men left the headquarters and walked toward the commissary, followed at a short distance by Pally John. As they neared, Hart saw the platoon of troops lined up before the big doors, with Lieutenant Marshall at one side, and in front of them a long table with some chairs behind it. On the ground at the near end of the table lay a brown carton, its top leaves opened to reveal a lining of white wrapping paper. Another box, still sealed, was on the ground at the other end. Several dozen Apache men sat in a group before the table.

When they reached the table, Jenkins sat in a chair by the closed box, and Hart stood before the table at the other end, removing his hat and setting it on the table, then motioning Pally John forward. "My name is Mr. Hart," he said after a few seconds of stern surveying. "I am your agent now. The old agent did bad by you, and the government has sent him away." Hart nodded to Pally John, who translated the sentences into Apache.

Casador jumped to his feet. "Who is this interpreter? We don't know him. He talks like a Papago."

Hart looked at him evenly. "Sit down, please."

Casador pointed to the interpreter with a yank. "He says bad things about Nantan Batunni-ka-yeh. We don't trust anyone who talks like that."

"Sit down."

"Six years ago his people killed a lot of us. We don't want him here."

Hart pointed sharply to the ground and Casador sank glaring to his haunches, as Hart leaned back, resting against the table. "You people have been doing all kinds of things that will not be tolerated anymore. I have heard that some of you have been stealing from the commissary. Well," he gestured behind him, "I have brought the soldiers back to guard it."

Even in his crouch Casador stiffened his back. "Which of us do you say took food from the storehouse?"

Hart was surprised by the dispute. "If I knew that he would be in the guardhouse."

"How do you know it was not one of your men, or a soldier, or that Papago there?"

Hart was silent for a second or two. "I will do the talking here today." Theatrically his tone softened. "I do not wish to be strict with you. It is for your own good. To show you that I want to be your friend, I have released your chief, Geronimo, from the guardhouse. He said he would try to speak to you, but he, uh, sends word that his family does not want him to leave again."

Sad glances of knowledge flickered among the Indians, too subtle to catch Hart's notice.

"As long as each of you follows orders I'm sure we'll get along fine. Now, I have brought something for you." He reached into the brown carton lined with white paper and pulled out a tiny black book. "I have one of these books for each of you. In it is the revealed word of the living God. It tells you everything you need to know about how to live."

Eskiminzin was seated next to Casador and saw him bury his mouth in his shirt collar, muttering in Apache, "Not around here, it doesn't."

"I want each of you to take a Bible home with you. I want you to talk about what it says. When you come back on issue day I will ask you questions about what is in it. I will have presents for those who can tell me what the book says. Now, you, Eskiminzin, I hear you're about the biggest chief around here, so you come up here."

Eskiminzin looked around in surprise. "I not chief. Diablo, my wife's uncle. He chief."

"No, Diablo is not a chief anymore."

Eskiminzin looked slowly around the circle, seeing clearly the insulted amazement that escaped the white men altogether. He stood up and went silently forward, his face becoming as stiff and grainy as the mountain mahogany of his bow. "You say Diablo not chief, you make big trouble." He said it sternly, but low, where no one else could hear.

Hart gazed across the seated Indians, asking Eskiminzin quietly, "Why isn't he here?"

"White men came yesterday, with a paper from the soldier chief at Fort Grant. They took him down there for a talk."

Out loud across the gathering Hart said, "No, he has no business in Fort Grant. Diablo has caused too much trouble. This is why the government will no longer recognize him as a chief. Now, because so many of you have been cheating on your ration tickets, in the future I am going to know who has been issued supplies."

Hart nodded to Jenkins, who reached down and broke open the sealed carton, as Hart continued, "Each of you men is going to be issued a tag to wear around your neck. You must wear your tags when you come in for rations. Only you with tags will be given food. This is what they look like." Hart took from Jenkins and held up a large, shiny tin rectangle, with a letter and number stamped onto it. A chain was looped through holes in the upper corners.

Eskiminzin made no protest as Hart slipped the tag around his neck and turned him around so the other chiefs could get a good look, as Jenkins made an entry in a large, leatherbound logbook.

Even after Hart gave him a little black Bible and dismissed him, Eskiminzin stood rooted to the spot, fingering the tag profoundly, feeling as a free horse must feel the first time a bit is shoved into its mouth, aware that he was now controlled but unsure how to move in order to avoid punishment.

Each of the headmen received a tag and Bible, just as silently, as Jenkins wrote down phonetic approximations of their names next to their tag numbers, with a note of how many families each represented. As Hart was finishing, the unkempt youth named Gurney came out of the headquarters building and approached him. "Excuse me, Mr. Hart. There is a man here from Tucson to see you, says his name's Reeble, says he represents the beef contractor. Wants to talk to you about some inequities in the meat weighing procedures instituted by the former agent."

Hart shook hands with the last of the chiefs. "Well, give him a drink;

tell him I'm sure we can reach a mutually agreeable accommodation.
I'll be along in a minute."

When the last of the Apaches had gone the soldiers were dismissed to
return to their camp, and Hart and Jenkins walked together back to the
headquarters. The nearly empty carton of books was left where it lay
for the hot little ground swirls to catch and rattle the white wrapping
paper. As the sun rose higher a vinegarroon squeezed through a crack
in the carton near the ground, to rest among the remaining Bibles.

Ethel didn't know Eskiminzin was in the wickiup when she entered,
struggling under a *tuts-ah* burden basket lumpy with wild potatoes she
had been digging.

He was seated cross-legged on the low wicker bed frame, facing away
from the canvas-flap door. He had drawn John's great Navajo blanket
completely over his head, and she could hear him sobbing quietly.
Without setting the basket down she backed noiselessly out of the wickiup and set the potatoes in the shade of the ramada. She put her hands
on her hips to straighten up to her full height, and took a deep breath as
she looked around, her black little eyes taking in the spare, pebbly earth
and brilliant sunshine. She turned her face into the low wind that
picked up heat and pungency from the desert floor and rattled the dry
leaves of the ramada with them. "Let it be good with him," she whispered.

Ethel removed the oak leaves from the mouth of the wicker jug and
drank some water, then adjusted her moccasins, picked up a smaller
basket, and walked toward the river. It was almost August, and she
knew a place upstream where the wood sorrel would be ready for picking.

EPILOGUE

Mr. Clum and I bought gasoline in Globe, and stopped in Peridot long enough to drink a Coke. "You know," he said at the soda fountain, "that fellow Hart was waiting in Tucson before I even got fired in San Carlos. It was just a *coup d'état,* pure and simple. I was running probably the only Indian reservation in these United States where nobody was cheating the Indians, and that was unthinkable. They sent me out after Geronimo hoping he would kill me, but if he didn't it was still okay, because I'd be out of San Carlos long enough to snatch it out from under me. I gotta hand it to 'em, it was a hell of a plan, and it worked."

He shook his head. "For what we did to these Indians, God on the Judgment Day is going to be either just, or He's going to be merciful. There is no way he could be both."

"So you've spent your retirement writing your articles, to set the record straight."

"It could have worked. I know it could have worked, if they had just let me alone."

Mr. Clum's eyes looked far away into his own wistfulness when I asked about Eskiminzin. "He died about fifteen, no, seventeen years ago. Some of his kids learned to write letters so we kept in some touch. He never did understand how he could try so hard to do right and get kicked in the chops every time he turned around. God, that was sad."

I asked about his wife and his answer was barely audible. "She passed away some years ago." I reached for my back pocket, but he laid a hand, still strong, on my arm. "No, Mudpies, you've been a good audience. I'm going to buy your Coke."

It was wearing late into the afternoon when Mr. Clum and I finally drove up to the Gila River dam. We picked up a couple of Bureau of Reclamation officials and continued on to the agency compound at Old San Carlos. The Gila flats, soon to be underwater, were just as pebbly and sterile as Mr. Clum had described them, the road being a mere visible trace of tread marks in the sandy places.

It was Mr. Clum who saw the buildings first, from a distance, square squat ruins that he recognized instantly and pointed out to me by name —the headquarters building, the commissary, the guardhouse where he threw Geronimo. The pole roofs of the old buildings had long since collapsed, but the thick adobe walls still reared upward, as yellow-brown as the ground out of which they grew as though rooted. Only at the top were they rounded, as they began that slow, slow melting of neglected adobe under the pelting of the rare desert thunderstorms. Mr. Clum said, "I built 'em good, didn't I?" His satisfaction was evident, and I smiled.

Near the headquarters building were parked a couple of trucks with a knot of men standing around, the blasting crews who had been packing explosives beneath the walls. Apart from them a little were six or eight very brown old men, a couple in Levi's but the rest in loose white pantaloons. From their long white hair, wide red headbands, and toetab moccasins I took them for Apaches.

Mr. Clum spent as little time as he could get away with being introduced around the circle of white men before he and I moved over toward the Indians. He held out both hands to the nearest one. "Is that you, Tauclee?"

Quietly he answered, "Yes, Nantan Batunni-ka-yeh." At last I had heard an Apache call him by his Apache name, and it struck me that all during those hours on the road, he had not just been spinning a tale. It seemed like a ridiculously long name. I found myself wondering if in the old days the Apaches had to call him by all those syllables every time they wanted to talk to him, although Tauclee's facile non-English tongue rolled them off as easily as I might have said, "Hello, John." I wanted to ask about it, but it wasn't my place to intrude on the moment.

The two old men regarded each other in perfect silence for what seemed like an embarrassing length of time. I studied them studying each other's eyes, enjoying a whole conversation in that speechless Apache communication that Mr. Clum hadn't forgotten, but was indecipherable to me.

The blasting crew had been watching from around the trucks, when I saw two of them turn their backs to the warm breeze and light cigarettes. One of them muttered, "My God, ain't they got nothing to say to each other after all this time?" Farther away, a crooked black umbilicum of wires led a hundred yards or so out to a table under a canvas tarpaulin. Other men there were screwing the wires down to terminals on the plungers that Mr. Clum would press to detonate the charges, after he had made his tour.

At last Tauclee nodded almost imperceptibly. "It's been a long time, Nantan Batunni-ka-yeh."

Mr. Clum nodded, too. "Yep, sure has."

I couldn't help how badly I wanted them to say something profound, something that would move me, but they didn't even know I was there.

Mr. Clum stuck his hands in his pockets. "There's been a lot of changes in the world."

Tauclee pursed his lips and shook his head. "Not around here."

Mr. Clum chuckled with quiet understanding, and Tauclee inclined his head toward the other old men. "Got some Injuns here to see you," and they moved off out of my hearing.

ABOUT THE AUTHOR

James L. Haley is the author of three previous books published by Doubleday, *The Buffalo War, Apaches,* and *Texas, an Album of History.* All of his books have been highly praised for their scholarship and readability. THE KINGS OF SAN CARLOS is his first Double D Western.